SATURDAY NIGHT
AND SUNDAY MORNING

This is an exceptionally frank and vigorous novel about working-class life in Nottingham. Its chief character, Arthur Seaton, a young man of 22, is not, at first glance, an attractive character. Indeed he might at times fairly be described as amoral, cunning, dishonest, selfish, or unscrupulous. He earns good money in a factory, which he spends on clothes and drink. Women he usually gets on the cheap, and carrying on with the wives of both a workmate and a soldier involves him incidentally in a thoroughly grim and brutal beating-up. Yet despite his bad character, one almost gets to like him for his vitality and generosity, and it is somehow no surprise when he appears in the end to settle down.

SATURDAY NIGHT AND SUNDAY MORNING

Alan Sillitoe

CHIVERS LARGE PRINT
BATH

British Library Cataloguing in Publication Data available

This Large Print edition published by Chivers Press, Bath, 1994.

Published by arrangement with the author

U.K. Hardcover ISBN 0 7451 2133 0
U.K. Softcover   ISBN 0 7451 2145 4

Photoset, printed and bound in Great Britain by
Redwood Books, Trowbridge, Wiltshire

CONTENTS

INTRODUCTION
TO NEW EDITION (1970) OF
SATURDAY NIGHT
AND SUNDAY MORNING

Saturday Night and Sunday Morning was first published in the autumn of 1958.

No one was more surprised by its success than I was, not even the reviewers and critics. I wrote the final version in Majorca, in 1956–57, but many of the chapters and various parts of it had been composed from 1950 onwards, so that it was in progress for seven years before the final typed version was sent to London.

Some of the chapters were originally written as short stories, a few of which were sent to magazines, but not accepted. One or two items in the novel (including the reflections while fishing by the canal bank on Sunday morning) were written as poems. They were merely incidents, yet fitted well into the novel because they either concerned one character—Arthur Seaton—or centred around one city and one family.

These sketches and stories have been lost, because in moving from one part of Spain to another during those indigent years of apprenticeship I could not take into my suitcases the monstrous amount of paper that was constantly accumulating.

The novel was turned down by four publishers. I thought I would make £200 from it at most, with which sum I intended to return to Majorca, and live for a year until I had another novel ready for publication—which I also hoped would earn me the same amount. And so I would go on living and writing.

Many people make the mistake of assuming that the novel is autobiographical, as they did when it first appeared. It is not, at least not in the strictest sense of the word. When I was writing it I had not been in a factory for ten years. But the novel, while mirroring the sort of atmosphere I grew up in, is a work of the imagination in that all the actors in it are put together from jigsaw pieces assembled so that no identifiable characters came out at the end. I imagine novelists of the middle-class condition also perform in this way.

I had no theme in my head except the joy of writing, the sweat of writing clearly and truthfully, the work of trying to portray ordinary people as I knew them, and in such a way that they would recognise themselves. This took me a long time to achieve, and was more difficult than one might imagine.

It is not up to me to say whether I succeeded or not. I am a writer still, not a critic or reviewer. I am too engrossed in the construction of my own novels, as I was with this one, even to be a reader of them in the final sense. After all, *Saturday Night and Sunday Morning* was and remains a first novel, with all its liberties and limitations. Yet it was in this piece of work that I think I found my true voice, and if I still like it at all, it is for that reason. Beyond that point, it is in the reader's hands.

Alan Sillitoe

PART ONE

SATURDAY NIGHT

CHAPTER ONE

THE rowdy gang of singers who sat at the scattered tables saw Arthur walk unsteadily to the head of the stairs, and though they must all have known that he was dead drunk, and seen the danger he would soon be in, no one attempted to talk to him and lead him back to his seat. With eleven pints of beer and seven small gins playing hide-and-seek inside his stomach, he fell from the top-most stair to the bottom.

It was Benefit Night for the White Horse Club, and the pub had burst its contribution box and spread a riot through its rooms and between its four walls. Floors shook and windows rattled, and leaves of aspidistras wilted in the fumes of beer and smoke. Notts County had beaten the visiting team, and the members of the White Horse supporters club were quartered upstairs to receive a flow of victory. Arthur was not a member of the club, but Brenda was, and so he was drinking the share of her absent husband—as far as it would go—and when the club went bust and the shrewd publican put on the towels for those that couldn't pay, he laid eight half-crowns on the table, intending to fork out for his own.

For it was Saturday night, the best and bingiest glad-time of the week, one of the fifty-two holidays in the slow-turning Big Wheel of the year, a violent preamble to a prostrate Sabbath. Piled-up passions were exploded on Saturday night, and the effect of a week's monotonous graft in the factory was swilled out of your system in a burst of goodwill. You followed the motto of 'be drunk and be happy', kept your crafty arms around female waists, and felt the beer going beneficially down into the elastic capacity of your guts.

Brenda and two other women sitting at Arthur's table saw him push back his chair and stand up with a clatter, his grey eyes filmed over so that he looked like a tall, thin Druid about to begin a maniacal dance. Instead, he muttered something that they were too tight or far away to understand, and walked unsteadily to the top stair. Many people looked at him as he held on to the rail. He turned his head in a slow stare around the packed room, as if he did not know which foot to move first in order to start his body on the descent, or even know why he wanted to go down the stairs at that particular moment.

He felt electric light bulbs shining and

4

burning into the back of his head, and sensed in the opening and closing flash of a second that his mind and body were entirely separate entities inconsiderately intent on going their different ways. For some reason, the loud, cracked voice singing in the room behind seemed like a signal that he should begin descending at once, so he put one foot forward, watched it turn towards the next step in a hazy fashion, and felt the weight of his body bending towards it until pressure from above became so great that he started rolling down the stairs.

A high-octane fuel of seven gins and eleven pints had set him into motion like a machine, and had found its way into him because of a man's boast. A big, loud-mouthed bastard who said he had been a sailor—so Arthur later summed him up—was throwing his weight about and holding dominion over several tables, telling his listeners of all the places he had been to in the world, each anecdote pointing to the fact that he was a champion boozer and the palliest bloke in the pub. He was forty and in his prime, with a gut not too much gone to fat, wearing a brown waistcoated suit and a shirt with matching stripes whose cuffs came down to the hairs of self-assurance on the back of his beefy hand.

5

'Drink?' Brenda's friend exclaimed. 'I'll bet you can't drink like young Arthur Seaton there'—nodding to Arthur's end of the table. 'He's on'y twenty-one and 'e can tek it in like a fish. I don't know where 'e puts it all. It just goes in and in and you wonder when 'is guts are goin' ter go bust all over the room, but 'e duzn't even get fatter!'

Loudmouth grunted and tried to ignore her eulogy, but at the end of a fiery and vivid description of a brothel in Alexandria he called over to Arthur: 'I hear you drink a lot, matey?'

Arthur didn't like being called 'matey'. It put his back up straight away. 'Middlin'.' he answered modestly. 'Why?'

'What's the most you've ever drunk, then?' Loudmouth wanted to know. 'We used to have boozing matches on shoreleave,' he added with a wide, knowing smile to the aroused group of spectators. He reminded Arthur of a sergeant-major who once put him on a charge.

'I don't know,' Arthur told him. 'I can't count, you see.'

'Well,' Loudmouth rejoined, 'let's see how much you can drink now. Loser pays the bill.'

Arthur did not hesitate. Free booze was free booze. Anyway, he begrudged big talkers

6

their unearned glory, and hoped to show him up and take him down to his right size.

Loudmouth's tactics were skilful and sound, he had to admit that. Having won the toss-up for choice, he led off on gins, and after the seventh gin he switched to beer, pints. Arthur enjoyed the gins, and relished the beer. It seemed an even contest for a long time, as if they would sit there swilling it back for ever, until Loudmouth suddenly went green halfway through the tenth pint and had to rush outside. He must have paid the bill downstairs, because he didn't come back. Arthur, as if nothing had happened, went back to his beer.

He was laughing to himself as he rolled down the stairs, at the dull bumping going on behind his head and along his spine, as if it were happening miles away, like a vibration on another part of the earth's surface, and he an earthquake-machine on which it was faintly recorded. This rolling motion was so restful and soporific, in fact, that when he stopped travelling, having arrived at the bottom of the stairs—he kept his eyes closed and went to sleep. It was a pleasant and far-away feeling, and he wanted to stay in exactly the same position for the rest of his life.

Someone was poking him in the ribs: he

recognised it not as the vicious poke of someone who had beaten him in a fight, or the
gentle and playful poke of a woman whom he
had taken to bed, but the tentative poke of a
man who did not know whether he was
poking the ribs of someone who might suddenly spring up and give him a bigger poke
back. It seemed to Arthur that the man was
endeavouring to tell him something as well, so
he tried very hard, but unsuccessfully, to
make an answer, though he did not yet know
what the man was saying. Even had he been
able to make his lips move, the man would not
have understood him, because Arthur's face
was pulled down into his stomach, so that for
all the world he looked like a fully-dressed and
giant foetus curled up at the bottom of the
stairs on a plush-red carpet, hiding in the
shadow of two aspidistras that curved out
over him like arms of jungle foliage.

The man's pokes became more persistent,
and Arthur dimly realised that the fingers
must belong either to one of the waiters or to
the publican himself. It was a waiter, towel in
one hand and tray in the other, white jacket
open from overwork, a face normally blank
but now expressing some character because
he had begun to worry about this tall, iron-
faced, crop-haired youth lying senseless at his

feet.

'He's had a drop too much, poor bloke,' said an elderly man, stepping over Arthur's body and humming a hymn tune as he went up the stairs, thinking how jolly yet sinful it would be if he possessed the weakness yet strength of character to get so drunk and roll down the stairs in such a knocked-out state.

'Come on, Jack,' the waiter pleaded with Arthur. 'We don't want the pleece to come in and find you like that or we shall get summonsed. We had trubble wi' a man last week who had a fit and had to be taken to 't General Hospital in an amb'lance. We don't want any more trubble, or the pub'll get a bad name.'

As Arthur rolled over to consolidate and deepen his sleep a glaring overhead light caught his eyes and he opened them to see the waiter's white coat and pink face.

'Christ!' he mumbled.

'He won't help you,' the waiter said dispassionately. 'Come on, get up and go out for some fresh air, then you'll feel better.'

Arthur felt happy yet unco-operative when the waiter tried to get him to his feet: like being in hospital and having a nurse do everything for you with great exertion, and all the time warning you that you mustn't try to help

9

yourself in any way or else it would result in you being kept in bed for another week. Like after he had been knocked down by a lorry riding to Derby two years ago. But the waiter had a different point of view, and after pulling him into a sitting position cried, his heavy breath whistling against the aspidistra leaves:

'All right. That's enough. You aren't lifeless. Come on, get up yoursen now.'

When another man's legs opened and closed over Arthur—the retreating shoe knocked his shoulder—he shouted in a belligerent and fully-awake voice: 'Hey, mate, watch what yer doin', can't yer? Yo' an' yer bloody grett clod-'oppers.' He turned to the waiter: 'Some people love comin' out on a Saturday night in their pit-boots.'

The man turned from halfway up the stairs: 'You shouldn't go to sleep in everybody's way. Can't tek the drink, that's what's the matter wi' yo' young 'uns.'

'That's what yo' think,' Arthur retaliated, pulling himself up by the stair-rail and holding firmly on to it.

'You'll have to go out, you know,' the waiter said sadly, as if he had donned a black cap to pronounce sentence. 'We can't serve you any more ale in that condition.'

'There's nowt wrong wi' me,' Arthur

10

exclaimed, recognising a situation of extreme peril.

'No,' the waiter retorted, coolly sarcastic, 'I know there ain't, but it's a bit thick, you know, getting drunk like this.'

Arthur denied that he was drunk, speaking so clearly that the waiter was inclined to believe him.

'Have a fag, mate,' he said, and lit both cigarettes with a perfectly calm hand. 'You must be busy tonight,' he suggested, so sanely that he might just have walked in off the street and not yet sipped a shandy.

His remark touched the waiter's grievance. 'Not much we aren't. I'm so tired I can't feel my feet. These Saturday nights'll be the death o' me.'

'It ain't what yer might call a good job,' Arthur said with sympathy.

'Well, it's not that exactly,' the waiter began to complain, friendly and confiding all of a sudden. 'It's because we're short of staff. Nobody'll take on a job like this, you know, and . . .'

The publican came out of the saloon door, a small wiry man in a pin-striped suit whom no one would know as a publican unless they recognised the slight cast of authority and teetotalness in his right eye. 'Come on, Jim,' he

11

said sharply. 'I don't pay my waiters to talk to their pals. You know it's a busy night. Get back upstairs and keep 'em happy.'

Jim nodded towards Arthur: 'This bloke here'—but the publican was already carrying his fanatic stare to another department, and so the waiter saw no point in going on. He shrugged his shoulders and obeyed the order, leaving Arthur free to walk into the saloon bar.

*   *   *

Fixing an iron-grip on the brass rail, he shouted for a pint, the only sufficient liquid measure that could begin to swill away the tasteless ash-like thirst at the back of his mouth. After the rapid disposal of the pint, so long in coming, he would bluff his way back upstairs, dodge the waiter, and rejoin Brenda, the woman he had been sitting with before his fall. He could not believe that the descending frolic of the stairs had happened to him. His memory acted at first like a beneficial propaganda machine, a retainer and builder of morale, saying that he could not have been so drunk and rolled down the stairs in that way, and that what had really happened, yes, this was it for sure, was that he must have *walked* down and fallen asleep on the bottom step. It could happen to anybody, especially if they had been at work all day, standing near a capstan lathe in the dull roar of the turnery department. Yet this explanation was too tame. Perhaps he really had tripped down a few of the stairs; yes, he distinctly remembered bumping a few steps.

For the third time he demanded a pint. His eyes were glazed with fatigue, and he would have let go of the bar-rail had not an ever-ready instinct of self-preservation leapt into his fist at the weakest moment and forced him to tighten his grip. He was beginning to feel sick, and in fighting this temptation his tiredness increased. He did not know whether he would go back upstairs to Brenda afterwards, or have his pint and get home to bed, the best place when you feel done-in, he muttered to himself.

The bartender placed a pint before him. He paid one-and-eightpence and drank it almost in a single gulp. His strength magically returned, and he shouted out for another, thinking: the thirteenth. Unlucky for some, but we'll see how it turns out. He received the pint and drank a little more slowly, but halfway through it, the temptation to be sick became a necessity that beat insistently against the back of his throat. He fought it off and struggled to light a cigarette.

Smoke caught in his windpipe and he had just time enough to push his way back through the crush—nudging his elbow into standing people who unknowingly blocked his way, half choked by smoke now issuing from mouth and nostrils, feeling strangely taken up by a fierce power that he could not control— before he gave way to the temptation that had stood by him since falling down the stairs, and emitted a belching roar over a middle-aged man sitting with a woman on one of the green leather seats.

'My God!' the man cried. 'Look at this. Look at what the young bogger's gone and done. Would you believe it? My best suit. Only pressed and cleaned today. Who would credit such a thing? Oh dear. It cost me fifteen bob. As if money grows on trees. And suits as well. I wonder how I'll ever get the stains out? Oh dear.'

His whining voice went on for several minutes, and those who turned to look expected him with every word to break down into piteous sobs.

Arthur was stupefied, unable to believe that the tragedy before him could by any means be connected with himself and the

14

temptation to which he had just given way. Yet through the haze and smoke and shrill reproaches coming from the man's lady-friend, he gathered that he was to blame and that he should be feeling sorry for what had happened.

He stood up straight, rigid, swaying slightly, his eyes gleaming, his overcoat open. Automatically he felt for another cigarette, but remembering in time what his attempt to smoke the last one had caused, gave up the search and dropped his hands by his side.

'Look what yer've done, yer young bleeder,' the woman was shouting at him. 'Spewed all over Alf's bes' suit. And all you do is jus' stand there. Why don't yer do something? Eh? Why don't yer't least apologise for what yer've done?'

'Say summat, mate,' an onlooker called, and by the tone of his voice Arthur sensed that the crowd was not on his side, though he was unable to speak and defend himself. He looked at the woman, who continued shouting directly at him, while the victim fumbled ineffectually with a handkerchief trying to clean his suit.

The woman stood a foot away from Arthur. 'Look at him,' she jeered into his face. 'He's senseless. He can't say a word. He can't

15

even apologise. Why don't yet apologise, eh? *Can't* yer apologise? Dragged-up, I should think, getting drunk like this. Looks like one of them Teddy boys, allus making trouble. Go on, apologise.'

From her constant use of the word apologise it seemed as if she had either just learned its meaning—perhaps after a transmission breakdown on television—or as if she had first learned to say it by spelling it out with coloured bricks at school forty years ago.

'Apologise,' she cried, her maniacal face right against him. 'Go on, apologise.'

The beast inside Arthur's stomach gripped him again, and suddenly, mercilessly, before he could stop it or move out of the way, or warn anybody that it was coming, it leapt out of his mouth with an appalling growl.

She was astonished. Through the haze her face clarified. Arthur saw teeth between open lips, narrowed eyes, claws raised. She was a tigress.

He saw nothing else. Before she could spring he gathered all his strength and pushed through the crowd, impelled by a strong sense of survival towards the street-door, to take himself away from a scene of ridicule, disaster, and certain retribution.

He knocked softly on the front door of

16

Brenda's house. No answer. He had expected that. The kids were asleep, her husband Jack was at Long Eaton for the races—dog, horse, motor-bike—and not due back until Sunday midday, and Brenda had stayed at the pub. Now sitting on her front doorstep he remembered his journey to the house: a vague memory of battles with lamp-posts and walls and kerb stones, of knocking into people who told him to watch his step and threatened to drop him one, voices of anger and the hard unsympathetic stones of houses and pavements.

It was a mild autumn night, a wind playing the occasional sharp sound of someone slamming a door or closing a window. He lay across the doorstep, trying to avoid the pavement. A man passed, singing a happy song to himself, noticing nothing. Arthur was half asleep, but opened his eyes now and again to make sure that the street was still there, to convince himself that he was not in bed, because the hard stone step was as round and as soft as a pillow. He was blissfully happy, for he did not have the uncomfortable feeling of wanting to be sick any more, though at the same time he had retained enough alcohol to stay both high-spirited and sleepy. He made the curious experiment of speaking out loud to see whether or not he could hear his own voice. 'Couldn't care less, couldn't care less, couldn't care less'—in answer to questions that came into his mind regarding sleeping with a woman who had a husband and two kids, getting blind drunk on seven gins and umpteen pints, falling down a flight of stairs, and being sick over a man and a woman. Bliss and guilt joined forces in such a way that they caused no trouble but merely sunk his mind into a welcome nonchalance. The next thing he knew was Brenda bending over him and digging her fingers sharply in his ribs.

'Ugh!' he grunted, noting the yeast and hop-like smell of her breath. 'Yer've bin boozin'!'

''Ark at who's talkin',' she said, gesticulating as if she had brought an audience with her. 'I had two pints and three orange-squashes, and he talks about boozing. I heard all about what happened to you though at the pub, falling downstairs and being sick over people.'

He stood up, clear-headed and steady. 'I'm all right now, duck. I'm sorry I couldn't get back upstairs to you in the pub, but I don't know what went on.'

'I'll tell you some day,' she laughed. 'But let's be quiet as we go in, or we'll wake the

18

kids.'

Got to be careful, he said to himself. Nosy neighbours'll tell Jack. He lifted the band of hair from her coat collar and kissed her neck. She turned on him petulantly: 'Can't you wait till we get upstairs?'

'No,' he admitted, with a mock-gloating laugh.

'Well, you've got to wait,' she said, pushing the door open for him to go in.

He stood in the parlour while she fastened the locks and bolts, smelling faint odours of rubber and oil coming from Jack's bicycle leaning against a big dresser that took up nearly one whole side of the room. It was a small dark area of isolation, long familiar with another man's collection of wordly goods: old-fashioned chairs and a settee, fireplace, clock ticking on the mantelpiece, a smell of brown paper, soil from a plant-pot, ordinary aged dust, soot in the chimney left over from last winter's fires, and mustiness of rugs laid down under the table and by the fireplace. Brenda had known this room for seven married years, yet could not have become more intimate with it than did Arthur in the ten seconds while she fumbled with the key.

He knocked his leg on the bicycle pedal, swearing at the pain, complaining at Jack's barminess for leaving it in such an exposed position. 'How does he think I'm going to get in with that thing stuck there?' he joked. 'Tell him I said to leave it in the back-yard next week, out of 'arm's way.'

Brenda hissed and told him to be quiet, and they crept like two thieves into the living-room, where the electric light showed the supper things—teacups, plates, jam-pot, bread—still on the table. A howl of cats came from a nearby yard, and a dustbin lid clattered on to cobblestones.

'Oh well,' he said in a normal voice, standing up tall and straight, 'it's no use whisperin' when all that racket's going on.'

They stood between the table and firegrate, and Brenda put her arms around him. While kissing her he turned his head so that his own face stared back at him from an oval mirror above the shelf. His eyes grew large in looking at himself from such an angle, noticing his short disordered hair sticking out like the bristles of a blond porcupine, and the mark of an old pimple healing on his cheek.

'Don't let's stay down here long, Arthur,' she said softly.

He released her and, knowing every corner of the house and acting as if it belonged to him, stripped off his coat and shirt and went into the scullery to wash the tiredness from his eyes. Once in bed, they would not go to sleep at once: he wanted to be fresh for an hour before floating endlessly down into the warm bed beside Brenda's soft body.

*   *   *

It was ten o'clock, and she was still asleep. The sun came through the window, carrying street-noises on its beams, a Sunday morning clash of bottles from milkmen on their rounds, newspaper boys shouting to each other as they clattered along the pavement and pushed folded newspapers into letter-boxes, each bearing crossword puzzles, sports news and forecasts, and interesting scandal that would be struggled through with a curious and salacious indolence over plates of bacon and tomatoes and mugs of strong sweet tea.

He turned to Brenda heaped beside him, sitting up to look at her. She was breathing gently; her hair straggled untidily over the pillow, her breasts bulged out of her slip, a thick smooth arm over them as if she were trying to protect herself from something that had frightened her in a dream. He heard the two children playing in their bedroom across the landing. One was saying: 'It's my Teddy-bear, our Jacky. Gi' it me or else I's'll tell our mam.' Then a low threat from the boy who would not hand back his plunder.

He sank down contentedly into bed. 'Brenda,' he said in a low voice. 'Come on, duck, waken up.'

She turned and pressed her face into his groin.

'Nice,' he muttered.

'What's time?' she mumbled, her breath hot against his skin.

'Half-past eleven,' he lied.

She sprang up, showing the crease-marks of crumpled sheets down one side of her face, her brown eyes wide open. 'You're having me on again,' she cried. 'Of all the liars, you're the biggest I've ever known.'

'I allus was a liar,' he said, laughing at his joke. 'A good 'un an' all.'

'Liars don't prosper,' she retorted.

'It's on'y ten o'clock,' he admitted, lifting her hair and rolling it into a ball on top of her head.

'What a time we had last night,' she grinned, suddenly remembering.

It came back to him now. He had put away more swill than Loudmouth, had fallen down some stairs, had been sick over a man and a woman. He laughed. 'It seems years.' He took her by the shoulders and kissed her lips, then her neck and breasts, pressing his leg against her. 'You're lovely, Brenda. Let's get down in bed.'

'Mam,' a small plaintive voice cried.

She pushed Arthur away. 'Go back to bed, Jacky.'

'It's late,' he crooned tearfully through the door. 'I want some tea, our mam.'

'Go back.'

They heard the shuffling of a small foot behind the door. 'I want to see Uncle Arthur,' Jacky pleaded.

'Little bogger,' Arthur muttered, resigning himself to the disturbance. 'I can't have a bit o' peace on a Sunday morning.'

Brenda sat higher in the bed and straightened her slip. 'Leave him alone,' she said.

Jacky was insistent. He kicked the bottom of the door.

'Can I come in, Uncle Arthur?'

'You little bogger.'

He laughed, knowing now that it was all right.

'Go down to the parlour,' Arthur said, 'and get the *News of the World* that's just bin pushed in the letter-box. Then I'll let yer

23

come.'

His bare feet went thudding softly on the wooden stairs. They heard him hurrying through the parlour below, then running back and climbing the stairs with breathless haste. They drew apart as he burst in and threw the paper on the bed, jumping up and crushing it between his stomach and Arthur's legs. Arthur pulled it free and held him high in the air with one hand, until he began to gag and choke with laughter and Brenda said he was to be put down or else he would go into a fit.

'Young Jacky,' Arthur said, looking up at his animated face, five years old, with pink skin and fair hair, fresh in his shirt and clean from bath-night. 'You little bogger, young Jacky, you young jockey.' He let him down, and the child burrowed up against him like a passionate rabbit.

'Listen,' Arthur said to him, blowing in his ear between each word, 'go and get my trousers from that chair and I'll gi' yer a bob.'

'You'll spoil him,' Brenda said, touching him under the blankets. 'He gets enough money as it is.' She lifted herself out of bed and picked up a skirt draped over the bottom rail. Both Arthur and Jacky watched her intently as she dressed, deeply interested by

24

the various secrets of her that became hidden with the donning of each item of clothing.

'What does it matter?' Arthur demanded at being forced to justify his generosity. 'I give 'im money because I was lucky to get a ha'penny when I was a nipper.'

She was slovenly and easily dressed for Sunday morning: a white blouse open at the throat, a wide grey skirt, a slip-on pair of shoes, and hair pushed in strands to the back of her neck. 'Come on, get up, Arthur. It's nearly eleven o'clock. You've got to be out of the house before twelve. It wouldn't do for Jack to see you here.'

'That bastard,' he said, holding Jacky at arms' length and pulling a face at him. 'Who do you love?' he shouted with a laugh. 'Who do you love, young Jack Blud-Tub?'

'Yo', yo',' he screamed. 'Yo', Uncle Arthur'—and Arthur released him so that he fell with a thud on to the rumpled bed.

'Come on, then,' Brenda said impatiently, tired of watching, 'let's go downstairs.'

'Yo' goo down, duck,' he grinned, 'and cook me some breakfast. I'll come when I can smell the bacon and egg.'

Jack's head was turned and she bent over to kiss Arthur. He held her firmly by the neck, and was still kissing her when Jacky lifted his head and looked wonderingly at them.

★   ★   ★

At half-past eleven Arthur sat at the table with a plate of bacon-and-egg before him. He tore a piece of bread in half and dipped it in the fat around his plate, then took a long drink of tea. Jacky, already fed, stood on a nearby chair and followed every move with his blue eyes.

'It's thirsty work, fallin' downstairs,' Arthur said. 'Pour me some more tea, duck.'

She held the newspaper against her midriff with one hand, 'Plenty of sugar?'

He nodded and went on eating. 'You're good to me,' he said after a while, 'and don't think I don't appreciate it.'

'Yes, but it'll be your last breakfast in this house if you don't hurry. Jack'll be home soon.'

Tomorrow is work, and I'll be hard at it, sweating my guts out until next weekend. It's a hard life if you don't weaken. He told her what was on his mind.

'No rest for the wicked,' she laughed.

He passed a choice piece of bacon to Jacky. 'A present from Uncle Arthur.'

'Ta!' he said, relishing the honour before

his mouth closed over the fork.

Brenda suddenly stiffened in her chair and half turned her ear to the window, silent like an animal waiting to spring, an alertness that transformed her face to temporary ugliness. Arthur noticed it, and swilled down the last of his tea. 'He's coming,' she said. 'I heard the gate open.'

He picked Jacky up and kissed him on the lips, feeling his arms curl tight around his face and ears. He then stood him on a chair while he kissed Brenda.

'So long,' he said. 'See you next week'— and walked towards the parlour. He stood by the bicycle for a moment to light a cigarette.

'Get going,' Brenda hissed softly, seeing her husband open the gate and walk down the yard.

Arthur unlocked the front door and pulled it towards him, sniffing the fresh air of a bright Sunday morning as if to decide whether the day was fine enough to venture out in. It was. He clicked the door to and stepped into the street, as Brenda's husband Jack opened the back door and came in through the scullery.

CHAPTER TWO

HE lifted a pair of clean overalls from the bed-rail and pulled them over his big white feet, taking care not to disturb his brother Sam who, while still in the depths of sleep, rolled himself more advantageously into the large mound of blankets now that Arthur had left the bed. He had often heard Friday described as Black Friday—remembering a Boris Karloff film of years ago—and wondered why this should be. For Friday, being pay-day, was a good day, and 'black' would be more fitting if applied to Monday. Black Monday. Then there would be some sense in it, when you felt your head big from boozing, throat sore from singing, eyes fogged-up from seeing too many films or sitting in front of the television, and feeling black and wicked because the big grind was starting all over again.

The stairfoot door clicked open.

'Arthur,' his father called, in a deadly menacing Monday-morning voice that made your guts rattle, sounding as if it came from the grave, 'when are yer goin' ter get up? Yer'll be late fer wok.' He closed the stairfoot door quietly so as not to waken the mother and two other sons still at home.

Arthur took a half-empty fag-packet from the mantelpiece, his comb, a ten-shilling note and heap of coins that had survived the pubs, bookies' counters, and cadgers, and stuffed them into his pockets.

The bottom door opened again.

'Eh?'

'I 'eard yer the first time,' Arthur said in a whisper.

The door slammed, by way of reply.

A mug of tea was needed, then back to the treadmill. Monday was always the worst; by Wednesday he was broken-in, like a greyhound. Well, anyroad, he thought, there was always Brenda, lovely Brenda who was all right and looked after you well once she'd made up her mind to it. As long as Jack didn't find out and try to get his hands around my throat. That'd be the day. By Christ it would. Though my hands would be round his throat first, the nit-witted, dilat'ry, unlucky bastard.

He glanced once more around the small bedroom, seeing the wooden double-bed pushed under the window, the glint of a white pot, dilapidated shelves holding Sam's books—rulers, pencils, and rubbers—and a home-made table on which stood his portable wireless set. He lifted the latch as the stairfoot door opened again, and his father poked his head up, ready to tell him in his whispering, menacing Monday-morning gut-rattle that it was time to come down.

Despite the previous tone of his father's voice, Arthur found him sitting at the table happily supping tea. A bright fire burned in the modernised grate—the family had clubbed-up thirty quid to have it done—and the room was warm and cheerful, the table set, and tea mashed.

Seaton looked up from his cup. 'Come on, Arthur. You ain't got much time. It's ten past seven, and we've both got to be on by half-past. Sup a cup o' tea an' get crackin'.'

Arthur sat down and stretched his legs towards the fire. After a cup and a Woodbine his head was clearer. He didn't feel so bad. 'You'll go blind one day, dad,' he said, for nothing, taking words out of the air for sport, ready to play with the consequences of whatever he might cause.

Seaton turned to him uncomprehendingly, his older head still fuddled. It took ten cups of tea and as many Woodbines to set his temper right after the weekend. 'What do you mean?' he demanded, intractable at any time before ten in the morning.

'Sittin' in front of the TV. You stick to it

like glue from six to eleven every night. It can't be good for yer. You'll go blind one day. You're bound to. I read it in the *Post* last week that a lad from the Medders went blind. They might be able to save 'im though, because 'e goes to the Eye Infirmary every Monday, Wensday, an' Friday. But it's a risk.'

His father poured another cup of tea, his black brows taut with anger. Short, stocky Seaton was incapable of irritation or mild annoyance. He was either happy and fussy with everybody, or black-browed with a deep melancholy rage that chose its victims at random. In the last few years his choice of victims had grown less, for Arthur, with his brother Fred, had been through the mill of factory and army and now stood up to him, creating a balance of power that kept the house more or less peaceful.

'I'm sure it never did anybody any harm,' Seaton said. 'Anyway, yer never believe what the papers tell yer, do yer? If yer do then yer want yer brains testin'. They never tell owt but lies. That's one thing I do know.'

'I wouldn't be so sure of that,' Arthur said, flipping a dead Woodbine into the fire. 'Anyway, I know somebody who knows this kid as went blind, so the papers was right for a change. They said they saw this kid bein' led

31

to the Eye Infirmary by 'is mam. It was a rotten shame, they said. A kid of seven. She led 'im along wi' a lead, and the kid had a stick specially made for him, painted white. I heard they was getting him a dog as well to help him along, a wire-haired terrier. There was talk o' standin' him outside the Council House for the rest of his life wi' a tin mug if he don't get better. His dad's got cancer, an' 'is mam can't afford ter keep him in white sticks an' dogs.'

'Ye're barmy,' Seaton said. 'Go an' tell yer stories somewhere else. Not that I'm bothered wi' my eyes anyway. My eyes 'ave allus bin good, and allus will be. When I went for my medical in the war they were A1, but I swung the lead and got off 3C,' he added proudly.

The subject was dropped. His father cut several slices of bread and made sandwiches with cold meat left from Sunday dinner. Arthur teased him a lot, but in a way he was glad to see the TV standing in a corner of the living-room, a glossy panelled box looking, he thought, like something plundered from a space-ship. The old man was happy at last, anyway, and he deserved to be happy, after all the years before the war on the dole, five kids and the big miserying that went with no money and no way of getting any. And now he

32

had a sit-down job at the factory, all the Woodbines he could smoke, money for a pint if he wanted one, though he didn't as a rule drink, a holiday somewhere, a jaunt on the firm's trip to Blackpool, and a television-set to look into at home. The difference between before the war and after the war didn't bear thinking about. War was a marvellous thing in many ways, when you thought about how happy it had made so many people in England. There are no flies on me, Arthur thought.

He stuffed a packet of sandwiches and a flask of tea into his pocket, and waited while his father struggled into a jacket. Once out of doors they were more aware of the factory rumbling a hundred yards away over the high wall. Generators whined all night, and during the day giant milling-machines working away on cranks and pedals in the turnery gave to the terrace a sensation of living within breathing distance of some monstrous being that suffered from a disease of the stomach. Disinfectant-suds, grease, and newly-cut steel permeated the air over the suburb of four-roomed houses built around the factory, streets and terraces hanging on to its belly and flanks like calves sucking the udders of some great mother. The factory sent crated bicycles each year from the Despatch Department to waiting railway trucks over Eddison Road, boosting post-war (or perhaps pre-war, Arthur thought, because these days a war could start tomorrow) export trade and trying to sling pontoons over a turbulent unbridgeable river called the Sterling Balance. The thousands that worked there took home good wages. No more short-time like before the war, or getting the sack if you stood ten minutes in the lavatory reading your *Football Post*—if the gaffer got on to you now you could always tell him where to put the job and go somewhere else. And no more running out at dinnertime for a penny bag of chips to eat with your bread. Now, and about time too, you got fair wages if you worked your backbone to a string of conkers on piece-work, and there was a big canteen where you could get a hot dinner for two-bob. With the wages you got you could save up for a motor-bike or even an old car, or you could go on a ten-day binge and get rid of all you'd saved. Because it was no use saving your money year after year. A mug's game, since the value of it got less and less and in any case you never knew when the Yanks were going to do something daft like dropping the H-bomb on Moscow. And if they did then you could say ta-ta to everybody, burn your football coupons and betting-slips, and ring-up Billy Graham. If you believe in God, which I don't, he said to himself.

'It's a bit nippy,' his father remarked, buttoning his coat as they turned into the street. 'What do you expect for November?' Arthur said. Not that he didn't have an overcoat, but you never went to work in one, not even when snow was on the ground and it was freezing. An overcoat was for going out in at night when you had your Teddy-suit on. Living only five minutes from the factory, walking kept you warm on your way there, and once inside at your machine the working of it kept your blood running. Only those that came from Mansfield and Kirkby wore overcoats, because it was cold in the buses.

Fat Mrs. Bull the gossiper stood with her fat arms folded over her apron at the yard-end, watching people pass by on their way to work. With pink face and beady eyes, she was a tight-fisted defender of her tribe, queen of the yard because she had lived there for twenty-two years, earning names like 'The News of the World' and the 'Loudspeaker' because she watched the factory go in every morning and afternoon to glean choice gossip for retail later on. Neither Arthur nor his father greeted her as they passed, and neither did they speak to each other until they were halfway down the street.

It was long, straight, and cobble-stoned, with lamp-posts and intersections at regular intervals, terraces branching off here and there. You stepped out of the front door and found yourself on the pavement. Red-ochre had been blackened by soot, paint was faded and cracked, everything was a hundred years old except the furniture inside.

'What will they think on next!' Seaton said, after glancing upwards and seeing a television aerial hooked on to almost every chimney, like a string of radar stations, each installed on the never-never.

They turned on to Eddison Road by the big red-bricked canteen. The November sky was clear and dark-blue, with some stars still showing whitely. 'Everybody'll 'ave little baby 'elicopters,' Arthur answered readily. 'You'll see. Five-bob-a-week-and-misses for ten years and you can go and see your mate at Derby in lunch-hour.'

'Some 'opes,' the old man scoffed.

'I read it in the paper,' Arthur said. 'It was the one last Thursday, I think, because my snap was wrapped-up in it, that they'll get to the moon in five years. In ten they'll be having cheap-day returns. It's true right

36

enough.'

Seaton laughed. 'You're crackers, Arthur. You'll grow-up one day and stop telling these tales. You're nearly twenty-two. You should know better. I thought they'd a cured you on it in the army, but I can see they didn't.'

'The on'y thing the army cures you on,' Arthur retorted, 'is never to join the army again. They're dead good at that.'

'When I was a lad they din't even have wireless sets,' Seaton ruminated. 'And now look at what they've got: television. Pictures in your own 'ouse.'

They were caught by the main ingoing stream: bicycles, buses, motor-bikes, and pedestrians on a last-minute rush to breach one of the seven gates before half-past. Arthur and his father walked in by the hexagonal commissionaires' office, a building in the centre of a wide roadway dividing the factory into two unequal parts. Seaton was on viewing in the three-speed shop, so turned off after a hundred yards.

'See yer't dinnertime, Arthur.'

'Tarr-ar, Dad.'

*   *   *

Arthur walked into a huge corridor, searching an inside pocket for his clocking-in card and noticing, as on every morning since he was fifteen—except for a two-year break in the army—the factory smell of oil-suds, machinery, and shaved steel that surrounded you with an air in which pimples grew and prospered on your face and shoulders, that would have turned you into one big pimple if you did not spend half an hour over the scullery sink every night getting rid of the biggest bastards. What a life, he thought. Hard work and good wages, and a smell all day that turns your guts.

The bright Monday-morning ring of the clocking-in machine made a jarring note, different from the tune that played inside Arthur. It was dead on half-past seven. Once in the shop he allowed himself to be swallowed by its diverse noises, walked along lanes of capstan lathes and millers, drills and polishers and hand-presses, worked by a multiplicity of belts and pulleys turning and twisting and slapping on heavy well-oiled wheels overhead, dependent for power on a motor stooping at the far end of the hall like the black shining bulk of a stranded whale. Machines with their own small motors started with a jerk and a whine under the shadows of their operators, increasing a noise that made the brain reel and ache because the weekend had been too tranquil by contrast, a weekend that had terminated for Arthur in fishing for trout in the cool shade of a willow-sleeved canal near the Balloon Houses, miles away from the city. Motor-trolleys moved up and down the main gangways carrying boxes of work—pedals, hubs, nuts, and bolts—from one part of the shop to another. Robboe the foreman bent over a stack of new time-sheets behind his glass partition; women and girls wearing turbans and hair-nets and men and boys in clean blue overalls, settled down to their work, eager to get a good start on their day's stint; while sweepers and cleaners at everybody's beck and call already patrolled the gangways and looked busy.

Arthur reached his capstan lathe and took off his jacket, hanging it on a nearby nail so that he could keep an eye on his belongings. He pressed the starter button, and his motor came to life with a gentle thump. Looking around, it did not seem, despite the infernal noise of hurrying machinery, that anyone was working with particular speed. He smiled to himself and picked up a glittering steel cylinder from the top box of a pile beside him, and fixed it into the spindle. He jettisoned his cigarette into the sud-pan, drew back the capstan, and swung the turret on to its broadest drill. Two minutes passed while he contemplated the precise position of tools and cylinder; finally he spat on to both hands and rubbed them together, then switched on the sud-tap from the movable brass pipe, pressed a button that set the spindle running, and ran in the drill to a neat chamfer. Monday morning had lost its terror.

At a piecework rate of four-and-six a hundred you could make your money if you knocked-up fourteen hundred a day—possible without grabbing too much—and if you went all out for a thousand in the morning you could dawdle through the afternoon and lark about with the women and talk to your mates now and again. Such leisure often brought him near to trouble, for some weeks ago he stunned a mouse—that the overfed factory cats had missed—and laid it beneath a woman's drill, and Robboe the gaffer ran out of his office when he heard her screaming blue-murder, thinking that some bloody silly woman had gone and got her hair caught in a belt (big notices said that women must wear hair-nets, but who could tell with women?) and Robboe was glad that it was nothing more than a dead mouse she was kicking up such a fuss about. But he paced up and down the gangways asking who was responsible for the stunned mouse, and when he came to Arthur, who denied having anything to do with it, he said: 'I'll bet you did it, you young bogger.' 'Me, Mr. Robboe?' Arthur said, the picture of innocence, standing up tall with offended pride. 'I've got so much work to do I can't move from my lathe. Anyway, I don't believe in tormenting women, you know that. It's against my principles.' Robboe glared at him: 'Well, I don't know. Somebody did it, and I reckon it's you. You're a bit of a Red if you ask me, that's what you are.' 'Now then, that's slander,' Arthur said. 'I'll see my lawyers about you. There's tons of witnesses.' Robboe went back to his office, bearing a black look for the girl inside, and for any toolsetter that might require his advice in the next half-hour; and Arthur worked on his lathe like a model of industry.

Though you couldn't grumble at four-and-six a hundred the rate-checker sometimes came and watched you work, so that if he saw you knock up a hundred in less than an hour Robboe would come and tell you one fine morning that your rate had been dropped by sixpence or a bob. So when you felt the shadow of the rate-checker breathing down your neck you knew what to do if you had any brains at all: make every move more complicated, though not slow because that was cutting your own throat, and do everything deliberately yet with a crafty show of speed. Though cursed as public enemy number one the rate-checker was an innocuous-looking man who carried a slight stoop everywhere he went and wore spectacles, smoking the same fags as you were smoking, and protecting his blue pin-striped suit with a brown staff-overall, bald as a mushroom and as sly as a fox. They said he got commission on what reductions he recommended, but that was only a rumour, Arthur decided, something said out of rancour if you had just been done down for a bob. If you saw the rate-checker on your way home from work he might say good evening to you, and you responded to this according to whether or not your rate had been tampered with lately. Arthur always returned such signs with affability, for whenever the rate-checker stood behind him he switched his speed down to a normal hundred, though once he had averaged four hundred when late on his daily stint. He worked out for fun how high his wages would be if, like a madman, he pursued this cramp-inducing, back-breaking, knuckle-knocking undiplomatic speed of four hundred for a week, and his calculations on the *Daily Mirror* margins gave an answer of thirty-six pounds. Which would never do, he swore to himself, because they'd be down on me like a ton of bricks, and the next week I'd be grabbing at the same flat-out lick for next to nowt. So he settled for a comfortable wage of fourteen pounds. Anything bigger than that would be like shovelling hard-earned money into the big windows of the income-tax office—feeding pigs on cherries, as mam used to say—which is something else against my principles.

So you earned your living in spite of the firm, the rate-checker, the foreman, and the tool-setters, who always seemed to be at each others' throats except when they ganged-up to get at yours, though most of the time you didn't give a sod about them but worked quite happily for a cool fourteen nicker, spinning the turret to chamfer in a smell of suds and steel, actions without thought so that all through the day you filled your mind with vivid and more agreeable pictures than those round about. It was an easier job than driving a lorry for instance where you had to have your wits about you—spin the turret and ease in the blade-chamfer with your right hand— and you remembered the corporal in the army who said what a marvel it was the things you thought of when you were on the lavatory, which was the only time you ever had to think. But now whole days could be given up to wool-gathering. Hour after hour quickly disappeared when once you started thinking, and before you knew where you were a flashing light from the foreman's office signalled ten o'clock, time for white-overalled women to wheel in tea-urns and pour out their wicked mash as fast as they could from a row of shining taps.

Arthur refused the firm's tea because it was strong, not from best Ceylon tips but from sweepings-up in the tea warehouse and the soda they doused it with in the canteen. One day he spilled some of their orange brew on a bench—thus went his story—and tried for three hours to rub out the stain, and even the ingenuity of the mechanics could make no inroads against the faint testament of unswallowable tea that stayed there as a warning to all who saw it, telling them to bring their own drink to work, though few bothered to take the hint. 'If it makes that stain on an old wooden bench covered with oil, what do you think it does to your guts?' Arthur asked his mates. 'It don't bear thinking about.' He complained at the head office about it and they listened to him. A director examined the canteen tea urns and found the insides coated with an even depth of tea and soda sediment. Because Arthur stood up for his rights a big noise was made, and thereafter the quality improved, though not enough to induce Arthur to drink it. He still came to the factory with a flask sticking out of his pocket, and took it out now after switching off his machine, because the light began flashing from Robboe's office, and men were unwrapping packets of sandwiches.

*   *   *

He walked over to Brenda's husband, Jack, who sat on his tool-setter's bench between a clamped-on vice and a carborundum wheel, a mug of the firm's tea in one hand and a cheese sandwich in the other; half the cheese sandwich was already in his mouth, and the other half was on its way there.

''Udge-up,' Arthur said, sitting beside him on the bench. 'Mek room for a rabbit-arse!'

'Don't knock my tea over,' Jack said.

Arthur unscrewed the cap from his flask and poured out a cup of scalding tea. 'Try a drop,' he offered. 'That stuff you've got'll give yer a bilious-bout.'

Jack unwrapped another sandwich. Arthur

45

had a big enough pack himself, but he wished Jack would offer him one, cut and spread by Brenda's own hands. Even if he did, I wouldn't take it, he cursed to himself. Christ, I'll give myself away one of these days.

'This tea's good enough for the others,' Jack said, 'so it's good enough for me. I'm not fussy.' His Monday-morning overalls were stiff and clean, with as yet only a few file-stains near the breast pocket, and his collarless plain blue shirt was fastened loosely by a stud at the neck. He had a young fresh-looking face of twenty-nine or thirty, but marred by a continual frown that subjected him to pitiless teasing by the men whose machines he looked after.

'Then you should be fussy,' Arthur said with deep conviction. 'Everybody should be fussy. Some blokes 'ud drink piss if it was handed to 'em in China cups.'

Jack's face relaxed. Not swearing himself, it didn't put him out to hear it from other people. 'No,' he said, 'they wouldn't go that far. I suppose I could get Brenda to make me a flask up in the mornings, but I don't want to put her to the trouble.'

'It's no trouble,' Arthur said, snapping a piece out of his sandwich.

'It might be, with two kids to look after.

Young Jacky's a bogger. He fell down the stairs yesterday afternoon.'

More quickly than was necessary, Arthur asked: 'Did he do hisself any damage?'

'A few bruises and screaming for two hours. But he's all right. He's like iron, if you ask me.'

Time to change the subject. Like treading on a haystack, he told himself, you dirty sinner. Will this be a quick enough change?

'How did you go on at the races?'

'All right. I won five quid.'

It was. 'Lucky bastard,' he swore. 'I put ten bob each way on the three-thirty at Redcar on Sat'day and I didn't get a penny back. I'll smash that bookie one of these days.'

'Why smash the bookie?' reasonable Jack asked. 'You're too superstitious. You either win or you don't. I don't believe in luck.'

Arthur screwed his sandwich paper into a ball and threw it across the gangway into somebody's work-box. 'Spot-on,' he cried. 'See that, Jack? Couldn't a done better if I'd 'ave aimed.'

'I don't think luck ever did anybody any good, in the end,' Jack went on.

'I do,' Arthur affirmed. 'Mostly I'm lucky and all. But sometimes I get a smack between the eyes. Not often though. So I'm

47

superstitious and I believe in luck.'

'You was only telling me you believed in communism the other week,' Jack said reproachfully, 'and now you talk about luck and superstition. The comrades wouldn't like that,' he ended with a dry laugh.

'Well,' Arthur said, his mouth full of second sandwich and tea, 'if they don't like it, they can lump it.'

'That's because you've got nowt to do wi' 'em.'

'I said I was as good as anybody else in the world, didn't I?' Arthur demanded. 'And I mean it. Do you think if I won the football pools I'd gi' yo' a penny on it? Or gi' anybody else owt? Not likely. I'd keep it all mysen, except for seeing my family right. I'd buy 'em a house and set 'em up for life, but anybody else could whistle for it. I've 'eard that blokes as win football pools get thousands o' beggin' letters, but yer know what I'd do if I got 'em? I'll tell yer what I'd do: I'd mek a bonfire on 'em. Because I don't believe in share and share alike, Jack. Tek them blokes as spout on boxes outside the factory sometimes. I like to hear 'em talk about Russia, about farms and power-stations they've got, because it's inter-estin', but when they say that when they get in government everybody's got to share and

48

share alike, then that's another thing. I ain't a communist, I tell you. I like 'em though, because they're different from these big fat Tory bastards in parliament. And them Labour bleeders too. They rob our wage packets every week with insurance and income tax and try to tell us it's all for our own good. I know what I'd like to do with the government. I'd like ter go round every factory in England with books and books of little numbers and raffle off the 'Ouses o' Parliament. "Sixpence a time, lads," I'd say. "A nice big 'ouse for the winner"—and then when I'd made a big packet I'd settle down somewhere with fifteen women and fifteen cars, that I would.

'But did I tell yer, Jack, I voted communist at the last election? I did it because I thought the poor bloke wouldn't get any votes. I allus like to 'elp the losin' side. You see, I shouldn't have voted either, because I was under twenty-one, but I used dad's vote because he was in bed wi' a bad back. I took 'is votin' card out of 'is coat pocket wi'out 'im knowin', and at the booth I towd the copper outside and the bloke at the desk inside that I was 'Arold Seaton and they didn't even bother to look at the card, and I went in and voted. Just like that. I didn't believe it mysen till I was outside again. I'd do owt like that though, I would.'

'You'd have got ten years in clink if they'd caught you,' Jack said. 'It's a serious thing. You were lucky.'

Arthur was triumphant. 'I told yer I was. But that's what all these looney laws are for, yer know: to be broken by blokes like me.'

'Don't be too cocky though,' Jack rebuked him. 'You might cop it, one day.'

'What for? Like gettin' married, you mean? I'm not that daft.'

Jack defended where Arthur had made him feel vulnerable: 'I'm not saying you are. Neither was I daft when I got married. I wanted to do it, that's all. I went into it wi' my eyes open. I like it, and all. I like Brenda, and Brenda likes me, and we get on well together. If you're good to each other, married life is all right.'

'I'll believe you then. Thousands wouldn't, though.'

Who would believe anyway that I was carrying on with his missis? One day he'll know, I suppose, but don't be too cocky, you cocky bastard. If you're too cocky your luck changes, so be careful. The worst of it is that I like Jack. Jack is a good bloke, one of the best. It's a pity it's such a cruel world. But he's one up on me because he sleeps with Brenda every night. I suppose I should keep on hoping he gets knocked down by a double-decker bus so that I can marry Brenda and sleep with her every night, but somehow I don't want him to get knocked down by a bus.

'I haven't told you this, have I?' Jack said gravely after a long pause of munching, as though something big and heavy had suddenly climbed up to his conscience.

Arthur wondered. Has he? Was it possible? His face looked thoughtful. What was it? No one could have told Jack about his carryings-on. Or could they, the nosey gossiping spies? Not much they couldn't. He does seem a bit funny this morning.

'What about, Jack?' he asked, screwing the top back on his flask.

'Nothing much. Only Robboe came up to me the other day and told me that I was to start on nights next week in the Press Shop. They're short-handed there and want another tool-setter. A week on nights and a week on days.'

'That's a bastard,' Arthur commiserated, thinking he was saying the right thing under the circumstances. 'I'm sorry, Jack.'

Then he saw his mistake. Jack was really happy at his transfer. 'I don't know about that. It'll mean a bit more money. Brenda's

51

been on about a television set lately, and I might be able to get her one like that.'

He accepted a cigarette from Arthur, who said: 'All the same, who am I going to talk to in tea-break?'

Jack laughed, a curious laugh, since the frown managed somehow to stay on his face. 'You'll be all right,' and slapped him—not very hard—on the shoulder, saying:

'I'll see you again.'

The light flashed: tea-break over.

*   *   *

I'm just too lucky for this world, Arthur told himself as he set his lathe going, too lucky by half, so I'd better enjoy it while I can. I don't suppose Jack's told Brenda yet about going on nights, but I'll bet she'll die laughing at the good news when he does. I might not see her at weekends, but I'll get there every night, which is even better. Turn to chamfer, then to drill, then blade-chamfer. Done. Take out and fix in a new piece, checking now and again for size because I'd hate to do a thousand and get them slung back at me by the viewers. Forty-five bob don't grow on trees. Turn to chamfer and drill, then blade-chamfer, swing the turret until my arms are

52

heavy and dead. Quick as lightning. Take out and fix in, shout for the trolley to take it away and bring more on, jotting down another hundred, not noticing the sud smells any more or belts over my head that gave me the screaming abdabs when I first came in the factory at fifteen, slapping and twisting and thumping and changing direction like Robboe the foreman's mind. It's a hard life if you don't weaken, so you grab like owt to earn a few quid, to take Brenda boozing and back to bed, or to the footpaths and woods up Strelley, passing the big council estate where Margaret my sister has a house and three kids from her useless husband, taking Brenda by all that to a broken-down shepherd's cottage that I've known since I was a kid and laying her on the straw and both of us so loving to each other that we can hardly wait. Only less of this or there'll be another handle on the lathe that I won't know what to do with and another gallon of suds that will jam the works. Time flies and no mistake, and it's about time it did because I've done another two hundred and I'm ready to go home and get some snap and read the *Daily Mirror* or look at what's left of the bathing tarts in the *Weekend Mail*. But Brenda, I can't wait to get at her. It serves you right, ducks, for being so lush and loving. And now this chamfer-blade wants sharpening, so I'll give it to Jack this afternoon. And it's too bad about him, but he'll be going on nights soon which is too bad as well, for him, because Brenda and me'll play merry hell in all the beds and nooks we can find. Bloomers flying, and legs waving in Strelley Woods, no matter how cold it gets.

*   *   *

The minute you stepped out of the factory gates you thought no more about your work. But the funniest thing was that neither did you think about work when you were standing at your machine. You began the day by cutting and drilling steel cylinders with care, but gradually your actions became automatic and you forgot all about the machine and the quick working of your arms and hands and the fact that you were cutting and boring and rough-threading to within limits of only five-thousandths of an inch. The noise of motor-trolleys passing up and down the gangway and the excruciating din of flying and flapping belts slipped out of your consciousness after perhaps half an hour, without affecting the quality of the work you were turning out, and you forgot your past conflicts with the gaffer and turned to thinking of pleasant events that had at some time happened to you, or things that you hoped would happen to you in the future. If your machine was working well—the motor smooth, stops tight, jigs good—and you spring your actions into a favourable rhythm you became happy. You went off into pipe-dreams for the rest of the day. And in the evening, when admittedly you would be feeling as though your arms and legs had been stretched to breaking point on a torture-rack, you stepped out into a cosy world of pubs and noisy tarts that would one day provide you with the raw material for more pipe-dreams as you stood at your lathe.

It was marvellous the things you remembered while you worked on the lathe, things that you thought were forgotten and would never come back into your mind, often things that you hoped would stay forgotten. Time flew while you wore out the oil-soaked floor and worked furiously without knowing it: you lived in a compatible world of pictures that passed through your mind like a magic-lantern, often in vivid and glorious loony-colour, a world where memory and imagination ran free and did acrobatic tricks with your past and with what might be your future, an amok that produced all sorts of agreeable visions. Like the corporal said about sitting on the lavatory: it was the only time you have to think, and to quote him further, you thought of some lovely and marvellous things.

*   *   *

When Arthur went back to work in the afternoon he needed only four hundred cylinders to complete his daily stint. If he cared he could slow down, but he was unable to take it easy until every cylinder lay clean and finished in the box at his lathe, unwilling to drop off speed while work was yet to be done. He turned out the four hundred in three hours, in order to pass a pleasant time doing a well-disguised nothing, looking as though he were busy, perhaps cleaning his machine or talking to Jack during the ostensible business of getting his tools sharpened. Cunning, he told himself gleefully, as he began the first hundred, dropping them off one by one at a respectable speed. Don't let the bastards grind you down, as Fred used to say when he was in the navy. Something about a carborundum wheel when he spouted it in Latin, but good advice just the same, though he didn't need to tell *me*. I'll never let anybody grind me down because I'm worth as much as

56

any other man in the world, though when it comes to the lousy vote they give me I often feel like telling 'em where to shove it, for all the good using it'll do me. But if they said: 'Look, Arthur, here's a hundred-weight of dynamite and a brand-new plunger, now blow up the factory,' then I'd do it, because that'd be something worth doing. Action. I'd bale-out for Russia or the North Pole where I'd sit and laugh like a horse over what I'd done, at the wonderful sight of gaffers and machines and shining bikes going skyhigh one wonderful moonlit night. Not that I've got owt against 'em, but that's just how I feel now and again. Me, I couldn't care less if the world did blow up tomorrow, as long as I'm blown up with it. Not that I wouldn't like to win ninety-thousand quid beforehand. But I'm having a good life and don't care about anything, and it'd be a pity to leave Brenda, all said and done, especially now Jack's been put on nights. Not that he minds, which is the funny part about it, because he's happy about a bigger pay-packet and a change, and I'm happy, and I know Brenda's happy. Everybody's happy. It's a fine world sometimes, if you don't weaken, or if you don't give the bastards a chance to get cracking with that carborundum.

57

Robboe the Gaffer passed along the gangway talking to a tool-setter. Robboe was a bloke of about forty who had been with the firm since he was fourteen, having signed on as an apprentice and put in a lot of time at night-school, a man who had not suffered the rigours of short-time before the war—as my old man had, thought Arthur—and who had been in a 'reserved occupation' during the war so that he had kept out of the army. He now drew about twenty a week plus a good production bonus, a quiet man with a square face, tortured-looking eyes and brow, thin rubbery lips, and one hand always in his pocket twiddling on a micrometer. Robboe kept his job because he was clever at giving you the right answers, and took back-chat with a wry smile and a good face as long as you did it with a brutal couldn't-care-less attitude and didn't seem frightened of him. A terror to men like Jack, to Arthur he was a human being afflicted with the heavy lead-weight of authority when a rebellion always seemed on the point of breaking out.

Arthur started with the firm as a messenger boy, carrying samples of bicycle parts from one branch of the factory to another, or doing errands around the city on a carrier-bike. He was fifteen at the time and every Thursday morning Robboe sent him on a mysterious errand to a chemist's shop downtown, giving him a sealed envelope with a note and some money inside. Arthur reached the shop after an interesting and idling ride along canal banks and through narrow streets, and the chemist handed him a stronger brown envelope containing something flat and sponge-like, and the change from the money in the first envelope. After three months of such journeys Arthur discovered what Robboe sent him to buy, because one morning the chemist was in too much of a hurry to see that the envelope was firmly sealed. So Arthur was able to open it while waiting for the traffic-lights to change, to see what was inside, and seal it again, this time securely. He found what he had expected to find, and rode his bike back along Castle Boulevard laughing like a maniac, overtaking buses, milkcarts, even cars in his furious speed. Everyone stared at him, as if he had gone mad. 'Three packets!' he shouted out. 'The dirty bogger! He's got a fancy-woman! Nine times a week!' So the news broke in the shop, and long afterwards, when Arthur had been taken off the messenger job and put on a drill, if he left his machine to walk out to the lavatory, someone would shout: 'Where are you going, Arthur?'

And if Robboe was not in the shop he would yell back at the top of his voice: 'I'm going downtown to get Robboe's rubbers!'—in his broad, deliberately brutalised Robin Hood accent that brought screams of laughter from the women, and guffaws from the men.

Robboe stopped at his machine, picked up a piece of finished work, and checked its size carefully with a micrometer.

Arthur paused while turning the capstan. 'All right?' he asked belligerently.

Robboe, always with a cigarette in his mouth, blew smoke away from his eyes, and ash fell on to his brown overall-coat. He made the last measurement with a depth-gauge. 'Yes,' he said. 'Nothing wrong'—and walked off.

Arthur and Robboe tolerated and trusted each other. The enemy in them stayed dormant, a black animal stifling the noise of its growls as if commanded by a greater master to lie low, an animal that had perhaps been passed on for some generations from father to son on either side. They respected this lineage in each other, recognised it when they asked or answered tersely the few brusque questions that passed between them, speaking with loud mouths and passionless eyes.

Robboe had a car—admitted, an ancient

Morris—and a semi-detached in a posh district, and Arthur held these pretensions against him because basically they were of equal stock, and he would therefore have felt friendlier had Robboe lived in the same kind of four-roomed house as himself. For Robboe was in no way better than him, he ruminated, spinning the turret and lightly applying its chamfer-tool to one of the last dozen cylinders of the day, and no better than anybody else if it came to that. Arthur did not assess men on their knowledge or achievement, but by a blind and passionate method that weighed their more basic worth. It was an emotional gauge, always accurate when set by him, and those to whom it was applied either passed or did not pass the test. Within the limits of its narrow definitions he used it as a reliable guide as to who was and who was not his friend, and up to what point he could trust a person who might become his friend.

So when Arthur looked at a man, or heard the inflexion in his voice, or saw him walk, he made a snap judgment that turned out to be as accurate as one made after weeks of acquaintance. His first assessment of Robboe had never altered. In fact it had gained ground. His half-conscious conclusions proved to him that no one man was better than the other in this particular case, that they shared with plain openness a world of enmity that demanded a certain amount of trust. And Arthur did not doubt that Robboe had applied a similar test to him, with the same conclusions. So the respect they had for each other was based on a form of judgment that neither could give words to.

Whenever Arthur looked into somebody's face and screwed up his brows to look black and cunning, and shouted: 'I've got yo' weighed-up'—the chances were that he really did have their main characteristics balanced nicely on the scales in his mind, though he could explain neither the mechanism of the scales nor the nature of the goods that kept each pan level.

Reactions varied to his remark. When he said it to one of his mates, perhaps in a quarrel over a box of work rejected at the viewers' table, they would reply in an equally knowing and stentorian voice: 'That's what yo' think.' When someone said to Arthur: 'I've got yo' weighed-up,' his stock reply was: 'Oh, 'ev yer? Then ye'r bloody clever mate, because I ain't got meself weighed-up, I can tell yer'—which was equally effective in shutting them up, and perhaps equally truthful in that though everybody might have the ability to weigh-up others, it never occurred to them to attempt a weighing-up of themselves. Arthur had stumbled on this lack from which all seemed to suffer, though as yet he had not thought of applying it with any great force to himself.

But despite his aptitude for weighing people up, Arthur had never quite weighed-up Jack the tool-setter. Perhaps the fact that he was Brenda's husband made him appear more complicated than other men. Certainly he was of the same sort as Arthur, never pretended otherwise, and he might normally have weighed him up like a shot, but somehow the essential ramifications of Jack's character evaded him. Jack was timid in many ways, a self-contained man who did not give much of himself away. He chipped-in with his share of the talking, yet never shouted or swore or boozed like a fish, or even got mad no matter how much the gaffers got on his nerves; he never opened his mind so that you could take a squint inside and see what he was made of. Arthur did not even know whether or not Jack had any idea he was carrying-on with his wife. Perhaps he had, and perhaps he hadn't, but if he had, then he was a sly bastard for not speaking out. He was the sort that might suspect or even have definite proof that you were knocking-on with his wife for

63

months and not take you up on it until he was good and ready. In fact he might never take you up on it, a mistake on his part, for if ever he did Arthur would give Brenda back, which was one of the rules of his game.

But, all said and done, if he was carrying-on with Jack's wife then it served Jack right. Arthur classified husbands into two main categories: those that looked after their wives, and those that were slow. Jack fell into the latter class, one that Arthur, from experience, knew to be more extensive than the first. Having realised this quickly he had been lucky in love, and had his fun accordingly, making hay while the sun shone, growing-up from the age of seventeen with the idea that married women were certainly the best women to know. He had no pity for a 'slow' husband. There was something lacking in them, not like a man with one leg that could in no way be put right, but something that they, the slow husbands, could easily rectify if they became less selfish, brightened up their ideas, and looked after their wives a bit better. For Arthur, in his more tolerant moments, said that women were more than ornaments and skivvies: they were warm wonderful creatures that needed and deserved to be looked after, requiring all the attention a man could give, certainly more than the man's work and a man's own pleasure. A man gets a lot of pleasure anyway from being nice to a woman. Then on the other hand there were women who wouldn't let you be nice to them, women with battleship faces and hearts as tough as nails who rattle a big fist at you and roar: 'Do this, do that, do the other, or else'—and you could try all you liked to be kind to them, but they wouldn't have any of it. It'd been better if they'd have been born men, then they'd do less damage and cause less misery: they'd be called-up in a war and get killed, or get slung in clink for saying: 'Down with this, and down with that,' from soap-boxes. They were the sort of women who thought you were barmy if you tried to love 'em, and they just didn't understand what love was, and all you could do was end up by giving them a smack in the chops. Hopeless and barmy. But I reckon that mostly women want you to love 'em and be nice to 'em, and that even if they didn't they'd start to love you back after a bit. Make a woman enjoy being in bed with you—that's a big part of the battle—then you were well on the way to keeping her with you for good. Christ, that's the best thing I've ever done, to make sure a woman got her fun as well as me getting mine. God knows how it dawned on me. I don't. Then again though, a man likes a drink, and if a woman didn't like a man who drank, then it was going to be touch-and-go, whichever way you looked at it. Which is my big trouble, and why I'm not so cocksure about everything, in the end, and why I have to be careful and find the most loving women of all—nearly always married women who don't get much love, who have slow husbands.

And so it was possible to forget the factory, whether inside it sweating and straining your muscles by a machine, or whether swilling ale in a pub or loving Brenda in her big soft bed at the weekend. The factory did not matter. The factory could go on working until it blew itself up from too much speed, but I, he thought, already a couple of dozen above his daily stint, will be here after the factory's gone, and so will Brenda and all women like her still be here, the sort of women that are worth their weight in gold.

CHAPTER THREE

IN the few minutes that passed between regaining consciousness and opening his eyes he knew that he was too ill to go to work. From time to time he intended getting out of bed to see how he really felt, but it was eleven o'clock before this was possible. Downstairs he found the filled teapot cold on the table where his mother had left it before going shopping. He did not know what was wrong as he walked bare-footed around the room. He picked up the *Daily Mirror* and, seeing no good-looking women on the front page, turned to the middle. A nice bathing-suit, anyway. Throwing the paper down, he went into the coal-place under the stairs to fill the bucket.

His mother came in, her arms weighed down with groceries.

'I *thought* you was badly,' she said, seeing him sitting with a pale face by the fire, 'that's why I let you stay in bed.'

'My guts are rotten,' he complained.

'Bilious trouble,' she said, a common label given to all such complaints. A common cure, when she had unloaded her baskets in the scullery, was to fetch sixpennyworth of Indian brandy from the shop across the street.

She trudged hurriedly up the yard, her arms folded and drawn tightly together in the cold. In summer months they were held more loosely across her thin chest. This picture went through Arthur's mind as he stayed by the fire, hearing to himself the click of her black, glossy, underslung shoes as she crossed the cobbled street. 'Sixpennyworth of Indian brandy, Mr. Taylor,' she would say, entering the shop. Old Tightfist, thought Arthur. 'Nice thing to come for on a morning like this,' the shopkeeper would say, measuring it out in drops. Arthur knew his mother would rather have risked short measure than be kept waiting, but a dee-dahed tune and a blank look through his frosted window would speed Tightfist's actions up for her. Unmade-up and thin, her face at fifty-odd had enough lines, not scored with age like an old woman's, but crease-marked in the right places through too much laughing and crying. By God she had worked and hadn't had a good life until the war, and Arthur knew it. When Seaton's face grew black for lack of fags she had trotted around to the various shops asking for some on tick till Thursday dole-day. But just as Seaton nowadays had endless packets of

Woodbines and a TV panel, so she had access to week after week of solid wages that stopped worry at the source and gave her a good enough life, and put real brightness into her bright blue-grey eyes as she asked, whenever she felt like it at the Co-op, for a pound of this and a pound of that. 'Anybody badly, Mrs. Seaton?' Arthur could imagine Old Tightfist asking her. He had a blank face of forty, was dead-set in his ways, and nosy like a nark. She would unfold her arms and take the purse from her pina-pocket: 'It's Arthur's stomach again. That factory's not a bit o' good to anybody on God's earth.' Young-looking and hair-creamed, Tightfist would hold up the sixpennorth of brandy and tell himself he must put more water in it when she'd gone. 'I wouldn't think so,' he no doubt said, slipping the glass-stopper back. 'I've never worked there myself. I was a traveller, you know. But grease is bad, I will say that.' She was only half grey as yet. Halfway between fair and brown, Arthur said her hair was. His old man's had been as black as the ace of spades. 'Do you think this'll do him much good?' she would ask. 'The poor bogger woks too 'ard, if you ask me. He's a good lad, though. Allus 'as bin. Don't know what I'd do wi'out 'im.' That's what Arthur knew she would say.

'Don't know of owt better.' Tightfist would think about the time Arthur came in his shop and played on the fruit-machine. I stuffed penny after penny into the slot, Arthur at the fire thought, and when it stopped at three lemons at last, the kitty didn't fall out. Not a farthing. So when Old Tightfist said he couldn't do owt about it I thumped it in the side until it started coughing, and twelve-and-fourpence crashed into my lap.

He waited for her, saw her walk down the yard, heard the latch click as she came in with her small medicinal load.

'Here you are,' she said. 'I'll soon get yer well.'

He drank the brandy and felt doubly better by giving an imitation before the mirror of Bill Hickock knocking it back in a Wild West saloon, and the sickness brought on by too much breathing of suds and grease in the factory gradually left him. He called out urgently for a chaser of tea, and his mother made a hot strong cup with plenty of sugar and rich Co-op cream from the pint-bottle top that she took from the outside window-ledge, an efficient mash through two dozen years of practice. He stayed by the fire while she cooked the dinner, reading the *Daily Mirror* in a smell of cabbage, and looking occasionally out of the breath and frost-smeared window at the long ramshackle backyards, at women coming home with their shopping, and at his mother nipping out through the scullery door now and again to tip some rubbish into the dustbin, or to have a few-minute gossip at the yard-end with old Ma Bull.

It was a good, comfortable life if you didn't weaken, safe from the freezing world in a warm snug kitchen, watching the pink and prominent houses of the opposite terrace. He could have laughed. From time to time it was fine to feel unwell and have a day off work, to sit by the fire reading and drinking tea, waiting for them to get cracking with something good on television. He did not know why he felt ill. Last night he was drinking with Brenda at the Athletic Club, though he hadn't put back enough to cause an upset stomach. This made him ask: Did I really feel badly this morning? But his conscience was untroubled: his wages would not suffer, and he always kept his work at the factory at least one day's supply ahead of those who waited for it. So there was nothing to worry about. His stomach was better now, and he drew his white bony foot back from the red heat of the blazing fire.

With a silk-scarf covering his Windsor-knotted tie he walked towards Wollaton hoping to meet Brenda on her way to the Athletic Club. He preferred to lean against a fence rather than trudge around dismal lanes, and from where he stood he saw that the surface of Martin's Pond was frozen. Last night Brenda did not know whether she would come or not: only perhaps, and the wording sounded so uncertain in the soft tenderness of saying good-bye that he had forgotten all about her until tea-time.

Five struck by Wollaton clock, its sound chipping the cold air, nipping in strides over the pond where children, on their way home from school, shouted and slid and threw stones at astonished ducks that rose up from clumps of reed-grass and flew with flapping wings into trees and the hedges of allotment gardens. He stood by the fence looking along the side of the wood, one hand thrust deep into the pocket of his long draped overcoat. Nearly always, while waiting for a woman to turn up, he played a game, saying to himself: 'Well, I don't suppose she'll come.' Or: 'Well, she won't be on *this* bus'—as it came around the bend and drew into the stop. Or: 'She won't come for another quarter of an hour yet'—expecting a pleasant surprise as she walked suddenly towards him. Sometimes he won, and sometimes he didn't.

Several people alighted from the bus, yet he could not see her. He tried to penetrate the window, top deck and lower deck, but they were steamed over with breath and smoke. Perhaps Jack will get off: the possibility amused him, and he laughed outright at the thought of it. More than a month ago Brenda had said: 'What shall I say to Jack if he asks me why I go to the club so often?' And he answered jokingly: 'Tell him you're in the darts team.' When next they met, she had said: 'I told him I play darts at the club, and he seemed to think it was all right.' 'Anything satisfies them if they get jealous,' he had replied. But some weeks later she had told him: 'Jack said he would come up to the club one of these nights to see if I really played darts. He joked about wanting to see me win the championship cup.' 'Let him come, then,' Arthur said.

And he thought the same now. She was not on it. The engine revved-up so loudly that the brittle twigs and tree branches seemed afraid of the silence that followed, making Arthur feel colder still and unable to hear the kids playing on the pond. Brenda came three times a week to the club when Jack was on nights, leaving Jacky and his sister with a neighbour's girl who earned a shilling for her trouble and was given a wink that told her not to say anything to a living soul. Arthur hoped that the dart story would be good for another few weeks. Turning his back on the bus that drove towards Wollaton, he stared again at the kids hooting and ice-sliding in the dusk.

She stepped off the next bus, paused at the roadside for a car to pass, then made her way across to him. He knew she had seen him but he stayed in the shadow of the hedge. She walked in short quick steps, coat fastened tight, hands in pockets, a woollen scarf drawn incongruously around her neck. He didn't go too far out of the hedge's cover but called her name when she was a few yards off. He wanted to be careful. You never knew. Jack might be trailing her. Not that he was afraid for himself—if it came to a show he knew he could hold his own with anybody: over six feet tall, just turned twenty-two, and bags of strength always to be drawn from somewhere—but if they were caught Brenda would be the one to pay. Be careful, and you won't go far wrong, he thought.

He went out to meet her, taking hold of her and drawing her into the shadows. 'Hello, duck,' he said, kissing her on the cheek. 'How are you?'

She came close and he put his arms around her. 'I'm all right, Arthur,' she said softly, as if she would have given the same answer had she not been all right. A white blouse showed below her scarf when he put his hand down near her warm breasts. She carried the easy and comfortable smell of a woman who had been in a hurry and was now relaxing from the worry of it, exuding warmth and a slight powdery perspiration that excited him. She must be thirty, he thought if she's a day. 'Did you get away from Jack all right?' he asked, releasing her.

'Of course. I told him I was going to the club to play darts again.' She was ill at ease, so he pulled her to him and held her more gently than before. It did not seem right that a woman should worry overmuch. He wanted all her troubles for himself at that moment. It was easy. He had only to take them and, having no use for them, throw them away.

'What did he say?'

'That he might be down later.' She spoke with her warm breath against his mouth.

'He allus says that, but he never comes.

75

Besides, he's on nights, ain't he?'

'Yes.' She would not have felt safe had he been ten thousand miles away. It's only natural though, he thought, putting both arms around her and kissing her tenderly on the mouth.

'Don't worry, duck, he wain't come. You'll be all right wi' me.' He pulled up her coat collar and fastened the scarf properly around her neck, then lit two cigarettes, placing one between her lips. They walked up the dark quiet tree-lined lane on their way to the club building. He told her how long he stood there before she came, making a joke of it, saying it was like waiting for a football match to start on the wrong day, saying many wild things to make her laugh. There was a wood on one side of the lane, and after more jokes and kisses, they went into it through a gap in the hedge.

Arthur prided himself on knowing the wood like the back of his hand. There was a lake in the middle where he used to swim when young. A sawmill on the wood's flank was set like the camp of an invader that ate slowly into it, though a jungle of trees still remained, that could be put to good use by Arthur on such nights as these.

He knew he was hurting her, squeezing her

wrist as he led her deeper into the wood, but it did not occur to him to relax his hold. Trees and bushes crowding around in the darkness made him melancholy. One minute he thought he was holding her wrist so tightly because he was in a hurry to find a good dry place; then he felt it was because there was something about her and the whole situation that made him want to hurt her, something to do with the way she was deceiving Jack. Even though he, now leading her to a spot that suddenly came into his mind, would soon be enjoying it, he thought: 'Women are all the same. If they do it to their husbands they would do it to you if you gave them half the chance.' He trod on a twig that sent a cracking sound circling the osier-lined indistinct banks of dark water below. Brenda gasped as some bush-leaves swept by her face; he had not bothered to warn her.

The ground was hard and dry. They walked over a hump clear of bushes, the roof of a concealed tunnel burrowed into the earth and strengthened with pit-props, an air-raid shelter for the sawmill men during the war. He now held her hand lightly as she walked behind, considerate and tender again, telling her when to avoid a bush, or a tree-root sticking out of the ground.

There were no more paths in the wood than the clear and definite lines on Arthur's palms, and he easily found the dry and enclosed place he had in mind. He took off his overcoat and laid it on the ground. 'We's'll be comfortable 'ere,' he said softly.

Brenda spoke, the first time since entering the wood: 'Won't you be cold?'

Hearing her so solicitous, he could hardly wait for what was to come. He laughed out loud. 'No fear. This is nothing to what we had to put up with in the army. And I hadn't got you with me then to keep me warm, duck!'

She put her arms around him, and allowed him to unbutton her coat. He smelled again the smell of a woman whose excitement at doing something she considered not quite right was but one step from the hasty abandonment of making love. He felt the hardness of the imitation pearl brooch against her blouse, and then the buttons themselves, and they lay down on the spot where he had carefully placed his overcoat. They forgot the cold soil and towering trees, and lost themselves in a warm passion in the comfortable silence of a wood at night, that smelled of primeval vegetation, a wood wherein no one could discover your secrets, or kill the delight that a man and a woman generate between them on an overcoat in the darkness.

*   *   *

Back on the lane it needed a few hundred yards to reach the club-house, through a tunnel of bent-over trees with the lights of paradise at the other end. Brenda took his arm, and they joked, talked, smoked cigarettes, felt lovable and agreeable towards each other, as though a great deal of care had been lifted from them.

But Arthur's gaiety lapsed by the tennis courts, and both became sad, as if they had taken on a happiness that could not be sustained. Brenda walked with head slightly bent, starting when she stepped on a patch of ice. Arthur thought again about Jack, this time with a feeling of irritation that he should be so weak as to allow his wife to go off with other men. It was funny how often you felt guilty at taking weak men's wives; with the strong men's you have too much to fear, he reasoned.

Did Jack know? he wondered. Of course he did. Of course he did not. Yet if he doesn't know by now he will never know. He must know: no man is that batchy. He must have been told. Arthur had no positive reason for thinking that he knew, yet relied on the accuracy of his total 'weighings-up' from meetings with Jack and the reports of Brenda. But you could never be sure. Not that it would matter either way, as long as Jack didn't object to it. There wasn't much he could do about it: he would never make a divorce. It would cost too much, one way or another. And no woman is worth making a divorce over.

He felt that Jack might be trying to find out for sure what was going on, and that perhaps he might already be at the club waiting for Brenda to arrive. The idea grew stronger, surfaced like a definite warning to his lips. Near the last turn of the hedge he said: 'Look, duck, I'm just going on in front to see if Jack's at the club. He won't be there, I suppose, but I'm going to make sure, so wait for me. I won't be long.'

She did not argue, but stayed behind, smoking a cigarette he had lit for her. He walked along the gravel drive and in through the gates. He stood by the bottom step, tall enough to look in the windows, trying to see as far as the bar, glad at his good luck that he could see everybody inside, while they could not see him standing there in the darkness. Jack sat by the far window—looking straight at him, as a matter of fact—alone at a table, his hand resting by a half-finished pint. Arthur watched him, feeling a sudden deep interest that would not let him move. He saw a man walk up to Jack, pat him on the back, say something to him in true matey style, and walk away again. Jack shrugged his shoulders, and picked up the glass in a desultory fashion to finish his pint.

So the bastard had really come at last! Arthur was unable to move. Surprise and curiosity fastened him to the hard soil, his eyes a camera that slowly fitted the picture into his brain. Then he remembered Brenda waiting for him down the lane, and with a sudden movement turned and walked away, feeling sprightly and happy as his blood raced once more and his shoes crunched on the gravel, as if he were just coming away from a long and satisfying part.

He found her where he had left her, standing like a shadow among the other shadows of the hedge. He would not have seen her in fact had she not moved slightly to indicate that she was there. He was so happy he would have walked right back to the main road without knowing what he was doing. He turned towards the hedge in a half-circle, as though he was a vehicle being steered by another person.

'I was freezing,' she said, half morosely, half regretfully, as though she had been blaming him for it and was now sorry. He told her to start walking with him along the lane, back towards the bus stop. 'Why?' she wanted to know.

'Because Jack's in the club.'

She didn't seem surprised. 'Did he see you?'

'Not me,' he said. She asked what they would do now. 'You're going home,' he said firmly. 'It's the best thing to do. I'll put you on the bus, then go back myself to the club for a drink or two, just to show my face.'

'What if Jack asks where I went tonight?'

'Say you went to your sister's for an hour, that you had a headache and didn't feel like going to the club.'

It was simple and explicit, because he had not thought about it. If he gave things too much thought they did not turn out so well. She understood, and they kissed good night near the end of the lane. She was warm again after the quick walk from the club. 'I'm sorry it went wrong,' he said at the bus stop, 'but I'll see you tomorrer night, duck.'

'That's all right. We had our bit of love, though, didn't we?'

'We did,' he whispered. 'I love you, Brenda.'

82

The bus came, stopped, sped away down the dark road, and he watched until its rear-light turned a corner.

He walked back up the lane, alone, with a tremendous feeling of elation and freedom, hardly able to believe it belonged to him, wanting to dance between the tree-shadows. Through gaps in over-arching branches he could see the stars. He sang and whistled and his happiness showed him the way like a lighted candle and protected him from the blackening frost of the night.

He was feeling so good in fact that it took him a mere ten minutes to get back to the club. He walked up the wooden steps—that felt unsafe because he seemed giant-sized with optimism—and pushed open the door, seeing at once that Jack was still sitting in the same place, the only difference being that his pint jar was now empty and he had not yet bothered to have it refilled.

There weren't more than a dozen men in the club, because it was a late week-day night, and wages had spilled out of the bottomless can of beer and cigarette prices. The bar-keeper and caretaker, dressed sprucely in a white jacket provided by the firm, was playing darts, a popular man at the game not because he had a particularly good aim, but because he had a fine head for keeping scores, a gift that he had developed in his job. Arthur had once reckoned-up the dart scores, and the barkeeper at the end of the evening had detected several mistakes, all very much to Arthur's advantage. 'I don't know,' the barkeeper had cried, 'you can't reckon owt up for tuffey-apples. I thought you'd come down from three-o-one too quick.' 'That's because I'm a numb-skull,' Arthur winked. 'I was never any good outside a bookie's shop.'

He now unhesitatingly walked across the room and sat at Jack's table, patting him warmly on the shoulder before taking off his overcoat and settling down for a drink. The good feeling from the lane had diminished in intensity, though the backwash of its elation lingered. 'How are you, Jack? I haven't seen you for two years: two weeks, at least.'

Jack greeted him coldly, looking up and giving a brief hello. If he one day thought to rip the mask of anxiety from his face he would be good-looking, for he had regular features and should have looked young for his age. Arthur noticed his bicycle clips, fastened in neatly to his overalls at the ankle. 'I thought you were on nights?' he demanded in gruff friendliness.

'I am.' Like all worried men Jack gave a

forthright answer to questions, too busy worrying to equivocate. 'Only I thought I'd come up here for a drink first. I can go in at ten o'clock. I'm not so busy as I was in the turnery.'

And also, for the same reason, it was hard to get him to talk much. 'How's Brenda these days?' No use not asking about her, he thought. Otherwise he'd twig something.

Jack looked at him, then turned his eyes away to the bar when Arthur met his stare with ingenuous grey eyes and a half, know-nothing smile. 'She's all right.'

'Is her cold better?' Arthur wondered whether he should have said this, whether he had not overdone it.

'She hasn't got a cold,' Jack said with a trace of resentment. He hardly ever looked at the person to whom he was talking, always at the bar, at other empty tables, at a row of machines, or a blank wall.

Arthur said: 'I thought somebody said she had,' and asked the barkeeper to bring two pints of beer, one for Jack, and one for himself.

'Thanks,' Jack said, not so cool now. 'I mustn't drink too much though, because I don't want to fall asleep on the job.'

Arthur had so many different feelings at

85

first, sitting with Jack after having been into the wood with his wife, that he did not know what feeling was the most definite. It was hard to know what to say next with such varied thoughts coming into your head. He asked how the kids were these days, and thought again that perhaps he was overdoing it.

'They're all right,' Jack told him. 'The eldest'll be at school soon. Less for Brenda to do.'

That's a good thing, Arthur thought, and couldn't stop himself from saying it. He took a long drink of beer.

'She'll have more time to herself,' Jack agreed.

'This ale's like piss,' Arthur said loudly, hoping to draw the dart players into some diverting banter and force the conversation away from Brenda and Jack's kids. It struck him as strange that when you were with a man whose wife you were doing you couldn't stop talking about her, though it occurred to him that Jack was doing a good half of it too. They were both to blame. I suppose he knows something then, he thought sadly.

The dart players would not bite the bait he had thrown out, so he was left to cope with the compact mass of Jack's mind himself, and it suddenly began to bother him, almost to the point of making him wish he had got on the same bus and gone home with Brenda. They talked about fishing, Arthur saying he hoped the thaw would come soon so that he could get on his bike of a Sunday morning and go out to Cotgrave, or beyond Trowel Bridge. 'You can't beat it up there,' he said, 'the fish bite like hungry niggers. They can't wait to get their chops on the 'ook. Queue for miles. I know a place with some owd lime-kilns where you can go if it rains.'

But Jack, unlike the fish, like the dart players, did not bite either. It was certainly taking something on to get him to talk. Arthur shouted out for two more pints, but the more Jack drank, he discovered, the less he opened his mouth to say things. 'What's up, Jack, my owd bird?' he exclaimed loudly, leaning across and patting him again on the shoulder, as he often did at work when Jack was bent over his bench sharpening somebody's drill. 'Why don't yer cheer up? You look as if you've got summat on yer mind.'

It was apparently the right thing to do and say, because Jack smiled, the first time that evening, and the tight expression of worry momentarily left his face. 'I'm all right,' he said in a friendly voice. Arthur wondered what would be said and done if he suddenly told Jack how the position really stood between himself and Brenda. Out of friendship, out of the feeling of being pals, he almost made up his mind to it. It's a rotten trick, he argued to himself, to play on your mate. Just for a bit of love.

The worried expression returned to Jack's face, as if he was weighing the balance of some trouble—what trouble? wondered Arthur—one minute, and trying to guess whether or not anything were really happening the next. Arthur wanted to shake his hand and tell him everything, tell him how good he thought he—Jack—was, that he had guts and that he was all right, that he didn't like to see him suffer because of a looney thing like this, of a woman coming between them.

Instead, he drew him into a conversation about football, and over their third pint Jack was declaiming on how Notts would get into the second division next year. Everyone at the club put in their various pieces of knowledge, using imagination when knowledge failed. Arthur had little to say, and ordered more pints for himself and Jack, feeling good and generous at buying beer for Brenda's husband. All the same he kept on thinking, Jack's a good bloke. It's hard luck that things stand the way they do.

'Bolton's centre-forward's got the best kick and aim o' the lot on 'em, I don't care what you say' Jack cried, up to his neck in it now. Arthur had never seen him less worried.

The bartender cried back, shaking his thin face: 'I don't believe yer, Jack. It stands ter reason they can't get it this year.'

'No more do I,' the other dart player put in. 'They can play for another ten years and they wain't get it, I can tell yer that, Jack.'

They were warmed-up to the argument, supping at pints and friendly in their speculations, each full of hope that he would be the man with the right prophecy.

'But you've got to think of last week's transfer from Hull,' Jack said, arguing skilfully, taking the other pint that the barkeeper passed to his table. Arthur watched him, thankful that certain laws existed to prevent you from seeing into each other's mind, that things were marvellous that way.

'It don't mek no bit o' difference,' the barkeeper insisted, 'not wi' fifty bloody transfers.'

'What about Worrel and Jackson? You can't say they wain't mek any difference.'

Arthur listened in a dreamlike way, happy from the beer he had drunk, dimly remembering the cold earth of the dark wood where he had lain with Brenda, hours ago: he had heard all about football before.

He reflected, fingering what he decided would have to be his last pint if he were not to begin a real bout and fall into a hedge-bottom on the way home, that it was just Jack's bad luck. Either you had it in for you, or you didn't He told himself that he would make the best of it, stack hay while the sun shone. Brenda was a good woman to know, and he wouldn't stop until things cracked up, as they must, he didn't doubt, sometime, one way or another.

He was easier in his mind now that Jack had forgotten his troubles and was arguing on football. Life indeed seemed to be more rosy. He put on his overcoat, ready to leave, saying good night to the others, then to Jack. But Jack had forgotten him, was so lost in brilliant and defiant debate that he hardly noticed him go.

The cold air bit into Arthur as he stood on the steps fastening his coat buttons. It was even colder now—good weather for steadying the few pints in your stomach—but soon the gate of the new year would swing open and it would be fine enough to take Brenda out on long walks to Strelley Woods and Cossal

Fields, to spend secretive long evenings together in warm spring air.

The club steps creaked as he descended on to the path. Looking behind, he saw them still going at it hammer-and-tongs, gesticulating over the tables, laughing and drinking, their voices floating over the grass lawns and tennis courts, strangled there by the bitter cold.

Walking out of the lights, he couldn't help giving one great horse-laugh in the darkness. Its sound echoed around him, seemed to rest upon the tarpaulined roof of the club-house, and slide out of sight down the other side of its sloping roof. He would be seeing Brenda to-morrow night. He lit a cigarette and whistled a tune as he walked. The thought made him feel good.

Too deeply engrossed in it, and straying too close to the side of the lane, he tripped over a tree-root. A dozen curses raced from between his lips as he righted himself. Then he laughed, and walked on.

CHAPTER FOUR

ROBBOE came in with the wages, walking from bench to bench, machine to machine, with hundreds of small brown envelopes packed one against the other in a long narrow box. It was a friendly hour: he smiled and made dry jokes, was a different man from the stern efficient mechanic who at other times walked the gangways twiddling a micrometer in his wide deep pocket. Groaning belts and pulley-wheels slackened, as though feeling the approach of a weekend's silence and idleness, and despite their still overpowering noise Arthur fancied he could hear traffic passing by on Eddison Road, and loaded trucks struggling out of the nearby marshalling yard.

Pressing the stop-button of his motor, production ceased, and with broad calloused hands he scooped steel shavings from the tray and crushed them into a wooden box with his boot, ready for the trolley to take away and deposit on the lane outside. He set to cleaning his machine: army spit-and-polish that left it gleaming, flicking half-hidden shavings into the light, and drawing a length of clean cotton waste between drills and chamfer-chucks. He rubbed hard on the feed-pipe, unfolding an attractive utility grey, polishing the turret and lathe handles, his long body bending, working leisurely but whistling a quick-jig tune, thinking of the world outside, of shining sun at dinnertime, and wondering if it would have any guts left when he knocked-off at half-past five. It was impossible to tell from where he was: the small windows placed high up along the wall were too black to show much daylight.

'Now then,' Robboe said, suddenly by his side. 'If you'll just spare me a minute I'll give you your wages.'

Arthur stood up to wipe his hands clean with a piece of cotton waste, smiling sardonically. 'I shan't say no, Mester Robboe.'

'You'll be the first one as ever did,' he laughed.

'How much this week?'—though like all pieceworkers he knew the exact number of pound notes folded into his packet.

Robboe spoke in a hushed voice: 'Fourteen. It's more than the tool-setters get. I'll be in trouble one of these days for letting you earn so much. They'll be lowering your price if you're not careful.'

It was a subtle warning, and Arthur braced himself against it, saying gruffly: 'Not if I know it, they wain't.'

Robboe went chuntering on: 'When I first started here I went home on a Friday night with seven-and-tuppence in my pocket. And now look at you. Fourteen quid. It's a fortune.'

'That's what yo' think. In them days yer could get a packet o' fags for tuppence, and a pint of ale for threepence. And just look at what the sods do to me'—he held up his wage-packet and read: '"Income Tax, two pounds eighteen and a tanner." It ain't right. That's munney I've earned. I know what I'd like to do wi' 'em.'

'You can't blame the firm for that, though,' Robboe said, lighting a cigarette now that he was at the end of his work. 'You shouldn't grab so much.'

'Grab be boggered. I earn it. Every penny on it. You can't deny that.'

Robboe had a genuine respect for hard work. 'I'm not saying you don't. But just keep it quiet. I wouldn't like anybody to know what you're taking home. They'd all be at my throat asking for a wage raise. Then I'd get my cards, I can tell you.'

He walked away, and Arthur slipped the wage-packet into his overall pocket. Truce time was over. The enemy's scout was no longer near. For such was Robboe's label in Arthur's mind, a policy passed on by his father. Though no strong cause for open belligerence existed as in the bad days talked about, it persisted for more subtle reasons that could hardly be understood but were nevertheless felt, and Friday afternoon was a time when different species met beneath white flags, with wage-packets as mediators, when those who worked in the factory were handed proof of their worth, which had increased considerably in market value since the above-mentioned cat-and-dog ideas had with reason taken root.

When the light flashed at half-past five Arthur joined the thousands that poured out through the factory gates. The sun was pale and weak, barely shining in the chill April air. He walked without thinking towards home, and caught up with his father as he turned in by the yard-end. The round full face of Mrs. Bull, the flattened nose, thin wide lips, and short greying hair, made a permanent gargoyle at the yard-end, a sardonic fixture familiar to everybody that passed. She lived in one of the terrace houses, nearer the factory, and stood waiting for her bricklayer husband, to snatch the wage-packet from his hand, Arthur thought, and at the same time to watch the factory turn out, something she never grew tired of doing.

Arthur and his father walked via the scullery into the living-room, where a hundred-watt bulb burned from the ceiling. Five people sat in the small room, and Margaret moved her chair back from the fire as Arthur hung up his coat before taking his place at the table. William stood by her knee, a legginged and pom-pom hatted five-year-old who shouted out: 'Hey-up, Uncle Arthur. Hey-up, Grandad,' as they came in. The mother laid a special pay-day treat of bacon-and-beans before them.

'I can see yer've mashed, Vera,' Seaton said fussily. 'It's pay-night, yer know!'

'Why,' she said, 'you cheeky sod. I mash every night for you. I know yer'd go mad without yer cup o' tea.' They never touched a bit until two cups stood emptied by their unwashed hands.

'Now then, Vera, my ducks, don't get like that,' he called out, bending over his plate and intently scooping up beans with a fork. She stood by the mantelpiece watching them eat, and after a few minutes' reflection walked to the table and cut two thick slices of bread, saying: 'This'll fill you up.'

Margaret sat dreamily by the fire, a young

full-busted woman of twenty-nine. William fidgeted on her knee, trying to sing a song, stopping to puzzle over the meaning of Arthur's loudly thrown-out statements, and finding them always indecipherable, went back to his song, glancing under the table from time to time to make sure that neither Arthur nor his father accidentally put their feet on his red-painted toy wagon. Arthur took him from Margaret's knee, lifted him up, and settled him firmly on to his own.

'Now then, yer little bogger, let me tell yer a story.' He accentuated his gruff voice. 'Once upon a time—sit still then, or I wain't tell yer. Tek yer fingers out o' my tea—there was a bad man who lived in a dark wood, in a gret big castle, wi' water drippin' down the walls, and spider-webs as big as eiderdowns in every corner, winders that creaked and trapdoors everywhere that swallered people up if they made a false move. . . .'

Margaret interrupted him. 'All right then, our Arthur, you'll frighten the poor little bogger to death.'

'No, he's enjoyin' it, aren't yer, old Bill?' William looked at him, waiting for more. 'Well, this man's name was Boris Karloff. He was a mad doctor who looked after thousands of vampire bats that ripped people's throats

97

out every night as they walked through pitch-black woods and swampy fields. Because, yer see, this doctor, Boris, let vampire bats out every night, and from his castle walls he could hear people screamin' as these bats got to work. He used to stand on a tower, laughin' an' showin' 'is fangs as he chewed up a couple o' kids for supper.' Arthur made weird sounds with his throat. 'An' one night he was in his laborat'ry, along all his glass bottles with shrunk 'eads in 'em, when all of a sudden . . .' William looked at him with full white eyes, hands curling and uncurling near an empty place, his face round and pale, his lips parting wider and wider as the story unfolded.

'Well,' Arthur suddenly jerked back at the climax, and everyone in the room, having stopped talking to listen, twitched at the word, 'it was the Devil who had come to visit him. They were great pals, you see, and after they talked about murder, and how to get rid of bodies at six bob a hundred . . .'

Margaret drew the line at the Devil, and sprang out of her reverie: 'He'll think ye'r talking about his father,' she said tearfully, taking William, who looked relieved, back on to her knee. 'You'll frighten the life out on him, wain't he, Bill?'

'Has he bin on to you again?' Arthur

questioned.

There was an awkward tension in the room.

'He's allus on,' the mother said, a voice of hatred and accusation. 'She's sleeping here tonight, away from the drunken swine.'

'I'll drop him one, one day,' Arthur promised. Yes, he thought, it's bad luck when you marry a man that drinks too much and knocks you around. One day though, he'll get it. He'll get killed at the pit, I hope. He took the clean wage-packet from his overall pocket and passed three pound notes to his mother. 'Here yer are, my board, mam.'

'Thanks, Arthur, my owd duck.'

William observed the crossing of the pound notes, saw them with glinting eyes, already knowing what they meant—sweets, bus fare, biscuits, endless rides on the Goose Fair— hanging idly from Arthur's fingers, then taken up into his grandmother's hand. His mouth opened at the pricelessness of it, at the vital Friday-night transaction going on before him, a stupefying amount of money swinging in all its power and glory over the table.

Arthur saw his excitement. 'Look at the young bogger,' he called out. 'Peein' 'issen to see it. You'd better keep your hairgrips locked up, our Margaret, or else he'll be opening the gas meter for all them shillin's.'

'He won't do no such thing,' she exclaimed, 'unless yo' put ideas into his head, stupid sod.'

Arthur took a five-pound note from his wage-packet. William stood at the table, his nose resting on the rim, his small hands gripping the tablecloth. Arthur dangled the note before him: 'Here yer are, Bill, run to Taylor's and get some Dolly Mixtures.'

William trembled, saw a multi-coloured mountain of Dolly Mixtures swaying and swimming before his eyes, an insane yet accepted exchange for a bit of crinkly black-and-white paper, such a piece as had paid the down-payment on his mother's washing-machine that morning. His eyes swung towards the watching faces, then turned slowly back to Arthur's hand that moved the note pendulum-fashion above him. He snatched for it, and missed. In his mind, while everyone laughed at his failure, and Arthur went on waving the money slowly, he made allowance for its angle of movement.

His arm went up and down like a piston, and clutched the note. He feverishly rattled the back-door latch, and in a second was running up the yard before anyone could stop him, gripping the five-pound note.

'Serves yer right,' the mother screamed at

Arthur, holding her heart from the shock.

Arthur reached the door, and chased the losses of his playfulness. A few strides of his long legs took him outside, after William who was toddling doggedly through the dusk a few yards in front, swaying slightly in his hampering leggings.

'Bill!' Arthur cried. 'Come back, you sod!'

The house behind was an uproar of laughter.

'Come back wi' that fiver and I'll gi' yer a tanner!'

William turned the corner into the street, running towards the shop, his steel-capped shoes clicking on the pavement, his breath going like a traction engine as he tightened his grip on the money.

Arthur caught him around the waist and picked him up, kissed him on the cheeks while removing the note from his now relaxed fingers. 'Run off wi' my fiver would you, young bogger-lugs? My 'ard-earned lolly. A fiver's worth o' Dolly Mixtures! Christ Almighty! You'd a made yoursen sick, I'm sure you would!'

William's young brain had known all the time that it was only a game, that you could not snatch a five-pound note and hope to achieve your goal of buying a mountain of sweets with it. So instead of weeping he threw his arms around Arthur's neck, loving his rich uncle who came from the towering world of work and sent pound notes across the dazzling air of the Friday-night kitchen. Arthur carried him to the shop, pushed his way towards the door where children, flushed with issues of spending money, shouted and played excitedly.

'We's'll see'f Taylors' 'ave some tuffeys, shall we? But you're a bit of a lead weight, our Bill. What does Margaret feed you on? Cannon-balls? Ye'r a ton-weight, and no mistake. The tuffeys wain't mek yer any lighter, I do know that!'

Treading on the bell, he carried plump William into the shop. Several women were paying weekly bills. They've all got TV's, Arthur thought, but they still get grub on tick. William looked at the jars, his blue eyes roaming slowly, his flat nose sniffing delectable peppermint and ham odours rising from the counter.

'What goo buy me, Unc Arf?'

'If yer a good lad I'll buy yer three pennorth o' caramels,' he said, setting him down on the floor. The five-pound note went back in his trousers pocket, and he sorted through a handful of small change for pennies. William clutched the caramels and pocketed the sixpence, and Arthur carried him shoulder-high back to the house.

Arthur washed loudly in the scullery, swilling waves of warm soapy water over his chest and face, blundering his way back to the fire to dry himself. Upstairs he flung his greasy overalls aside and selected a suit from a line of hangers. Brown paper protected them from dust, and he stood for some minutes in the cold, digging his hands into pockets and turning back lapels, sampling the good hundred pounds' worth of property hanging from an iron-bar. These were his riches, and he told himself that money paid-out on clothes was a sensible investment because it made him feel good as well as look good. He took a shirt from another series of hangers near the window and slipped it over his soiled underwear, fastening the buttons and pursing his lips in a whistle that made a shrill split in the room's silence.

A soft drizzling rain fell as he hurried to the bus stop. Clean-shaven and smart, fair hair short on top and weighed-down with undue length at the back sent out a whiff of hair cream. From below the overcoat came narrow-bottomed trousers, falling with good creases to the tops of black, shining square-toed shoes. His tall frame was slightly round-shouldered from stooping day in and day out at his lathe, but all memory of work had gone from him as, with head down in the darkness, and tramping shoes making a distinct sound on the wet pavement, he crossed the wide road to join a bus queue.

He sat on the top deck and smoked a cigarette. The trolley-bus pulled itself up the road, and he handed out money for his ticket. The stink of a man's pipe drifted from a nearby seat, and he drove it away with a noisy blast of air. People shouldn't be allowed to smoke pipes, he thought. Pipe-smoking men are a menace, to themselves as well as to everybody else. Though if you start going out with a woman whose husband smokes a pipe, you're sure to be on a good thing, because pipe-smoking husbands are the slowest in the world, the easiest of all to do the dirty on. Like Joyce's husband five years ago. They just puff their hubble-bubbles all day long like a baby sucking a dummy, and don't think about anybody else. They're too selfish to bother with wives, and that's where blokes like me step in.

He was ten minutes early, and saw himself waiting a long time for Brenda, but she was already standing in the shadow of the public house. It was four days since they had met,

104

and a multitude of different hours had passed slowly for each of them. A smash of skittles sounded from behind the pub lights. You could never tell what mood she would be in, he cogitated, or what mood I'm going to be in after she's either got funny or laughed. He took her hand, but she drew it away, saying with a frown: 'Don't let's hang around. Let's get going somewhere.'

'What's wrong with her?' he wondered.

They walked slowly along the Ropewalk, into a quiet, ill-lit district of hospitals and doctors' houses. There was a smell of trees and bushes, and over a low wall the Park mansions built by last-century lace manufacturers stood unlighted in a vale of gloom, with the vari-coloured lights of a marshalling yard beyond.

Arthur knew she was worried even before she spoke. Something is up, he told himself. He felt the agony of her worry clinging about them, thick and tangible.

'Why don't you tell me what's up?' He stopped her and, seeing her pale blue blouse showing through her coat, began to fasten it: one, two, three, four large brown buttons. 'Pull up your collar as well,' he ordered.

'You make too much fuss,' she said.

He put his arms around her and kissed her.

'You're all right, Brenda,' he said. 'I like you a lot.' She was handsome because for some reason she was afraid. Then the muscles of her face relaxed and the glow of her soft features was framed and accentuated by an aureole of silence backed by the sound of the city. 'Why don't you tell me what's up then, duck?'

Her face hardened. She turned away. 'The same old story,' she cried.

He didn't understand. She never told him outright what was the matter, as if to do so directly would inflame the wound. Perhaps she hoped that by coming upon it in a roundabout way she would not anger those fates that had the power to confirm the fact that something was wrong, or make whatever it was even worse.

'What old story?' he demanded. 'We've had so many old stories lately.'

'Well,' she said, 'if you want to know, I'm pregnant, good and proper this time.'

He wanted to say: So what? What does it matter if you are? You're married, aren't you? So what's the odds? It ain't as if you was a young girl.

'And it's your fault,' she said acrimoniously. 'You never will take any care when we're doing it. You just don't bother. I allus said this would happen one day.'

'It's bound to be my fault,' he said with sharp irony. 'Everything's my fault. I know that.' What a wonderful Friday night! Yet if it wasn't one thing, it was another. 'I can't see yer swellin' up yet,' he said.

'You're barmy,' she retorted. 'That doesn't happen for ages.'

'Then how do you know?' There was always a chance that she was wrong, that she didn't know what she was talking about. Hope to the very end, he told himself, even when you've slipped into the fires of Hell and the flames are searing your guts.

'You'll never believe owt, will you, Arthur?' she cried. 'I suppose you have to see the kid before you believe me?' She stopped by the wall. It rained no longer, and they looked at the distant lights.

'But how do you know?' he insisted.

'Because I'm twelve days late. That means it's dead sure.'

'Nothing's dead sure,' he said.

'But this is.'

He knew she was right. Had it not been certain she would be weeping and hysterical with hope. He could tell by her voice that she was resigned to it. Hope had failed in the last few days, and she had become fatalistic.

'All right,' he said, 'what shall we do?' She wants me to feel guilty about it, but I don't feel bad at all. It's an act of God, like a pit disaster. I should have been careful, I suppose, but what's the good 'o going wi' a married woman if you've got to use a frenchie? They spoil everything. Then he thought of something else. He was brutal and exultant: 'How do you know it's mine?'

She pulled her arm away and thumped him. 'Why? Don't you want to take the blame? Are you backing out now?'

'What blame? There's no blame on me. Only I just wondered whether it's mine. It's not forced to be, is it?'

'Yes,' she said, 'it's yourn right enough. I haven't done owt like that wi' Jack for a couple o' months or more.'

I'll tek that wi' a dose o' salts, he thought. Yet you never know. 'What shall we do, then?'

'I'm sure I don't want it, I can tell you that.'

'Have yer tried owt yet? Took owt, I mean?'

'Some pills, but they didn't work. Thirty-five bob they cost me. I hadn't got it, but I borrowed it from Em'ler, one of my old work-mates. Right down the drain though.'

He took two crumpled pound notes from his pocket and folded her hand over them.

She thrust them back: 'That isn't what I meant, and you know it.'

But he dipped his hand into her pocket and left them there. 'I know it ain't, but keep 'em anyway.' He cursed out loud, both because he wanted her to think he was suffering with her, and to force himself into an unhappy mood. It was Friday night, and being so fixed into contentment by that fact alone, a major tragedy or a ton of dynamite was needed to blast him out of it.

'It's no use swearing,' she said. 'You'd better think of something.'

'Don't you want to have it?' he said hopefully.

Her laugh went echoing bitterly along the empty road, leaping over the dark houses. 'You want your brains testing,' she retorted.

'I know I do,' he said. 'I've thought of going to the doctor's many a time, but I don't like standing in queues.'

'I suppose you'd like me to have a kid by you?' she scoffed. 'It'd make you feel good, I suppose. But no fear. Not me. You can find somebody else if you want kids. I've got two already.'

'Another one wain't mek any difference then,' he argued. 'Will it, duck?' He took her arm, pressing her elbow. A sudden wind blew

109

a dead cigarette packet over her shoe, and she kicked it back into the gutter.

'You're looney,' she said. 'What do you think having a kid means? You're doped for nine months. Your breasts get big, and suddenly you're swelling. Then one fine day you're yelling out and you've got a kid. That's easy enough though. Nowt wrong wi' that. The thing is, you've got ter look after it every minute for fifteen years. You want to try it sometimes!'

'Not me,' he said gloomily. 'Anyway, if that's how you feel.'

'What do you expect?'

They walked on again, towards the great wall of windows of the General Hospital. 'I'll see an aunt of mine,' he said. 'She'll know how to get rid of it. She's had fourteen of her own, and I'm sure she got rid of as many others.'

'I hope she knows something then, because there'll be a hell of a row if I don't get rid of it, I can tell you.'

He still could not worry with her and take it seriously; and he did not like the way she was carrying on about it. That was a sure way to get nothing done.

'Don't worry, Brenda, duck, you'll be as right as rain in a week. I'll go and see about it on Sunday.'

But the night was young yet, as they said on the pictures.

CHAPTER FIVE

RAIN and sunshine, rain and sunshine, with a blue sky now on the following Sunday, and full clouds drifting like an aerial continent of milk-white mountains above the summit of Castle Rock, a crowned brownstone shaggy lion-head slouching its big snout out of the city, poised as if to gobble up uncouth suburbs hemmed in by an elbow of the turgid Trent. Two smart Sunday-afternoon couples on their way to the pictures stepped out of the cold dank air on to a double-decker trolley-bus, which left the road empty of all but Arthur when it turned off by the tight-shut front of the Horse and Groom.

He walked along Ruddington Road, hands plunged ever deeper into spacious pockets with dejection, wishing he could turn his back on the worry that Brenda had thrown into his face on Friday as easily as he had turned his back on the castle at the last corner, and wishing also that he could separate himself from the headache that had come to him through trying to wash his worry away in the pale ale of the Midlands. Who would have thought it? Brenda on the tub, up the stick, with a bun in the oven, and now he had to pump Aunt Ada and find out how to empty the tub, throw Brenda to the bottom of the stick, and sling that half-cooked bun from the stoked-up oven. At any price, she said. It's got to be done. It was nature's way, he argued. Yes, she replied sarcastically, and his bad luck. But he could see no need of all the fuss, and understood once more why in these happy days men joined the army: to escape the smoke that came from other people's fires. People made too much fuss about useless things, but you have to get caught by it, or at least join in the chorus of their moans and groans, otherwise life would not go on and you would be left in some old doss-house, neglected like an apple-coking by everybody in the world. And that's how they got you. Last night Brenda cried like a baby and he mopped the tears from her eyes with one hand and caught the runnings of his own cold with the other, so that she thought he was crying too, and went into the house somewhat contented. But as soon as he was out of earshot he started laughing, drunk to himself and all the world, until he crept upstairs in his stockinged-feet, set his Teddy-suit on the number-one hanger, and slept sounder than any log.

From the hump of the railway bridge he

turned around and saw the squat front-end of the castle still sneering at him. I hate that castle, he said to himself, more than I've ever hated owt in my life before, and I'd like to plant a thousand tons of bone-dry T.N.T. in the tunnel called Mortimer's Hole and send it to Kingdom Cum, so's nob'dy 'ud ever see it again. He walked on with held-in wrath between the blackened shops and houses of Ruddington Road, through the fresh wind that did his cold no good.

He kicked open the entry-gate that led to Ada's back door. Perhaps the twenty kids—or however many it was she'd got—will be in and I won't be able to get a word in edgeways, but then again maybe the house'll be empty and I can have a nice quiet talk. All the same I'd better not blab my mouth and tell her why I want the advice. The whole family 'ud know in five minutes. News gets around so quick you'd think they'd got tom-toms on every roof.

He saw through the open door that the lavatory-bowl was cracked. The coal-house was ruined because they'd once kept chickens there and had smashed part of the wall down to put wire netting in its place, and the asphalt paving had been dug-up to make a V-for-Victory garden during the war. Window

curtains were torn at one corner but otherwise clean, though the back door at the top of
the three steps had been left slightly ajar day
and night for years because the landlord
wouldn't repair the uneven floor tiles. Even
though they pay the rent, Arthur thought.
Landlords today are so lucky they don't know
they're born. The on'y way they got our rent
before the war was through County Court.

'Anybody in?' he shouted from the scullery.
'Bring out your dead, Aunt Ada.'

'Come in, Arthur,' she called out. Waves of
heat, rising from an enormous coal-fire built-
up in the grate, met him as he entered. 'I can
see Dave still woks at pit,' he said, racing to
unbutton his overcoat before he stifled to
death. 'Where's the Tribe?'

'Gone to't pictures.' The table was laden
with the débris of Sunday dinner, and she sat
by it, Arthur's entry taking her gaze from the
burning heart of the coal-fire, that acted like
a crystal ball in which she saw a past whose
incidents however black could never be anything but fascinating now that they had
buried themselves behind her. She was a
woman of fifty-odd dressed in a grey frock,
with a face attractively made-up, a face that
Arthur remembered being plump but now
narrowing and showing her features more as

they had been when she was a young girl, but with a mask of age imposed.

'How are yer, my owd bird? Why don't yer mam come and see me any more? Has owd Blackclock bin on to her again?' She reached into the hearth for the kettle and settled it skilfully on the blazing coals.

He laid his overcoat on the sofa. 'No, Dad's all right these days. He don't get on to her now. Not since me and Fred's grown-up.'

'Sit down then, duck,' she said. 'I'll make you a cup of tea in ten minutes. I'm glad you've come though. Sunday afternoon's the only time I get a bit of peace, and I like somebody to talk to. I like the house to be empty now and again. It's a treat the way you look after your clo'es, Arthur. Every young man should, that's what I say. But you know, it's like living in a different house, when the kid's aren't fighting and running over everywhere. Eddie's gone up Clifton with Pam and Mike, and they won't be back till six, thank God. They lead me such a dance all week that I'm allus glad to get shut on 'em at weekend. Last night we went to't Flying Fox and I had so many gin and Its I thought I'd never get home. Our Betty clicked wi' a bloke, and he bought the whole gang of us drinks all night. He must a got through a good five quid, the

116

bloody fool. He had a car though, so I suppose he could afford it, and he thought he was on a good thing with our Betty, but you should a seen his face drop when she came home wi' us instead of going off with him! He was going to start some trouble, but our Dave—he was wi' us as well—got up and said he'd smash him if he didn't clear off. The poor bloke went deathly white and drove off in his car. "What a bleddy fool I was," our Betty said when he'd gone, "I should a got 'im to drive us all home!"'

Arthur laughed. 'I wish I'd 'ave bin there,' he said, happy sitting with Aunt Ada and waiting for the kettle to boil on a cold April afternoon—until the big worry started thumping away once more inside his brain. He wanted above all to go to sleep, feeling as if he hadn't seen a bed for a month. The heat from the big fire beat against his eyes, and the marble clock on the mantelpiece clacked away like a bird in the last five minutes of its life, while Ada poked the fire and reset the kettle. The sideboard along one side of the room sloped down away from the wall because of a subsidence in the tiles, indicating too much space between the living-room floor and the cellar roof, in which Ada's three sons, on the run from the army during the war, had stowed much of their loot whenever they did a job, a credit and debit bank on which they had worked their living in snatches of freedom from glasshouse and gaol. Above the dresser hung two pictures in oblong frames, bearing an antique ring for the family because their father, now dead, had plundered them from France in the war before the last, a boozing bombardier sergeant of the artillery who had stayed on till nineteen-twenty, thrown out of the army for, so Ada said, using such foul language that even soldiers couldn't stand it. The pictures he gave Ada were of two beautiful girls standing by a marble balustrade, wearing chiffon stoles over creamy shoulders against a background of soft full-blown roses. Doddoe had been killed three years ago, when his powerful side-carred motor-bike burst like a bullet into a draper's shop at the bottom of a hill, with grinning and goggled Doddoe gripping the handlebars and knowing, when it was too late, that he should have taken the turn sooner, spouting like buckshot all the bad language he had ever known in the second before crashing. That's the way to do it, Arthur thought, sitting stupefied by the fire's heat and the fever from his cold. Doddoe knew what he was up to when he forgot that turning.

Ada now had another husband, but in taking him on, the tribe from her womb was not increased beyond the eleven children she had already borne from Doddoe. Nowadays she was both too old or too wise to have any more, rested on her laurels and relished the twilight of retirement in which she found herself. For Doddoe had come upon her like a scourge of God and fired her through a life of dole, boozing, bailiffs, and a horde of children who grew up learning to fend for themselves in such a wild free manner that Borstal had been their education and a congenial jungle their only hope. Ralph, Ada's present husband, was a mild man who brought her five children of his own—thus the rumour that she had twenty—and who was himself wanting a peaceful life after seeing his first wife die of consumption and his eighteen-year-old daughter settled on the same downward blood-spitting track. But Ada's sons and daughters had not been bred to peace, and led him a worse life than before, for he discovered that he was jealous of Ada. At fifty she still had the personality of a promiscuous barmaid, a kindness to listen to any man's tale and sob like a twin-soul into his beer, even to bring him home to bed if she thought it would make him feel better. And Ralph showed resentment at this, bearing an ingrown agony that came so strongly because the same thing had happened to him—only he had called in his shackles of furniture and five children and stayed with her—and he had an uneasy premonition that she might in the future favour other unfortunate men. Ada's eldest son Dave bought a record of 'Jealousy' and every time Ralph mentioned the softness of her heart and the fact that she spoke to too many men when they were at club or pub, the invidious disc began to wheel around the turntable and beat out its howling damnable tango that drove his mild heart to frenzy. One Saturday night, among moans of despair from Ada, he fought with Dave when the tune was played, and Dave quickly knocked him down, though as he fell Ralph clutched both gramophone and record and sent them smashing to bits on the floor. Thereafter Dave and the others merely contented themselves with turning the volume of the wireless full on whenever 'Jealousy' was played on Family or Forces Favourites. Ralph was a considerate man who gave Ada—as far as he was able, for her sons were true chips off Doddoe's block—the sort of quiet life she had never known. Since the end of the war, when the Redcaps ceased their eternal hounding of

120

her sons, life had calmed down. Everyone had work, and regular money had been coming into the house for so long that she no more worried about what would happen when times stopped being good. The greatest excitement of the house these days was when it was rabidly divided by the football results on Saturday night. Even then, it was more or less united by Family Favourites on Sunday morning.

While Arthur looked into the fire Ada reset the table for tea, then opened the sideboard cupboard and took out a roll of cooked meat, asking him how he was, how he felt these days, as if he had been ill at some time. She questioned everyone in this way when they came to see her or when she met them on the street, so that one might think she had lived among sickness all her life, which she had not. Arthur replied that he was feeling all right, though admitted that he had something on his mind.

'Why,' she exclaimed, emerging from the scullery with a bottle of sauce and setting it by his place, 'what would a nice-looking young chap like you have to worry about?'

He lifted the kettle from its rosy bed of coals and poured scalding water into the teapot: 'Well, it ain't that I'm worryin', Aunt

Ada. I never worry, you know that. It's a mate o' mine at wok. You see, he's got a young woman into trouble, and he don't know what to do. He wanted me to help him, but I don't know what to do either. So I thought I'd come and see you.'

Ada tut-tutted as she sat down. 'That's bad luck for the poor bogger,' she commented with a fatalistic expression. 'What a daft thing to do, to get a girl into trouble. Couldn't he have bin more careful? He'll just have to face the music, like our Dave did.' Arthur remembered: Dave got a woman into trouble who had turned out to be the worst kind of tart, a thin, vicious, rat-faced whore who tried to skin him for every penny he'd got—until he threatened to chuck her over Trent Bridge one dark night, and she settled for a quid a week out of court.

'Well,' he said, 'ain't there summat as can be done? I mean to say'—but he didn't know how to say it; he had never spoken so openly to her before, and wondered why he had expected it to be so easy—'well, sometimes people do things to stop it. They get rid of it by taking pills or something, don't they?'

She poured tea into a big white cup, and stopped abruptly at his last remark, holding a spoon in the sugar basin, an inquisitive look

122

on her ageing face. He noticed for the first time that she hadn't got her teeth in. 'How did you know about things like that?'

'I read it in the Sunday papers'—he smiled, but felt like a criminal, recalled the up-ended sensation when first walking into an army camp after getting his papers.

'You don't want to mess about with things like that,' she cautioned. 'You never know where it can lead.'

'It's for my mate,' he said. 'He's in a mess, and I'd do owt to help him. You can't let your mate down when he's in trouble. He's a good bloke, and he'd do owt for me if I was in the same hole.'

She looked at him suspiciously. 'Are you sure it ain't you as is in this mess?'

He met her investigation with an ingenuous, almost startled face at the injustice of it. Lie until you're blue in the face, was his motto, and you'll always be believed, sooner or later. 'I wish it was me that was in trouble, rather than my mate,' he said seriously, 'then I wouldn't feel so bad about it. But it's him that's in trouble, and I've got to help him. That's what pals are for.'

'I'm sure I don't know what to tell you,' she said, softening before his display of loyalty. 'It's dangerous to mess with such things. I

123

once knew a woman as got sent to prison for a thing like that.'

She sipped slowly at a cup of tea, and Arthur explained: 'This girl's about a fortnight past her monthlies. She's taken pills, but they didn't work.'

'The only thing she can try, as far as I know,' Ada told him 'is, to take a hot bath with hot gin. Tell her to stay there for two hours, as hot as she can bear it, and drink a pint of gin. That should bring it off. If it don't, then she'll just have to have the kid, that's all.'

The front door opened to a tramping of feet, was pushed to with a heavy slam, and a multitude of boots came kicking through the hall. The Tribe's advance-guard was struggling out of its coats, breathing hard after having run too quickly from the bus.

'They're back,' Ada said laconically.

Jane, Pam, Mike, and Eddie came into the room crying for their tea. Arthur pushed his empty plate and cup away. Just in time, he thought jubilantly.

'Tek your sweat,' Ada shouted. 'The pot's empty. Wait till the kettle boils.' Big ginger-haired Jane threw herself on to the sofa, and Arthur noted the bouncing of large sweater-covered breasts as she landed. 'I suppose yo' lot of 'ogs 'ave swallered all the tea?' she cried with a flush on her indignant face.

''Eve less o' yer cheek,' Ada said, brandishing her fist, 'or yer'll get no tea.' The fight was on again. Doddoe had left a fiery enough rearguard to keep his ghost still tangible in the house. If they were my kids, Arthur thought, they wouldn't get away with this.

Pamela was tackled next for turning the wireless up too loud. She was a fourteen-year-old version of Jane, but with a milder face and smaller breasts, with the same shade of freckles on her arms and the same flaming ginger in her hair. Bert and Dave came in, back from the pictures, and in trying to restore Jane and Pam to order turned the room into a box of catcalls and shouts to mind your own business and demands that you keep your big dirty plates of meat to yourself. Ralph came downstairs in his stockinged-feet, turfed out of his nap by the eruptions below. 'Why don't yer mek less bleddy noise?' he cried from the stairfoot door, boots in one hand and sports page in the other, his face bewildered and filled with frustrated wrath. But nobody took a blind bit of notice of him—as he was quick to point out—so he pushed through to the fire and sat disconsolately by the range to pull on his boots while Ada

125

poured him a cup of tea.

Arthur went into the front room with his cousins for a game of poker. With locked door—to foil any spontaneous and mischievous migration from the living-room—they switched on the light and sat around the smooth polished table. Dave lifted the plant-pot from the centre and set it on the floor beneath the window.

'No cheating,' Bert said.

'Anybody cheats in this 'ouse, and they get smashed,' Dave shouted, smarting from some previous injury. 'And that means yo', Bert. Yer got seven bob out o' me las' week because o' them three extra kings.' He snatched the cards from Bert, who was about to deal, and began counting through the pack, his thin red face bent close to them.

'I'll deal,' Arthur volunteered, taking the cards. 'You can trust me, can't yer? I've never cheated in my life, I'll tell yer that now.'

'Never trust a bloke as says that,' Bert said, dejected. He turned to Dave, his fists clenched with fury: 'If ever yer tek them cards from me again like that, you'll get summat.'

'You shouldn't be such a bleedin' cheat,' Dave said. 'It serves yer right.'

Arthur dealt the cards, a regulation five to the others, and lucky seven to himself, without them seeing. The two lowest cards he dropped on to his lap before either Dave or Bert looked up from their argument. A series of thuds and shouts were heard from the living-room. 'Hark at them lot,' Arthur said innocently. 'Fightin' over the crusts now.'

Dave gave a great guffaw. 'The trough, you mean'—then scowled when he saw his cards.

'Bluffin',' Bert said. 'That means he's got a royal flush.'

'Royal flush, my arse,' Dave said, throwing them down without waiting for a second helping. Bert took two from the pack, smiled and pushed a shilling to the middle of the table. Arthur sorted his cards and raised him half a crown.

'Steady on,' Dave said, umpire now. 'That's big money. You can't play like that.'

'He's bluffin', that I do know,' Bert said, cocksure, and raised him another lump-sum.

But Arthur was not bluffing. 'Take that,' he said, spreading them out on the table.

Jack-queen-king-ace of clubs. He cleared seven shillings.

'How many cards yo' got?' Bert demanded suspiciously.

'Same as yo',' Arthur retorted, lips set tight against such mistrust. He raised his cash-pile to fifteen shillings on the last game. They took his luck with humour and resentment, to which Arthur replied: 'Cheat? Of course I cheat. I allus cheat. Don't you know that?' From which they gathered that he did not. He shuffled his half-dozen secreted cards back into the pack.

Arthur went with Bert to the town centre for a drink. It was dark on the bridge. The Castle was invisible, hiding behind a night-screen of mist, smoke, and darkness. A wind ascended from low-lying marshalling yards, from swampy canal banks and minnow streams, causing Bert to swear at the rawness of it, and Arthur to button his coat.

Bert was a short, ferocious, blue-eyed son of Doddoe, who knew that danger meant un-pleasant things but threw himself head-first into it until only his fair and curly hair was visible above the rum-scruffle. Such methods of attack had been his education, in Remand Homes and Borstal. His brothers, in fighting to clear themselves of the police, had shown as much—if not more—courage than if they had been shovelled with rifle and bayonet on to a battlefront. But Bert, for some unknown reason, was most like Doddoe and had not

128

tried to escape the army. In fact he joined too young by giving a false age and at seventeen had been thrown into the last offensive over the Rhine, emerging from the mêlée with less wounds than his brothers who had served in the forlorn ranks of the deserters. Bert was the spit-and-image of his father, Ada said, and she loved him for it and for his sharp intelligence and sentimentality that was part of herself. Bert had never allowed Ralph to replace Doddoe. Doddoe had been bully and dictator, and now in his place Ada reigned on a stable throne, with Ralph as ineffectual consort, whom Bert the realm protector threatened to knock down whenever he spoke to her with raised voice.

They walked down the bridge-slope in silence, crossing Castle Boulevard, passing a darkly windowed Woolworth's to a pub on the edge of a backstreet wasteground for the first pint of the night. Bert said they should try to pick up a couple of tarts, and as the dimly lit Match showed nothing of interest they progressed by slow stages to the Nottingham Rose. They seemed luckier there, but the two loving and hilarious girls who battened on to them, after consuming thirty-bob's worth of drinks up to closing time, gave them the slip and hopped on to a bus. So Arthur and Bert made their way through animated Slab Square and descended homewards to the Meadows.

With the canal dampness came misery, and Arthur meditated on the weight of Brenda's trouble hanging over him, which now seemed heavier than ever.

'We'll go back to the house,' Bert said, 'and get some supper. I expect mam'll get a bit o' meat for us.'

Arthur could think of nothing better. The streets were almost empty. A late bus rumbled by on its way to the depot, all lights shining, the conductress sitting on a back seat looking tired to death.

'If ever I see them tarts agen'—Bert lit a nub-end found among the burrows of his overcoat pockets—'I'll paste their bloody heads, I can tell you.' They stepped off the curb and crossed the cobbled road.

'All they want is ale,' Arthur said. 'But what can you expect? When you pick a tart up in a pub you tek a big chance. Sometimes they give and sometimes they don't.'

Bert raved that they'd skin a bloke dry, but Arthur's big worry had come back, and when he passed the horse-trough by the labour exchange he felt a drunken impulse to lie down in it and drown himself. He laughed.

Not deep enough. And it's cold. And besides, hadn't Ada given him some good advice? He hoped to Christ she had, and that it could be brought off. Latest sports models gleamed faintly behind the window of a bicycle shop, with the shadowy cardboard form of Sir Walter Raleigh bowing nobly from their midst. Bert, whose senses were more acute after an evening of disappointment, stopped and turned, attracted by something lying on the ground: a half smell, a faint sound, the animal knowledge that someone was sprawled out on the stone floor of the doorway. Arthur, who wanted his cold-meat supper, asked impatiently what was up? Bert had forgotten the sponging tarts. 'Some poor sod's come a cropper,' he said, bending to look at the prostrate body. 'Drunk as a lord,' he grinned. 'Smells it as well.'

Arthur prodded the body with his boots, and Bert told the man to get up. 'You can't lay there like this. Yo'll catch yer death o' cowd.' Showing more interest, Arthur noted that his head was bare, that his clothes were old and worn at the elbows. Though a cold night he wore no overcoat, and his trousers were pulled up above his ankles by the twisted position into which he had fallen, showing that he wore boots but no socks. About fifty,

131

Arthur guessed.

'We'll get 'im on 'is feet,' Bert said, but on trying to lift him found they could move no more than head and shoulders. He grunted, but would not get up. 'Come on, mate, the cops'll get you if you don't start movin'.'

He grunted again, his eyes rolling as if to shake away the fifteen pints he must have drunk. Suddenly he shook from head to foot and made a great effort to get up but, breathing heavily, lay back with a sigh. Arthur looked up and down the road to make sure a policeman wasn't in sight. 'If we don't get 'im up 'e'll find 'issen in a cell, and get a fine in the mornin'. Ranklin's the magistrate these days, and he's a real bastard.'

Bert shook him until he gurgled and opened his eyes. 'Where's yer digs, mate? Where do yer live?'

The man folded up slowly, like a jackknife, and rolled sideways. Bert levered a fist under his armpits, and dug him sharply in the ribs until he stood on his feet. By the lamplight they saw that his eyes were swollen: Bert said it looked as though he had been knocked down. Each took a firm hold and walked him along the road, up the hump of the bridge. At the next lamp-post Arthur stopped and bawled right into the man's ear:

'Where do you live, mate? We might as well tek 'im 'ome,' he added to Bert. The man's lips were thick and clumsy with drink, and he could not manipulate them into any sound that might be understood. His lips moved. He lifted his hand, then let it fall. They made out the name of the street, but could get no number. Had his eyes been open, the movement his lips made would have resembled a smile. Still supporting him, they walked on. When they let go, thinking he might be able to walk, he fell on to the pavement and they had the hard trouble of getting him up again. Bert talked to him, as though he was not drunk at all, asking if he had had a good night and drunk plenty of booze. Bert said he was a Mick, and called him Paddy, asking what part of Ireland he came from, if he had ever kissed the Blarney Stone, and whether he had worked at Guinness's brewery in Dublin.

He lived on a long straight road leading from the railway station to Trent Bridge, and Arthur hooted into his ear once more and asked the number of the house he lodged at. No reply. 'I know,' Bert said. 'Doddoe stayed at a boarding-house one night when mam locked the door on 'im. There's some down this way.' The man was no longer a deadweight, his boots not dragging so heavily on

133

the pavement. When they came to the boarding-houses Bert thumped him: 'Which one Paddy?'

'Thish wun,' emerged from his bronchial voice, and he turned forcefully towards the iron gate. Arthur steered him along the gravel path, Bert holding on to the gate so that it wouldn't grind on its hinges and crash to.

The man pulled his arm away. 'Lemme go,' he said, leaning against the door and fumbling with the knob. Arthur searched for it, feeling the pulsating heat of the man's body pressed on to his fist, and when he turned the handle the man slumped indoors. He'll waken up in an hour or two from the cold, he thought, then go to bed. He pushed him inside, closed the door, and walked back to the road.

Bert fell into step by his side. 'That'll save 'im a night in clink,' Arthur said, opening a packet of cigarettes. 'The bastard worn't very thankful, though.'

Bert passed the man's wallet over, 'I frisked 'im, but it's stone empty.'

It was a cheap blue one, smelling of sweat as if it had rested for years against the sweating chest of a nigger-driven navvy, smelling also of tobacco, one of its compartments having served as a pouch for flat dark flakes of some strong mixture. Bert was right. There was nothing in it except a tiny newspaper clipping cut neatly from the 'situations vacant' column, which Arthur screwed up and sent rolling over the cobblestones into the gutter.

CHAPTER SIX

THE ample lower portions of Brenda's body slid further down into the long zinc bath. The water was becoming too hot to bear, but she gave a sigh, signifying that it was better this way than the other, and said:

'Another saucepanful, Em'ler.'

Arthur leaned against the sideboard, morose and angry, as if he could not bring himself to unbutton his overcoat in the stifling room because it seemed to give protection against steam, gin fumes, and unpredictable women. Having rushed through tea, he had changed clothes and caught a bus to Brenda's, complying with her stern request that he should be present at the ceremony of 'bringing it off'. Em'ler, Brenda's old companion at the stocking factory, had been called in to help on the big night, and she was said to be a bit touched. No sooner had Jack left for the nightshift and the kids been despatched to the pictures with a well-paid neighbour's girl till ten, than a bath appeared from the coal-house, gin-bottles from the sideboard cupboard, and Em'ler sidled through the scullery to stoke up the fire for water. When she opened the back door Arthur recognised her, drawing back in surprise because he had expected a stranger. She was known as a blabmouth in all the pubs, and in a one-second flash he pictured her tomorrow spreading the news of tonight through every jug-and-bottle in town. But he remembered that she was a bit touched, and that even if anybody believed her information it would be so ravelled-up that they wouldn't be able to make head or tail of her tittle-tattle. So he smiled and said: 'Hey-up, duck,' as he came into the large kitchen where the table had been pushed beneath the window and the zinc bath set square in the middle of the floor.

Em'ler stood by the bucket of boiling water that was balanced on the coal-fire. She sighed in sympathy with Brenda's ordeal in the bath, repeating: 'I don't know,' again and again, in a tone that got so much on Arthur's nerves that he wanted to throttle her, 'I don't know'—dipping the aluminium saucepan into the bucket and pouring a thin trickle into the bath, so that fresh clouds of rising steam spread in all directions over the ceiling. 'I don't know, I really don't.'

'Shut yer rattle,' Arthur said.

'It won't do the paper any good,' Brenda remarked, winking at him. 'The last time, it all peeled off afterwards, and Jack was ever so mad,' she laughed.

'He stood need to be,' Em'ler said angrily. 'If he'd use his noddle a bit he'd know that he was the cause of all this. But how can you expect any man to use his noddle?' Arthur grinned: she thought it was Jack's they were trying to get rid of. It was impossible to tell how the twilight workings of her mind accounted for his presence in the house.

Brenda looked across at him. 'Cheer-up, duck. It'll be all right. Have a drink of gin. Em'ler, pour Arthur a drink.' Half a tumbler-ful was thrust into his hand, but after the first sip he set the glass down, screwing up his mouth. 'You don't like it?' Brenda shouted from the bath, waving a hand to him.

'Poison,' he said.

'Mothers' Ruin,' she called out, an ecstatic look on her face that was high-lighted in the glare of the electric-bulb. 'It's wonderful.'

'I'm not surprised,' he said, 'the way Em'ler drinks it. She'll be dafter than ever if she goes on like this.' Em'ler had finished a glassful since he came in.

'She's like me,' Brenda said, 'she can take it.'

'I am an' all,' Em'ler agreed, heaping more coal on the fire. 'I was brought-up on it.'

'That's what sent her crackers,' Arthur said.

Em'ler resented this: 'I'm not so daft as you think. Not half as daft as you men, I can tell yer.'

Brenda reached out for a glass of warm gin on the chair, and as she turned fresh trickles of sweat broke out on her forehead, ran down her face and neck, and hastened between her breasts into the water. After a liberal drink she let her hand fall back heavily, shivering as it disturbed the placid water that rippled its heat against her flesh.

'I don't know,' Em'ler moaned, 'I don't know, I'm sure. I don't like to see you suffer like this.' But Brenda saw a threat to deflect her from her purpose and became as angry as the hot water would allow. 'It's got to be done,' she said.

Arthur glared at Em'ler: 'Why don't you shut your mouth?'

She stared back. 'It's you as wants to shut your gob,' she said with a sneer. Arthur lit a cigarette and threw the still lighted match by her face and into the hearth. She turned to force more gin on Brenda: 'Drink this, duck. It'll do you good.'

Brenda took a few sips and put it on the chair. 'It's too hot,' she complained.

139

'Shall I put some more water in?'

'A drop.'

Em'ler let the boiling water trickle slowly into the bath. 'Another?'

'I suppose so.'

'It breaks my heart to do this,' Em'ler said. 'I do wish the other stuff'd 'ave worked.'

Brenda reached for the gin: 'I took it as long as I could, but it's over a fortnight now, you know.'

'I'd rather you'd 'ave the kid,' Em'ler said. 'I'd look after it. You could give it to me. I'd bring it up and love it, I can tell you.'

'I know you would,' Brenda said. 'You're as good as gold, Em'ler, but I can't do it. It'd cause a lot of trouble.' She drank the gin, her lips twisting as it went into her stomach. Em'ler took a cork-tipped fag from her red handbag, and Brenda refused her offer to light one and put it into her mouth. 'It'd on'y get wet. Put some more water in.' Her eyes rolled and she slurred her words. 'That's enough,' she said at the fourth ladle, the water now above her waist.

Arthur took off his coat and sat with legs stretched out over the mat, smoking cigarette after cigarette. He watched Brenda's face disintegrating, her features mixing beneath the fire of hot gin and a sea of water. Never again, he kept saying to himself, never again. No more bubble-baths for Brenda. Never again. I'd rather cut my throat. He felt drunk, though he had taken no more than a sip of the gin. Sometimes he was part of the scene, sitting among the two women, warmed by the fire, choked by the steaming bath; then he was looking down on it, like watching the telly with no part in what he was seeing. He was only real inside himself. That did not change, proved by the agony of fatigue that lingered from his day's work, intensified by the fever, swelling through him. Cigarettes tasted like manure, but he smoked. A glass of beer attracted him, but there was none in the house, and he couldn't go out to the pub because he was unable to drag himself away from the scene that held him like an adjustable spanner. And when he forced it loose he felt that if he tried to leave the two women would leap on him and rip him to bits.

Em'ler was crying out that she wanted to take Brenda to bed. 'I do wish you'd give it up. It's going to be all right now.'

Brenda opened her eyes wide; they were brown and turned good-naturedly on the room around her, as if she were taking her normal Saturday-night bath. 'No,' she cried thickly, 'don't be daft. It's not that easy, I'm sure.' She turned, as if to fix herself into firmer resolution, but the slight movement disturbed the water so that she groaned and closed her eyes from its heat.

Arthur walked over and kissed her damp forehead and mouth. 'You'll be all right soon, love.'

'Yes,' she said, 'yes, I know I shall. You're a good-hearted lad, Arthur.' Never again, he said to himself, and wondered whether such fuss was necessary, unable to understand how they had let such a thing happen. Never again.

'Come on, duck,' Em'ler said in a voice of anguish, 'drink this.' Brenda put it mutely to her lips, then thrust it aside without tasting it.

'Drink-up, duck,' Arthur called out. She obeyed, sipping it slowly. Em'ler talked, to stop Brenda closing her eyes and being sick, asking her when she had last had her hair permed and where Jack was, saying that this was his job and that he should be here at a time like this. Brenda opened her eyes and lifted her head: 'No he shouldn't,' she argued. 'It wouldn't be right. Tek the hair from my eyes, my owd duck. Jack likes to be at wok when this goes on.'

'It's not right, though,' Em'ler said angrily. 'Men think they can get away with murder.'

She glared wickedly at Arthur, her grey eyes filled with a rancid hate. He grinned, and she dropped her glance, passing more gin to Brenda.

'How much left?' Brenda asked.

Em'ler looked into the pot. 'Half a glass,' she lied. Brenda's skin turned salmon-pink below the water-line, and she drank slowly. She rolled her head back but, finding nothing on which to rest it, brought it forward again, finally leaving it a little to one side. Arthur could not worry any more. The fever of his cold put him into a half-sleep. Brenda's face was hidden by steam, and the air was so warm and gin-smelling that for minutes at a time he did not know where he was. The stumpy table-supports under the checked-cloth looked like a cook's legs below an apron, and the heavy dresser, whose mirror was steamed over, resembled the back of a coal-barge disappearing through the evening mist. The chairs, the sofa on which Brenda had spread out her clothes, became beads of moisture on the window panes. He woke up as the gin-glass slipped through Brenda's perspiring fingertips, and Em'ler, in a mad dash that scattered a frail chair in her way, saved the gin from falling on to the rug, wiped Brenda's fingers dry with a towel, and gave the glass back to her. 'You haven't got much more to drink now, duck,' she said kindly.

Brenda pushed her hand away. 'Don't want it. I'll be sick.'

'It's for your own good,' Em'ler insisted firmly.

'Drink it,' Arthur said gently. 'A drop more, duck.' The smell of gin penetrated the barrier of his cold and made him feel slightly ill.

'I'm going dizzy,' Brenda said.

Em'ler poured more water into the bath. 'Keep your eyes open,' she said, watching her closely, 'then you won't feel dizzy, duck.'

'I can't keep 'em open.' She tried to drink more gin, but it spilled from the corners of her mouth. 'My mother didn't teach me this,' she drawled, repeating the phrase until it became unrecognisable. Then she began to sing in a thin caterwauling voice.

'Shut up, duck,' Em'ler said gently. She turned on Arthur: 'You bastard. You dirty bastard.'

'Whose a bastard?' he cried, jumping up with surprise. 'You're daft, you ugly bitch.'

'Drink this, duck,' she said. 'Come on. Just a drop more. Keep your eyes open, then you'll feel better.' Brenda tilted the glass upwards and drank, then stared blankly before her, saying nothing, face pale and mouth set hard. Em'ler wiped sweat away with a towel, pushed back strands of hair from her forehead, then poured more hot water into the bath. 'Only this left,' she said, passing the rest of the gin.

'I thought it was all gone!' Brenda's lips twisted. 'I'm getting out,' she wept. Em'ler looked at the drop of gin left.

'Let her get out,' Arthur said. 'It's done the trick by now.'

'You shut up,' she said cuttingly, 'this is my job.'

'Then get on wi' it,' he said, and lit another cigarette. Brenda stood up suddenly, her pink steaming body unfolding before him like a rose in full bloom. She swayed, as if about to fall, then stepped with a splash on to the rug. Em'ler wiped her dry with one hand and held her up with the other.

'Want any help?' Arthur volunteered.

The retort was quick: 'No thank you. I can manage all right without *your* help, thank you very much.' She reached for a dressing-gown on the sofa back, and when she turned the towels fell from Brenda, leaving her naked, swaying towards the fire.

Arthur reached her first, then Em'ler pushed him jealously away and caught up

145

Brenda's formidable weight, holding her up-right and trying at the same time to get the dressing-gown on her. 'Hold still, Brenda. Please hold still while I fasten this.'

'Tell me if you want any help,' Arthur said, sitting relaxed in his chair.

'Shirrup, you bastard, you,' Em'ler snapped back. 'I'll pay you out one day.'

'Christ, I've never known anybody as daft as yo', you cross-eyed gett,' he said in an even voice.

Brenda rolled slightly, closed her lids over the staring eyes and slipped down on to the rug unconscious. Em'ler ran into the scullery for a cup of cold water which she sprinkled lavishly until Brenda's eyes opened. With tremendous strength and skill she lifted Brenda back on her feet and walked her to the stairfoot door, which she pulled open so that they could climb the steps. 'Come on to bed, duck,' she coaxed. 'It's all over now. Come on to bed and sleep it off.' They went up the stairs with snail-like slowness. At times Em'ler had to lift Brenda's feet and legs and place them on the steps above, cleverly econ-omising her strength, and Arthur watching from behind, thanked God that Em'ler had done all this for them, and in one sentimental moment forgave her all the times she had called him a bastard. 'Come on, Brenda,' she kept saying. 'Come on, duck. Just another step. That's right. Now one more. Now another. We shall soon be at the top. I'm sure we've brought it off. Just one more step.'

A clear laugh came out of Brenda's drunkenness: 'I don't care whether it comes off or not. I don't care now.'

Em'ler sat her down on the bed. She fell back and lay perfectly still, giving a sigh and going immediately to sleep. Arthur stood in the doorway, watched Em'ler shaking her head and pulling the sheets over Brenda. 'Is she all right?' he asked.

Em'ler's face came closer to a smile than he had ever seen it. 'Nowt to worry about,' she told him.

He took a pound note from his pocket. 'Buy yourself something with this, Em.'

She pushed his hand away. 'I don't want your money. You keep it. You'll need it one day.'

'Don't be daft,' he retorted. 'Buy yourself a blouse or some stockings. Yer've done us a good turn tonight.'

She smoothed her hair back. 'No, I don't want any of your money'—her voice becoming hard again. He pushed the pound note into her apron pocket but she thrust it back into his coat.

'All right,' he said. 'If you won't let me thank you.'

She leaned over to switch off the light. 'Who do you think you are? Trying to thank me for this? You've got a cheek, mate, I can tell you.'

'Bogger you then,' he swore, and turned to walk out of the room. He changed his mind and went back, kissing her on the lips. 'Thanks,' he said.

She lifted her fist to hit him, but he caught the strong wrist and stopped her. 'You touch me,' he said, 'and see what you get.' He pressed her arm back until the pain of it showed in her face.

'Let me go, you bastard,' she said. 'Somebody's coming down the yard.' He heard a knocking at the back door, and released her. The light out, they ran downstairs.

'Brenda?' Jack called out. 'Let me in. I forgot my snap.'

Arthur caught hold of Em'ler and whispered: 'Keep 'im talkin'. I'm going out by the front door.'

'I'll do as I think fit,' she answered in her normally loud, idiotic voice. 'I might keep 'im talkin' and I might not. You can't make me. It's up to me to say whether I'll do it or not, let me tell you.'

'You bastard,' Arthur hissed. 'Keep quiet.'

'I'm not a bastard,' she cried.

'All right then. But for Christ's sake don't yap so loud.' Jack hammered on the door, shouting: 'Open up, Brenda. Who's in there with you?'

'*You* might be a bastard,' Em'ler went on, as if she hadn't heard the knocking, 'whatever your name is, but I'm not one. If you think I'm a bastard I'll show you my birth certificate to prove it.'

'You're worse,' Arthur said, and left her talking and fumbling in her apron pocket as if she really did carry a birth certificate with her. He walked quietly through the parlour, and heard Em'ler lift the latch and ask Jack gruffly what he wanted, saying that she couldn't find her birth certificate now but would show it him tomorrow. Holding the parlour door open, Arthur laughed as he heard Jack stammering out his excuses to the fierce Em'ler who continued to bar his way for reasons best known to herself. Brenda slept obliviously upstairs, and Arthur did not care now whether the night's work had been successful or not. Feverish and weary, he couldn't have cared less—standing on the doorstep trying to decide on the best direction to the nearest pub—if he had made twenty thousand women pregnant and all their husbands were at his back, brandishing sickles and after his blood.

He walked down the long empty street, his head clearing with the sudden onset of fresh air, his mind lighter, his troubles weighing less since he was no more face to face with them. Market Square lights danced around him. Each pavement threw back the sound of his shoes walking. Draughts of beer and smoke-smells came out of pub doors. He dodged between tall green buses that scooped up loads of darkness as they went by with all lights shining, pushed his way through crowds gathered around Slab Square Bible-punchers and soap-box orators. The evening dug a slit-trench in his brain, and he couldn't throw off the vivid and blood-like scene of Brenda's white body reclining in the bath, and Em'ler's idiot face passing glass after glass of gin until Brenda was hopeless and helpless in her swill-tippling and unable to speak or recognise anybody in the room. It's her fault for letting such a thing happen, he cursed. The stupid bloody woman.

He stumped on to the Peach Tree and sat down to a double rum, feeling easier, his cold giving less trouble. Someone sang in a wailing, off-key voice, a snake-head swaying before a microphone on a stage at the room's far end. He stared glumly at the backs lined at the bar, listened to the businesslike clink of the till, and the crisp brandy-snap tone of the barmaid. The floating demoniac voice sent into the microphone came through smoke-haze and wheeled around Arthur so that he wanted to get his hands at the insane throat causing all the noise. Other people felt like-wise. Arthur watched a man make his way through the crowd. 'Pardon me, Pardon me'—and walk up to the youth who was singing. They spoke to each other like two friends meeting on the street, the singer holding a cigarette, the other man his lapel. The singer's cigarette was unlighted, and he seemed to be offering it to the man. Then, suddenly, the man who had seemed so meek hit the singer, dealing him a violent crack on the lower half of his face. The singer's feet caught in the microphone wires, and when he tried to get up and retaliate, he fell down again.

Arthur was glad it had happened, laugh-ing so loud that he began to choke from the pain in his ribs. Perhaps the singer hadn't realised he was making such a terrible racket, thinking he sounded like Gene Autry or Nelson Eddy. Anyway there was no need to make a noise like that and it served him right that he had been clobbered. With a red, bruised, and bewildered face the singer walked by Arthur, out through the swing doors. The same doors were pushed inwards while his eyes were still on them, and in came Winnie, Brenda's younger sister.

She looked around the bar and at the tables near the wall, opening her black coat because of the sudden heat. Arthur noted a coloured scarf like a turban, high-heeled shoes, stockings, and a black handbag.

'Hey, Winnie,' he called out, 'are you lost?'

She didn't hear him. He had met her once before, at Jack's birthday party last year, which she broke up at two in the morning by flying into a temper at Jack and smashing every pot and bottle on the table with a poker because he accidentally spilled half a pint over Brenda's best dress. Such an act of destruction fascinated Arthur. He had wanted to get to know her. She was a small woman of twenty-five who seemed to Arthur only half the size of himself. At Jack's party he had called her Gyp because of her long black hair, a nickname that enraged her, and she threatened to biff him one if he didn't stop. He asked her to come outside and do it then, so that they wouldn't make a mess of Jack's party, but she refused and said that if he didn't behave himself she'd tell her husband about him when he came home on leave from Germany. 'All right, Gyp,' he had answered, and this remark was the cause of her temper that led her to smash up the party, using Jack's spilled beer as an excuse.

He stood up and walked across to her. 'Hey up, Winnie,' he said. The Gyp would come later.

She turned to him and smiled, giving no sign of the fire for which he was prepared. 'I'm looking for a friend of mine,' she said.

'Maybe he's in the Trip,' he suggested.

'It's a *she*, cleverdick,' came the retort.

He took her arm. 'Come and have a drink then.'

'No,' she said, 'I've got to get going. I haven't finished cleaning the house up yet for when Bill comes home. He'll be in tomorrow night, and if the house's scruffy he'll have a fit and black my eyes.'

He persuaded her to sit down. 'I'll have a gin-and-orange,' she said.

'How long's he got?'

'Ten days this time, but he'll be back again next month. He's a sergeant now, in the

153

M.Ps.'

He watched her drink; her full small lips seemed spiteful and charged with trouble; her breasts, large and out of proportion in size to the rest of her body, pushed the folds of her purple jumper forward. You touch me, they said, and see what a smack you get. Mounds of mischief. You'd never think she was Brenda's sister, he said to himself. A bit of funny business went on in the family twenty-odd years ago. Some gypsy selling clothes pegs got hold of her mother and gave her what for, I'm sure, when she offered him a cup of tea. You've only got to look at her eyes and them high cheeks and that coal-black hair and the beaky little nose. A nice change though from a bread-pudding face with spotted-dick eyes and ginger-pink tabs.

'When does Bill get his ticket then?' he spoke out.

'Only another ten months. And I'll be glad as well. He'll be better out of it. I might just as well not be married, with him in the army.' She had a tiny endearing gap between two front teeth, which intensified any emotion showed on her face, making her look more annoyed than she really was, or sadder, or happier, a physical accretion to her personality that fascinated Arthur.

'No,' he said, 'it's no life for a woman. Nobody to look after her and take her out when she feels like a good time. It must be miserable for you. A woman wants a bloke to look after her, not to be stuck in Germany. I can't understand a bloke as signs on for the army, especially when he's married, and never could. And when he's got a nice sweet little woman like you I reckon it's even bar-mier. Leaving you behind in Nottingham. I don't know what the world's coming to, I don't an' all. Have another drink duck, then you'll feel better. You will, I mean it. Being in the army's no life even at the best of times. I know, because I've been in. No, duck, the sooner he's home the better, then he can look after you as a bloke should. He can get a job and settle down, and bring a regular pay-packet into the house every Friday. There's nowt like it. You write and tell him to get home as quick as he can, and to get out of the army for good. Gin-and-orange? I'll have a black-and-tan.' He talked in a low voice, his tone suggesting that he did not know he was being sympathetic. It was as effective as the drink, his words rolling out a theme of pity for a deserted woman until she felt sorry for her-self, at which he began to cheer her up with crude jokes and slapstick actions, so that

155

when he called her Gyp she was so happy that there was no objection to it.

'How's Brenda?' he said later, when she was sipping her third gin-and-orange.

'You should know,' she laughed. 'You're her fancy-man.'

With a mutual grin the subject changed. He felt happy. Whether Brenda's trouble had been resolved or not did not matter: he was relieved that she was asleep and that it was settled one way or another, and this sense of relief made him unquenchable in his tenderness to her sister Winnie. By ten of the pub clock he was holding her hand and merely looked up to order a last round before 'time' was shouted. The more he talked the less he noticed the noise, and they sat in a magic ring of quiet speech that no disturbance could enter.

'I'll see you home, duck, if you like,' he said, when the last drinks had gone and they stood up to fasten their coats.

'All right,' she answered. Locked in the fevered fastness of his cold he could hardly remember Brenda, thinking that perhaps he had dreamed about her sometime, but nothing more. She had vanished behind a veil of fever, sunk beneath the steaming waters of a zinc bath, gone to extinction carrying a bottle of boiling gin, arm-in-arm with batchy Em'ler. He was happy enough with Winnie, walking her up Derby Road towards home. She took his arm, having forgotten that she should have been cleaning her house for Bill tomorrow night, and Arthur didn't remind her. Loaded buses passed them. At Canning Circus she told him to walk across quickly so that they wouldn't be recognised by any of her neighbours also on their way home from long errands to public houses. He knew then what he was in for, telling himself what a lucky bastard he was, yet hoping with the same inward breath that his premonition would turn out well. She was small by his side, like a little girl. You bleedin' kidnapper, he laughed to himself as they swung into Winnie's street. They stopped talking, lightened their footsteps. 'I don't want the neighbours to twig anything,' she whispered, pressing his arm.

'You know what the neighbours can do?' he said derisively.

'Shut up,' she hissed. 'It's all right for you, but Bill's coming home tomorrow night. I'll be in big trouble if anybody sees me with you.'

Having a cold made him reckless, but her sharp sensible retort put him back on guard, and he kept quiet until they were in the house.

'I don't think anyone saw us come in,' she said, switching on the kitchen lights.

'You'll be all right.' He held her gently and bent down to kiss her. She threw her arms around him, taking his kisses with the greed of a passionate woman who had been parted too long from her husband. 'Shall we go upstairs, duck?' he said.

'Yes, but be quiet.'

He followed, loving her on every second stair, loins aching for her small wild body, remembering that he had recently ascended another set of stairs under different circumstances. The evening had begun, and the evening was about to end. She stripped to her underwear and lay in bed waiting for him. Never had an evening begun so sadly and ended so well, he reflected, peeling off his socks.

CHAPTER SEVEN

Jack took a short cut through the Frame Shop, for time was valuable since his promotion. Arthur was surprised at his appearance as he walked down the gangway: he seemed to have shrunk in size during the last month: he was sallow in the face, his lips were half open as if he were talking to himself, the black hair remembered as so glossy was now lank and dead, and he came into the shop looking as though he had no right there, nodding furtively to Robboe, and making his way between rows of machinery towards Arthur.

Arthur had tried to imagine the scene when Jack was finally let into the house last Monday night, into his living-room littered with wet towels, empty glasses and gin bottles, and a long zinc bath of still steaming water. What had Em'ler said to him? He would have offered his right arm to have been an invisible listener. Even Brenda did not know, for though the gin and hot bath had been successful she did not say much to Arthur, sitting glumly a few days later in the Royal Coach and being sarcastic when she spoke any word at all.

He stopped work when Jack approached, clapped him on the back, said how glad he was to see him, that he should come more often so that they could natter like old times. 'But I suppose you're too stuck up now you've got such a posh job. One of these days they'll make you a foreman and then you won't even speak to me when we pass on the street.'

Jack received these sallies frigidly, his dark eyes taking in the familiar details of the lathe, darting into the sud-bin, up to the pulley-wheels, on to the turret—everywhere but at Arthur's face. 'You should be glad to see me,' he said, 'because I've got something to tell you.'

'You've won the pools, I suppose?'

His face became earnest and sad. 'I wish you'd be serious and listen to what I'm going to say. I haven't got much time. I've got to be back at my job in ten minutes.'

'What is it then?' Arthur was annoyed and uneasy because Jack was nervous, and he didn't get on well with people who threw their nervousness in his face.

'I've come to give you fair warning,' Jack went on. 'I shouldn't be telling you this, but being as we're supposed to be friends, I will. You'd better be on your guard for the next couple of days because two big swaddies are after you. They're going to bash you up, so don't say I didn't warn you, though God knows, you don't deserve to be warned after what you've done. You should have had more sense, at your age.'

Arthur thought: in a case like this, say nothing. Let him do all the talking. Encourage him by: 'I don't know why two swaddies should be after my guts. But thanks for telling me anyway.'

Jack almost looked at him, but couldn't quite fix his gaze. It moved to a stack of work, and he said: 'You're a crafty bogger, Arthur. I think you know very well why they're after you, but in case you don't I'll tell you. One of the swaddies is Bill, Winnie's husband. He says you've been carrying on with his wife. He says as well that you've been carrying on with Brenda. Well, I don't know about his wife. You may have been carrying on with her for all I know. But I think he was wrong about Brenda. I like to know things in black and white, straight, and I know what black is and what white is in this case. I'm sure he's wrong about Brenda. But if he wasn't, I'll give you fair warning, Arthur. I'll cause trouble for you if you do carry on with Brenda. But then, I think you're my friend, and wouldn't do such a thing. I think you're all right, deep down.'

Jack clenched and unfolded his fist all through his long speech, and at the end of it Arthur passed him a piece of clean rag, which was accepted to wipe sweat slowly from his mouth and forehead. 'You can be dead sure there's nowt between me and Brenda,' Arthur said. He was not worried by what he had just heard, yet felt that after his triumphant night with Winnie the forces of righteousness were closing-in, spoiling the fangs and blunting the claws of his existence. But one could never say that. Luck was always changing. It thumped you with knuckledusters on the back of the neck one minute, and stuffed your gob with sugar the next. The thing was: not to weaken. Like Jack, for instance.

'You know,' Arthur said, 'these two big swaddies might be after me, but if it comes to a fight I'll give 'em a run for their money. They want to be careful. I shan't run away from 'em.'

Jack shook his head. 'No, I know you wain't. I wish you would, though, because if you don't keep out of their way it'll mean trouble for you.'

'And trouble for them bastards,' Arthur swore, feeling his back pressed too close to the wall. He did not like to fight, and would avoid it by all means possible: only the stupid fought with their fists, when they hadn't the brains to argue: it was a poor way out of any problem. Yet when you were cornered, with two big swaddies after blood—two big heathens who had no brains and couldn't listen to argument—then you could only lash out with your fists and smash whatever hundredweight sacks of coal came for you.

'Don't say I didn't warn you,' Jack said.

'I won't. Thanks for the favour. I'll look out.'

'See you another time then.' He was already on his way down the gangway.

'So long,' Arthur called, twisting the turret with such force that its noisy clack echoed above the sound of other machinery.

*　　　*　　　*

At knocking-off time he walked along Eddison Road with his head high, unnoticed in the crowd, thinking how right Jack had been, for he could swear that two swaddies had trailed him a few evenings ago. He had thought that perhaps they were policemen, but concluded this to be impossible because as far as he knew he had snatched no bags, burst no gas meters, coshed no shopkeepers. And so

163

Jack had explained it all. He made up the story as he walked along: Bill had arrived from Germany, and the same night had called at the beer-off by the street-end, and stood talking to one of the tight-lipped women that passed for neighbours, who had lost no time in saying what a good woman and wife Winnie had been while Bill was away, yet at the same time hinting that something fishy had been going on the night before, adding that Winnie had been seen in the Peach Tree with a young chap who was tall and had fair hair. In the knocking-about that took place when Bill got back to the house Winnie had ended up with a black eye and Bill with the claw-marks of a tiger down one side of his face, and Winnie said that of course she had been in the Peach Tree with Arthur, but that he had been waiting to see Brenda, her sister, who had turned up after ten minutes, during which time she had only taken advantage of one measly gin-and-orange. As for bringing him back to the house he could ask Brenda whose bed he had gone back to, though he was to say nothing about it to Jack on pain of another fanciful tiger-claw dèsign down the other side of his face. But Bill had been so enraged at this trouble when he had expected bliss to be his lot after a rough crossing from the Hook that he was determined to make Arthur pay for it. A young man that carried on with two married woman should be stopped dead in his tracks. He had tackled Jack on the question: a bloke called Arthur who works at your factory is carrying on with your wife, Jack. Jack hadn't believed him, but Bill said he could prove that Arthur went back home with Brenda last Monday night. Jack had laughed in his face, saying that he was home last Monday night and that Brenda had been in all evening with a friend of hers called Em'ler, an old mate from the stocking factory. He must have felt sheepish in adding that Em'ler had been drunk—not quite the right sort of friend to have—and that his wife was upstairs in a dead stupor in which she lay until morning. Bill swore that Jack was a bloody fool. Jack had smiled. Bill had said, all right, then. He was home for ten days and was going to get this young bastard who wanted to break up their happy married lives. A mate of his was on leave at the same time and they would shadow him, and bash him up one of these nights. Jack had seen that Bill was in earnest, and so had warned Arthur.

He turned in at the yard-end. Dusk was spreading between the houses, turning into a cold, windy April evening. His heavy boots clobbered their way down the yard. Lifting the back-door latch he passed through the scullery and hung his coat in the parlour. He usually said: 'Hey-up,' to the rest of the family, but this evening he was too preoccupied for politeness, seating himself morosely at the table and waiting for his mother to pour him a cup of tea. The wireless was drumming away, and the first thing he said was:

'Turn that thing off.'

But it was playing some Old Time waltzes that his mother liked. 'Leave it on,' she said. 'It's nice music.'

'Well, pour me a cup o' tea, then,' he demanded.

She looked up at him. 'What's up wi' yo' tonight? Pullin' a megrim like that.'

He didn't answer. The wireless was left on. His elder brother Fred sat at the table doing a crossword. He wondered what was on Arthur's mind, seeing him drink his cup of tea without saying a word. 'I'm going upstairs to listen to the wireless,' Fred announced.

Arthur followed him, and sat on the bed.

'You don't seem very happy,' Fred said. 'What's the trouble?'

He didn't want to explain his worries. 'Nowt,' he answered in the last stages of dejection. Lighting a cigarette he walked to the

166

window and hurled the dead match outside as if it were a stone and he wanted it to hit someone; stood for a moment to watch kids playing beneath the lighted streetlamps, hearing the distant hooting of traffic and the soft throbbing of factory engines at the end of the terrace. 'If you want to know what's up,' he said, 'two blokes are after me, a couple of swaddies'—and he told everything. 'Winnie's husband's on leave from Germany, and he's out with one of his pals to get me before they go back.'

'Keep out of their way for a bit, then,' Fred advised him. 'Are you going out tonight?'

'I was thinking about it.'

'I'll go with you. I'd like a walk.' If I can't help him much in a fight I can at least see that he doesn't get into one, Fred told himself.

'Are you sure you want to come?' He didn't feel like leading Fred into any trouble. With himself, it didn't matter.

'I said I wanted a walk, didn't I?'

'It's your funeral then,' Arthur warned him.

'And yours,' Fred retorted, 'for getting mixed-up in a thing like this.'

Neither used overcoats, hoping to warm themselves by a quick walk to the pub, and then to be re-stoked by a pint or two. Fred admitted, walking up the yard, that he was broke as usual—thirty-bob sickness benefit didn't go far—and Arthur said that the drinks would be on him. Mrs. Bull stood at the yard-end, her moon-face a beacon scanning the street for news of established wrecks and for rumours of those next destined for the dogs, peering through half-darkness to find out who was nipping to Taylor's for a basket of grub on tick. Arthur unknowingly nudged her in passing.

'Mind what ye'r doin',' she shouted after him. 'Yer young bleeder.'

'I think you bumped into her,' Fred explained.

Arthur turned: 'I didn't see yer,' he cried. 'You stand there so often I thought you was a new pillar the builders had put up. You want to be careful: I might 'ave stopped and stubbed my fag out on you by accident. Though I don't suppose it'd have bin the first time that that's 'appened.'

She shook her fist. 'You cheeky sod. I've seen you carryin' on wi' married women. I copped you the other night down town, and don't say I didn't.' She kept a chock-a-block arsenal of blackmailing scandal ready to level with foresight and backsight at those that

crossed her path in the wrong direction, snip-
ing with tracer and dum-dum from sandbags
of ancient gossip.

'You want to mind yer own business, you
nosy bogger,' Arthur shouted.

'Ah!' she cried, in the sort of knowing voice
that maddened him, 'so as dirty people like
you can prosper!'

Fred pulled at his arm. 'She's barmy,' he
said. 'She's got the ox.'

They walked uphill to the Peacock, in
which few people sat because it was still early,
and found a table in a corner across from the
bar. Arthur fetched the drinks: stout for himself, and a pint for Fred.

Arthur drank eight bottles of stout, and
Fred realised, seeing him drink like this, how
much he was worried. Also, Arthur always
smoked heavily during boozing, but now he
was putting back pint after pint of stout without even noticing the packet of cigarettes that
Fred slid on to the table. 'You want to take it
easy,' he warned him.

'What for?' It was an uncompromising
request, implying that he wanted to be left
alone.

'Because you'll get drunk. You'll start
fighting.'

'No I wain't. I've got enough on my konk

wi'out getting into a fight.' It was a logical answer, but Fred knew that it meant nothing if a force of anger came up before he had time to think. At the seventh bottle he exclaimed. 'Look, stupid, I don't want to have to carry you home.'

'Who's askin' yer ter carry me 'ome?'

'Nobody. You never do. You just conk out.'

'How many times have yer seen me conk out from too much booze?' he asked truculently.

'Twice. But that was enough.'

Arthur gave him a black look, but Fred stared back until he relaxed and merely said: 'If I conk out it wain't be on yo', so don't worry yoursen.'

'I'll watch it,' Fred rejoined. 'I'm not going to lug you right down Ilkeston Road in the dark. Especially if you start spewin' all over the place.' He wasn't yet worried: eight bottles of stout were nothing to panic about.

'A drink'll do me good tonight,' Arthur said.

'A drink's all right, but not a bath in it.'

Arthur laughed, but it was the laugh of a man caught unawares by something funny at a time when he saw nothing to laugh at in the general situation. 'You aren't drinkin' much yoursen.'

Fred tapped the half-pint before him. 'Somebody's got to stay sober and look after you.'

'You insultin' bastard. I don't want no lookin' after.'

'Not much you don't.' Fred piled it on. 'Anybody who goes carryin'-on with two married women and lets their husbands find out about it wants lookin' after.'

Arthur disliked having the subject brought into the open. 'I didn't let them know about it. Some neighbours must have seen me, and opened their traps. They won't let a bloke live.'

'Them swaddies wain't let you live, when they get you.'

'I can look after myself,' he affirmed. 'Wait and see.'

'That what I'm doing. Only if they're around tonight I'll be here to help you. I don't want to have you rolling drunk all over the place and not be able to do anything when they see you. Anyway, if you do see 'em, take my tip, and run. It's the best thing to do. You told me they're both big bastards on leave from Germany. You can't stand up to 'em with all that piss inside you.'

'I can allus fight better when I've had summat to drink,' Arthur answered. 'It makes me mad. If I saw 'em when I was sober I might want to shake 'ands wi' 'em an' say: "How do, lads? Sorry, but you shun't 'ave bin such stupid bastards as to sign on for ten years wi' the army, then you could 'ave looked after yer wives a bit better." But if I've 'ad some drink I'll just lash into 'em.'

Four youths were amusing themselves at the dartboard, two teams coming excitedly down from three-o-one, shouting out each score with such vehemence that Fred thought ninety-thousand quid had been promised as a prize. They were either bad players, or drunk, for darts were hitting the wall and board-wires, falling over the floor like wounded birds. One dart player, with an exaggerated swing of his arm, slung a dart forcefully in the general direction of the board. Its steel tip clicked loudly on an outer wire, ricocheted, and turned a few graceful somersaults in the air above Arthur's leg.

Sitting at a table, Arthur always found difficulty in placing his legs in a comfortable position. He could only find accommodation for one of them beneath this particular table. The other was outstretched over the floor, showing a space of flesh between the top of his short socks and the pulled-up bottom of his trousers. The antics of the flying dart ended by plummeting downwards and sticking in the soft meaty part of his exposed ankle, then hanging down from his flesh.

His leg twitched, but he did not jump up from the sudden pain, being so busy thinking about his trouble that not even a brick on his head or a firework explosion would have roused him. He bent forward, plucked out the dart, and laid it on the table beside his glass.

Fred was always amazed at the way a fight started; a defective machine was set in motion and you knew it was going to break itself up unless you ran to the switch and stopped it. But at such moments he became too interested in the movement towards destruction, and the machine turned into a twisted mass of nuts and bolts on the floor.

The young man who had thrown the dart sported an electric-blue suit, brown shoes, yellow pullover, a brown tieless shirt, and several pimples on his face, a face all scrunched-up, with eyes half blind so that you could almost see the drink slooshing around behind them. 'Can I have my dart back?' he asked Arthur.

Arthur looked up, speaking quietly: 'Say you're sorry, then, because your dart stuck in my leg.'

Fred wanted to tell the youth: 'Do as he

says, then you'll be all right.' But he just sat there, placing bets with himself as to what would happen next. The youth looked down at Arthur: 'I want my dart,' he said. His friends shouted impatiently: 'Come on, Ted, get that dart back and have your throw. We're waiting.' The youth grinned at them, then said again with slightly more truculence: 'Give me back my dart.'

Arthur made a reasonable request: 'Just say you're sorry, and I'll give it back to you.'

'I say I'm sorry to nobody,' the youth cried, suddenly finding his way through the beer and bravado that clouded his brain. 'Give me back my bleedin' dart.'

Arthur stood up and hit him, putting into his fist all the bursting irritation of the past few weeks. It was such a blow that the youth went staggering against the bar, kept upright by his tripping feet that took him gracefully back like some trick dancer. He jogged through his friends, who moved out of his track and stared at him with bulging eyes as he passed. Then he rebounded and hit Arthur, and Arthur's fist burst out as if he were a robot and a button had been pressed in him by the youth's blow, and the youth followed the same track once more to the bar, only this time spinning slightly as he went. He returned again, with his friends.

Fred said later that it looked like a wonderful free-for-all in a cowboy film. He was able to give this objective picture because as soon as the fight started he made for the door that led outside to the lavatory. He felt bad about leaving his brother to fend for himself, but had to get out of the way of flying fists and upturned tables, not being allowed by the doctor to take part in fights because of his bronchitis.

Arthur was doing all right, he decided. The youth had apparently thought that Arthur wasn't as tall as he was when he saw him sitting down, and now realised his mistake: Arthur was so much bigger than the others that they could hardly get at him. He lashed out left, right, and centre, and was not averse to dealing occasional kicks with his heavy working boots. The barman and publican beat their way close to him. Fred shouted: 'Do a bunk, Arthur!' He watched him pause, look back and give him a nod, hit out once more at the youth who had caused it all, and rush for the swing doors.

They met outside. 'Let's bolt up this street,' Fred said. A lamp shone weakly, and one or two panes of yellow light came from an occasional window. They walked quickly along, and were turning the first corner when a commotion broke out behind. Fred said they should run, but Arthur replied that it was better to walk quietly so that no one could know which direction they had taken. They turned several corners in the maze of streets, and came out on to the lights of Alfreton Road. 'I think I could do with another drink,' Arthur said, fastening his coat.

*   *   *

After the ten o'clock turnout of public houses Canning Circus gave in to its curfew and became silent. Late cars changed gear as they ascended the hill, showed their dark snouts upon circling the island at the top, then disappeared into the oblivion of an opposite road. A moon illuminated the island's flowerless garden, and the junction's green lamp-poles were dimly lighted in comparison to such lunar brilliance.

Arthur and Fred walked by the almshouses talking about war, Fred gesticulating as he threw out his opinions on tactics, fluently comparing Korea to Libya, mountain to desert, 'human seas' to tanks. A light shone from a public house in which people were still washing-up. All other doorways and buildings stood empty, their windows darkened by blinds. A few people were about, one man stalking along in the shadows, another walking boldly across the island whistling the latest song hit. A third person came unsteadily out of the public house clutching a glass beer mug. 'See that?' Arthur said, pointing to him. 'What's that funny sod doin'?'

Fred saw only an interruption to his flow of speech, but on drawing closer heard the man humming an unrecognisable tune, as if to disguise the purpose of his expedition across the road. He stepped on to the pavement and looked intently into the window of an undertaker's shop.

'I wonder what he's up to?' Arthur repeated.

Having made up his mind, the man took three calculated strides back to the pavement edge and threw the beer mug with great force at the window. The smash sounded musical and carefree, and glass splashed on to the pavement, while the man adroitly dodged the chaos he had caused.

Arthur was stirred by the sound of breaking glass: it synthesised all the anarchism within him, was the most perfect and suitable noise to accompany the end of the world and himself. He ran towards the disturbance, each strike of his boots on the pavement sending an echo through the empty circle of buildings, rebounding from each deserted corner.

'Come on,' he called to Fred.

Several people already stood near the undertaker's window, as if they had sprung out of the ground, and by the doorway a woman held the bewildered culprit by his wrist. Arthur peered closer and saw that another woman, younger and wearing an army uniform—the colour of which immediately prejudiced him—had taken command, and had sent someone to fetch the police. Fred grinned at the jagged hole, at giant cracks running away from it in all directions, at head-stones, scrolls, and earthen flower vases splattered with glass. He laughed at the wreck, and pushed some glass into the gutter with his shoe cap.

'What's up, missis?' a raincoated pipe-smoker wanted to know. 'What's 'e done?'—nodding at the man held by the wrist, who grinned with great friendliness at each new arrival.

'Chucked a pint jar at that winder,' Arthur said.

'He did *that*,' the woman in khaki told him, pointing at the wrecked window like a

178

museum guide showing off a prize exhibit. She was a woman of about thirty-five, her prominent bosom emphasised by highly polished buttons. Arthur noted her thin lips, high cheekbones, eyes that did not open very wide, a low forehead, and hair that just curled out of the back of her peaked cap and rested on her shaved neck. Weighing her up, he wondered if she had ever been loved. He doubted it. She was the sort of woman who would spit in a man's eye if he tried to be nice to her, though at the same time he supposed her to be the sort who wanted most of all in the world to be loved. Only you could tell by her face that she would kick you if you tried. Old Rat Face, he said to himself, that's what she is. Potatoes and Horsemeat.

'She's a fawce bogger,' a man said, half in admiration, half in contempt. 'She knows what she's doing right enough.'

'You'll get a stripe for this,' Arthur cried. 'Right across your back.'

Most of the interest was focused on *him*, standing mutely by the woman who held his limp and resistless wrist. He was neither young nor middle-aged, a man who seemed to have a stake in two generations without being cradled and carried along by either one. His face seemed marked by some years of marriage, yet his bearing branded him as a single man, an odd, lonely person who gave off an air of belonging nowhere at all, which caused Arthur to think him half-witted. The uniformed woman looked as though she also had never had a home and belonged nowhere, but she had aligned herself with order and law, and sympathy was against her. The man turned slightly towards the window. He had brown hair that receded over a narrow forehead, and his pink face looked as though it had just been thoroughly washed. With the arm that was not held, he pointed through the glass to a black flower vase covered by a metal grid, and to a grey, partly inscribed headstone. 'In Loving Memory Of'.

'I only wanted one o' them,' he said, looking around for approval, 'and one o' these.' He spoke with a whine, as though he never really meant to smash the window, and that for this reason he should eventually be released by the elder woman at his side.

'Why did you do such a barmy thing, mate?' Arthur called out. 'That winder worn't worth smashin'.'

He looked at him as if he brought some hope, and pointed again to the two objects. 'I wanted that there,' he said with simple insistence.

Sympathetic voices gave him confidence, and while he still hoped for some sort of release, seemed pleased that he was such an attraction. From the look in his eyes and the grin on his face, it was as though he thought he might be dreaming, or did not quite believe where he was, or that the situation was some kind of game. 'I wanted them things for my mother'—inclining his head again to the window. The tone of his voice indicated that he should continue, but he stopped speaking, as if only capable of making one short sentence at a time, and in a moment of excitement he had thought to stray beyond this line.

'Let's go off home,' Fred suggested. 'Them owd 'ags'll 'and 'im over to the coppers. There's nowt ter wait for.'

Arthur preferred to stay, standing with a blank mind, as if he were at the theatre watching a play, fascinated but unable to participate. 'Where's your mother then?' several people called out at once.

The woman in khaki braced herself. 'Leave him alone. The police will ask him all the questions. He can do all his talking to them.' Some wit from the crowd asked him again where his mother was, and he turned to them with a grave look, saying solemnly: 'I buried her three months ago. I didn't mean no harm, missis,' he said gently to the woman holding him.

'All the same,' she said, 'you didn't need to do this.'

A woman called out that the police were coming. Fred edged closer to the prisoner. 'You was daft to do that,' he said, in a voice that precluded either hope or assistance.

'There are bigger and better winders ter smash downtown,' Arthur said. 'I know a clinker on Long Row, wi' furniture behind it!'

'I wanted it for my mother. I've only just buried her.'

'You'll get six months in Lincoln for this,' someone from the back shouted, showing a dual knowledge of geography and justice that made everybody laugh. The woman holding him asked them to be quiet and leave him alone: their taunts made him nervous.

'Let me go, missis,' he said to her secretively, as if her plea meant that she was now on his side. 'Go on, be a sport. I didn't mean no harm. I'd on'y had a pint or two.'

The woman in khaki turned on him sharply. 'Shut up, you. You'll stay where you are and wait for the police.'

''Ark at 'er,' somebody said. 'She talks to 'im as if 'e was dirt, the poor bogger.'

A new wave of curiosity caught every

member of the crowd at the same time, and interest moved to the vital statistics of the man himself. They asked where he lived, how many kids he had, where he worked, what his name was, and how old he was. But so many questions confused him, and he could not answer. In a loud voice the woman in khaki told them to leave the questions for the police, as though her only function on earth was to live until they came.

He still looked for salvation from the woman by his side. 'Let me off, missis, please,' he said. 'Be a sport.' She held him so loosely that it did not occur to him to snap his wrist free and run. Such a thought had been in Arthur's mind for some time. 'Why don't you run, mate?' he whispered. 'You'll be all right. I wain't stop yer, and my brother wain't.'

'Don't put ideas into his head,' the army woman barked.

'You shut yer bleedin' rattle, Rat Face,' he said contemptuously. 'You want a good pastin'. What good will it do you to hand him over to the coppers? Your sort won't let a bloke live. Just walk off,' he called to the man. 'Rat Face won't stop you.'

The man had so many allies that he looked at each new voice as it piped up, a radiant grin never leaving him, even when he again

183

mentioned the fact that he hadn't long ago buried his mother. The crowd began shouting that he be set free but, standing with her legs slightly apart, the woman in khaki held her ground. Arthur passed him a lighted cigarette, placing it between his trembling fingers. 'Run!' he whispered.

'I couldn't,' he said, puffing nervously. 'This woman won't let me.'

'She ain't got owt to do wi' it,' he argued. 'Get crackin' an' run.' A gangway opened through which he could escape. 'They'll shove you in clink,' Arthur said, 'and no mistake.'

Panic overspread his face, and with a sudden movement he snapped his wrist free.

'Stay where you are!' Rat Face roared.

He looked around, bewildered, not knowing what to do, unable to force the ratchet-claws of the trap from his brain. Arthur stood on the roadway so as not to obstruct his escape. Quick decision entered into all the lines of the man's face at once, and the grin that it had worn for so long left it like the flick of a shutter.

Rat Face attempted to hold him. She caught him by the arm but he pushed her roughly away. She tried to slap him but he held her wrist and twisted it, and encouragement from the crowd gave him strength to break finally from her grip. He stood trembling, ready to sprint clear of them.

As suddenly as his way of escape opened, the crowd for some reason closed their ranks. Hope never left a human face more quickly. A police officer stood facing him.

Questions were answered truthfully, briefly, and with alacrity, as if the man had been asked the same ones many times before, and as if he was now relieved that he did not have to make the decision whether or not to run away. He enjoyed giving the answers, as if his salvation lay in appearing pleased to do so, and in his smile was an all-embracing desire to satisfy the police with their clarity, and amuse the now silent crowd by their contents. The two women who held him made their statements.

'Any more of you like to witness?' the policeman said, looking around. No one moved. The squad car with the man inside circled the island and descended towards the city centre by a subsidiary street, its wireless antennae bending backwards and forwards from the sudden movement of starting.

Arthur felt as if he were coming out of a dream, and the first thing he noticed were his cold feet. He imagined Brenda now warmly in bed, snug and obliviously asleep, the two children perhaps with her. 'I could do wi' a pint,' he said, as they turned down Alfreston Road.

'I wouldn't have thought it possible,' Fred cried in a hopeless rage. 'How could anybody do a thing like that?'

'Because she's a bitch and a whore,' Arthur cursed. 'She's got no heart in her. She's a stone, a slab o' granite, a bastard, a Blood-tub, a potato face, a swivel-eyed gett, a Rat-clock. But the man was a spineless bastard, as well.' The broad road, banked by shops and work-yards, was well lighted by the moon and an occasional lamp. Arthur walked on the pavement edge, hands in pockets, thinking: They'd nark on their own mother, some people. You might as well live in a jungle with wild animals. You'd be better off, in fact. Fang-and-claw in the army was better than this. At least you knew you had to be on your guard. You could always fend for yourself there. A car raced down the middle of the road, followed by a motor-bike rattling away full-tilt towards Basford. A policeman, trying shop locks, followed them fifty yards down the road with his eyes. Fred walked steadily, but Arthur still held his arm. They turned on to Hartley Road, between a church and a school, both buildings standing deserted like unwanted corpses. Fred said he would like to fix his fingers around somebody's throat, any human throat, as long as he could press down hard and kill. The empty street was filled with a pleasant smell of tobacco from the Boulevard factory. At the next crossing Arthur suggested a short-cut home.

They stepped off the pavement and walked diagonally towards the opposite corner, on their way through the sleeping suburb. In the middle of the road, when each was locked in his separate thoughts, a small black car appeared from a side-street, primed to full speed on a quick journey home. They did not hear its approach in the dull silence; it skidded towards them on the tarmac, its driver trying at the last minute not to knock them down.

Fred was the most sleepy and preoccupied, yet the first to realise what was happening. Car tyres drummed on the road, but could not swerve clear. 'Look out, Arthur!'

Brakes screeched, and he leapt out of the way, feeling Arthur fall forward as he pulled his arm. Arthur was too late. A hammer-blow caught his thigh, a companion piece knocked him in the side, a hard sharp corner scratched his lagging hand, and he flattened on the road, palms and face pressed on to a solid cold surface, so that he felt as if a coal fire had been rammed into the back of his throat. Then a hand tried to push him underwater. The car stopped nearby.

Arthur was able to sit up. 'Where's that car?' he demanded, rubbing his leg.

Fred, whose knees were trembling, told him to stand. 'Are you all right, then?'

'Christ, it got me a good 'un,' he answered. 'That bastard wain't feel none too good when I get hold of him.' Fred hooked an arm beneath his brother's armpit and forced him to his feet. Walking to where the car stopped they heard the sharp click of a closing door. The man lit a cigarette as he walked towards them.

'You bloody young fools,' he shouted, defending through attack. 'Why didn't you look where you were going?' He made as if to knock Arthur down. His height was medium, his raincoat open, and a fierce chin jutted from an ordinary face. His tiny four-seater friend stood waiting at the curb. Arthur still felt the dull ache of a bruise on his thigh and side, and was forced to keep a rigorous control on legs that wanted to lead him in a direction he had no intention of taking. Neither he nor Fred spoke for a moment, and the man's offensive tactics seemed to be succeeding.

'I might have killed you both. Do you always walk about blind? Or were you too drunk to notice? You want to leave the ale alone, then you won't be a danger to people like me, and you'll be able to cross the road properly.'

Waves of whisky-breath came into their faces. Fred thought the only thing to do was to be sensible. We've been stone-cold sober since Canning Circus. 'You want to have less of it,' he cautioned, 'or we'll have you run in for drunken driving. Anybody can tell yer've had too much booze.'

The man leered, came close, and threw his newly-lighted cigarette to the ground. He ignored Arthur, who stood looking and listening with lips set tight. 'It was you that was at fault, and you bloody-well know it,' he went on, at receiving such a feeble retort from Fred, fists clenched by his raincoat pockets. 'You walked across the road with your eyes shut. I suppose you were practising to get a job as sleepwalkers on the Empire. I saw you and hooted till I was blue in the face. You must be deaf as well as blind.'

'You know your hand didn't get anywhere near that hooter,' Fred said quietly. 'In fact I'll bet you haven't got a hooter on a car like that. It's so small you can't get one in after your fat gut has been squeezed in there.'

He came closer and lifted his fist. 'If you don't have less o' your cheek,' he threatened. Fred glared back, hoping to avoid what he knew by now to be inevitable.

Arthur stepped in, pushed himself between them, gripped the astonished man by his raincoat lapels, and lifted him up. 'If yo' don't shurrup, and button yer gret gob,' he roared like a bull, his face livid with fury, his eyes swimming with blood, 'I'll SMASH yer ter smithereens.'

The man's mouth opened, said nothing, then shut slowly as he hung several inches above the ground. His eyes rolled emptily, his face a ghastly white as he angrily yet fearfully wondered how he came to be in such an awkward situation. When Arthur released him he staggered back towards the wall, pale, tired, hopelessly drunk.

A diabolical suggestion sprang inspired from Fred's agile brain: 'Let's tip his car over. It's no bigger than a baby's pram.' Arthur laughed, and agreed, regarding it as perfect justice, punishment both for the actual metal that had struck him, and for the cranky driver leaning against the wall.

They bent their backs against the car, one

at the front wheel, one at the back, straining and groaning, making a magnificent joke of it, pushing with their shoulders, majestically heaving at the weight as if it were a giant Wolseley, lifting at convenient places with their hands, fighting against door and running-board, wheel and mudguard.

It lifted slowly. It became lighter.

'Keep on,' Arthur encouraged.

The last effort, and:

'It's going,' Fred said with a radiant smile.

'Another shove,' Arthur called. 'I can feel it.'

They heard nothing more. Though locked in a revengeful act they felt a sublime team-spirit of effort filling their hearts with a radiant light of unique power and value, of achievement and hope for greater and better things. The weight was enormous at first, then became lighter and lighter, until the car was held gently, like a butterfly, on a thread, a perfect point of balance that made them want to laugh and cry-out and roar like ecstatic warriors, and they would have done so had it not meant the ruin of their project.

It swung away, and in a fraction of a second landed with a grinding crash on its side, settling tranquilly on to the paving. It looked more attractive in that position, quiet and dignified, four wheels poking decoratively from its chassis, like a mule that, after a hard day's graft, settles down in its stable to rest.

The man slept deeply near the wall.

Arthur did not notice the pain as they walked away. He felt more buoyant and mirthful and stocked with good spirits than for many months, hoping that the next few days would pass quickly, wanting Jack to return to his beloved night-shift, and Brenda to be free for his forays into her dimly-lit parlour after work. The maze of streets sleeping between tobacco factory and bicycle factory drew them into the enormous spread of its suburban bosom and embraced them in sympathetic darkness. Beyond the empires of new red-bricked houses lay fields and woods that rolled on to the Erewash valley and the hills of Derbyshire, and as they entered the house they were talking about the pleasure of cycling to Matlock on the first fine Sunday in spring.

CHAPTER EIGHT

MRS. BULL's malicious gossip travelled like electricity through a circuit, from one power-point to another, and the surprising thing was that a fuse was so rarely blown. One midday at the summer's beginning, when a low, quiet-looking sky was full of intimidation as before rain, she stood by the pillar to watch the factory turn out. Suddenly there was a soft pluck-like report from an air-gun, and she jumped a mile. Her fat arms sprang unfolded from her apron. With a hand to her face, she squealed out:

'Christ All-bleedin'-mighty! Somebody got me that one!'

She wailed in like fashion for some minutes, like a stuck pig, said old Mrs. Mackley who looked up at her bruised face, glad that Mrs. Bull had been shot but not daring to do anything but sympathise. 'Now I wonder what rotten sod's gone and done that?'

Cleverdick that she was, Mrs. Bull looked around after cursing, to discover who had taken a pot-shot at her. Deep-set beady eyes traversed the yard's length from street to factory, were then swivelled back from the

193

factory wall to where she was standing, ranging along upstairs and downstairs windows, no point of architecture or human movement escaping her. It was rumoured that the government had her name down for a reconnaissance unit in the next war.

'I've twigged it,' she said, jerking her chin at Mrs. Mackley: her eyes fixed dead at the last but one window from where she stood; it was slightly ajar. Bernard Griffin lived there with his divorced mother. He had an air-rifle. The biting pain in her face caused her to assume that he still had the air-rifle. Her memorised case-book came into action: sent to Borstal when a kid for breaking open gas meters and ripping lead from church roofs; deserted three times from the army; got a girl into trouble and did three months in gaol when he didn't pay for the baby; apart from all this he hates everybody's guts. She had a dossier on everyone in the yard.

With Witness Mackley she walked to the Griffins' backdoor, and thumped so hard on it that the neighbour opposite swore she would have broken the panel had she given just a single thump more. No one was at home. At least, no one came to the door.

Holding her bruised face she walked back to the yard-end. Half the workers had already passed, in a mad rush for cafés and fish-and-chip shops, and this loss of entertainment, together with the pain of the pellet-wound, promised her husband a miserable dinner-hour.

*   *   *

There were times when Fred was forced to admit that Arthur was not a very nice bloke. In fact sometimes, he swore to himself, he can be a real bastard. If anybody gets on the wrong side of him he can do what seem very dirty tricks indeed—if you didn't know that his motive was revenge. Mrs. Bull had been continually gossiping about Arthur carrying on with married women, and both Fred and Arthur considered this an unforgivable sin because she happened to be right. Arthur felt she was ruining his reputation apart from risking his neck, resenting her stares as he walked up and down the yard, and her half-muttered words of disgust that branded him a dirty old man. How Mrs. Bull had discovered so much about him he had no way of knowing, and did not care to find out. She was not above a little rum stuff herself, but he was not interested in this and it never entered his mind to hold it against her. So though he was

195

incapable of fighting fire with fire, he hit upon the idea one morning when he was off work with an upset stomach of fighting fire with a lead pellet. Despite Mrs. Bull's extraordinary powers of observation she did not hear him close the bedroom window after the shot simply because he did not need to close it: he had fired from a hole in the pane: his mother had been meaning to put a cardboard patch in it for several days but had not yet done so. Fred was in the same room when he fired, sitting at the table filling in his sickness benefit form. Arthur slid another pellet into the gun and let-fly at what remained of the plaster poodle on the mantelpiece, a handsome dumb-friend that, since Arthur had acquired the air-rifle from Bernard Griffin for ten shillings, had lost its head and breast in a storm of shell and shot, expert marksmanship that left only a shapeless stump of black and white plaster resting on four untouched paws.

By afternoon the news had spread by chimneygram: Mrs. Bull had been shot. Not with a real gun though, but with an air-rifle, the story-teller would add when the person laughed, or was sad, according to how friendly they were with the victim. Mrs. Bull's face had never looked so fierce and determined as she gesticulated: 'The wicked bogger. He didn't need to pick on me, a woman who's never done a ha-porth of harm to a living soul.'

She waylaid Bernard Griffin coming home from his window-cleaning job, and on tackling him about having shot her with his airgun he was even more incensed than if he had actually done it. 'How could I have shot you?' he stormed. 'For one thing I've been at work all morning. You can ask my boss if you don't believe me. And for another thing I sold my pellet gun last week to a pal o' mine at Mansfield.'

Arthur, in his shirt sleeves, leaned on the gate and looked at them with sympathy and interest, shaking his head sadly at some of the more violent pronouncements of Mrs. Bull. Fred listened from the bedroom window, knowing that Mrs. Bull, while going full-tilt at one person, could quite easily, for no obvious reason, swing around to an onlooker and accuse them of whatever crime needed vengeance. And whoever it was might be the guilty one. Which was why Fred thought that Arthur shouldn't stand too close.

'Anyway,' Bernard Griffin went on, 'how do you know it was somebody in this yard as done it? It could easy have come from up the street. An air-gun carries a long way, yer know.'

She decided he wasn't to blame, and looked away, her eyes more shifty, her mind seeming to roam up and down the street searching for another suspect. Not that you can blame her, Arthur thought, with that black mark on the side of her face, as though somebody slung a bottle of ink at her.

They went to a cheap matinée at the pictures, a cinema filled with old-age pensioners, truant children, shop assistants on half-day, shift-workers, and those off sick like themselves. An old man smoked foul twist behind; three rows further back a baby began bawling at the rowdy climax of a cowboy picture. Coming straight out of it, the sound of six-guns still blazing, thud of avenging hooves breaking through bleak sunshine and a thriving wind, he bumped into Brenda. Loaded with shopping baskets she looked fresh and innocent, red-cheeked and relaxed, saying with a Saturday-night sharpness that he should look where he was going. It was the first time for a week. 'Have a fag, duck,' he said, but she didn't like to smoke on the street.

'I'm fine,' she answered.

'How's Jack these days?' he asked. 'I haven't seen him for a long time.'

'He's looking better.'

He lit a cigarette. 'And Em'ler?'

'All right,' she laughed. 'Still thinks everybody's barmy.'

'The bleeder wants certifyin', if you ask me'—imagining her to be the cause of all his troubles.

'She's harmless. She was as good as gold to me that night.' It was the first time she had mentioned 'that night', and it pleased him, meaning that they could close their eyes over it and get to know each other once more.

'I tried to give her a quid for helping us, but she wouldn't take it. She nearly scratched my eyes out. I like Em'ler, you know that. She's one of the best sort. Only at times she makes me mad. I think she's a bit of a gossip, because some woman in our yard knows about me going out with a married woman and she's making my life a misery.'

She laughed out loud. 'Well, if you let a thing like that bother you, you want certifying, not Em'ler.'

'It's not that. I don't mind who knows about us. Only this woman goes out of her way to make trouble.' He told her of how he had shot Mrs. Bull, to which she replied that it was a barmy thing to have done and might have blinded her.

'She asked for it,' he said. 'You see, it'll do her a lot of good. She'll think twice about gossipin' at the yard-end again.'

'Well, let me know what happens. If you go to gaol, send a note, and I'll bring you a pie to Lincoln with a couple of files in it.'

'Thanks,' he said ironically. 'I knew you'd stand by me. How's Winnie and Bill these days?'

'Bill's gone back. I don't think he enjoyed his leave. He spent most nights chasing a bloke who went after Winnie. Somebody's been doing their best to break up his marriage. Winnie swore blind he was wrong about it all, and glad when he went back.'

Jack's a deep 'un, Arthur thought. He hadn't even told Brenda about Bill's ideas. Why not? It was funny when you thought about it. Jack knew about me and Winnie, and yet he didn't tell Brenda, not even as a man might tell his wife, to pass the time while the kettle boiled, or between one fag and the next. Neither had Winnie said anything to Brenda about him going to bed with her that night. Perhaps Jack didn't want to put ideas into her head. The jungle was safer than he thought. 'Can I come and see you tonight, duck?'

'Make it tomorrow, about nine, when the

kids are in bed. But don't let's get into any more fixes, eh?'

'I'll watch that. You can stop worryin' from now on.'

A strong wind blew down the road, and a bicycle propped by its pedal against the kerb crashed on to the pavement, and a man ran out of the barber's shop to pick it up. Brenda said she had to hurry home to make Jack something to eat. 'He goes on at half-past seven.'

'I'll see you tomorrow night, then.'

Fred had waited at the next corner reading a newspaper.

'Any news?' Arthur asked.

'Not much. A kid was drowned in Wollaton Cut. A man got three months hard for shoplifting. There was a road-smash at Radcliffe. A collier got killed in the pit, and there's going to be a Three Power meeting.'

'Is that all?'

*　　　*　　　*

House-roofs were flushed orange by the setting sun, and a green luminous light crossed the house-walls of the opposite terrace; a sudden silence was brought on by the heightened colours of dusk, reflecting the red-ochred bricks of lavatory walls as Mr. Bull knocked at the Seatons' back door. When Fred saw his pinched and harassed face he knew he had been bullied into the visit by his wife, and felt sorry for him standing on the doorstep in his factory overalls and not knowing what to say. Some women won't let their husbands live, he thought. Some won't let anybody live. While Mr. Bull was making up his mind how to begin, and Arthur was doing a one-act mime at him through the kitchen window, Fred wondered how Mrs. Bull had come to the conclusion that it was Arthur who shot her.

'Ar've 'eerd yer've bin shootin' at my missis,' Bull said, sliding his foot nervously around the doorstep, causing Fred to wonder how it was that a shifty-eyed man always married a shifty-eyed woman. The muscles twitched on Bull's face: he wanted to be fierce, but was afraid to raise his voice above the quiet level of speech, only asking Fred to say with some conviction that no one in the house had shot his wife, then he would be satisfied and go back home. So Fred told him bluntly: 'I ain't shot your missis. I don't know what you're talking about. You'd better go and ask somewhere else.' He made to shut the door in Bull's face, but Bull was not prepared to leave. If he went back empty handed to his wife there would be an unpleasant scene. 'Listen,' Bull said, as if to strike some sort of bargain, 'my missis got shot at dinnertime wi' an air-gun and she reckons you've got one in your house.' He spoke in a whining voice whose tone grated against Fred's nerves. You can stand only so much from a bloke like this, he thought, who always knows he's wrong before he starts. 'Well, it ain't true,' he said. 'There ain't no gun in this house.'

'What do you think this is?' Arthur shouted from within. 'The 'eadquarters o' the Royal Corps o' Snipers?'

Bull's eyes opened wide, then half closed, and an expression of anger spread over his face. He began shouting about how they were a bloody pack of heathens, that they weren't civilised, that they all needed a good thumping, and that he'd give it to them if they stepped outside, one at a time.

Arthur left his chair by the fire. He stood over Bull like a lamp-post: 'Yo'll be the one to get a thumpin' if yer don't shut yer gret gob.' They faced each other, Bull looking as though he thought he had said his last word; then he turned and walked back up the yard, fumbling with the gate-latch to let himself out. 'The poor bleeder's got to face his missis now,'

Arthur said. 'Some blokes are born unlucky.'

Suddenly they saw her coming down the yard, walking with a swinging motion as if she had just come off a ship. The bruise was still visible on her cheek, though the swelling had decreased since dinnertime. 'It makes her look prettier, I'm sure it does,' Arthur remarked.

'She's up to no good,' Fred told him. 'When she walks like that it means trouble.' Arthur said he was going upstairs for his gun, and before Fred could ask him not to be bloody-well daft, the stairfoot door slammed and he was clobbering up to his bedroom like a pit-pony. Fred sat by the fire, waiting for the storm to break.

Mrs. Bull was at the door, rat-tat-tatting like a machine-gun. Fred went on smoking, and the knocks sounded again. 'They're in,' he heard Bull say. 'I know they're in.'

He went to the door and opened it slowly, asking them to come in, saying how sorry he was he hadn't seen them for such a long time, implying that they should call more often. Mrs. Bull entered the kitchen cautiously, as if fearing an ambush, and once inside her eyes darted everywhere, as though she were a bum-bailiff checking up the furniture for a quick sale. Fred considered it lucky that his father wasn't at home, for she would have been put out in no time. If there was anything the old man couldn't stand it was a gossiper, and Arthur was said to take after him in this respect.

'I'm sorry I can't ask you to have a cup o' tea,' he said, 'but it's stone-cold now.' She stood by the door with folded arms, as if to know whether the house was clean before coming right in, or as if trying to see into the cupboards and find out how much food they contained. But Fred was passing judgment on her too: she was the sort that let her rent lag three months in arrears even though it was only eleven bob a week, and stood at the pawnshop door every Monday morning, even though her husband had a good job.

She spoke at last, her heavy jaw moving slowly, firm determination in her small, deep-set eyes. 'I've come to see about that gun yer've got.'

'Gun?' Fred said, standing up with a shock at the word. 'We ain't got no gun 'ere. What do you think this is? Cammell Laird's?'

He could never understand why people lost their tempers so quickly. Perhaps it was the 'Cammell Laird's' that upset her, which was the name of a big gun factory in the Meadows.

Still not moving from the corner, she brandished her fist: 'Yo' 'ev less o' yer cheek, yer young bleeder. I got shot today with an air-gun, and I'm going to find out oo it was as done it.'

Fred faced her with a look of outraged innocence, afraid of the ructions that would ensue if the old man came back and caught them in the house. He had only gone up the street for a haircut. 'You're not the on'y one as got shot,' he said, as if it was the worst thing that could happen, and that such attacks should be ruthlessly put down. 'Mrs. Morris got hit as well, I heard, only an hour ago, just up the street as she was turning the corner on to Ilkeston Road. She was telling mam about it when she went out to get something for dad's tea. That's why I got mad at your mester just now, thinking I'd done it. I've never seen an air-gun in our house in my life. Dad wouldn't have one in the place.'

He saw her eyes changing their mind. She was almost convinced. 'Well, all right, then,' she said. Bull added: 'I told you they hadn't done it.' She turned on him: 'Yo' shut yer gap. I ain't found 'em yet, and I wain't rest tell I do.'

As they turned to leave, the tread of boots sounded behind the stairfoot door, and the loud rending voice of a laughing maniac filled the kitchen with a derisive cackle. Everyone looked across the room, waited with frozen expressions for some extraordinary event.

The door was kicked open, and Arthur was framed in the open space, standing with legs apart on the bottom step, a loaded air-rifle pointing at the Bulls.

Fred stared at the apparition. Shades of purple crept over Mrs. Bull's face. Mr. Bull trembled, afraid of being ordered by his wife to tackle him. 'That's it,' she screamed. 'He's got it, the brazen bleeder. He's the one that shot me.'

Arthur's face was fixed into firm lines to stop himself laughing. 'Get out,' he cried, 'or you'll get another, in yer fat guts this time.'

She raved about going to the police and having him sent to Lincoln, shouting that it should be against the law to have air-guns. Then she turned on her husband: 'Go on! What are yer standin' there for? 'It 'im, 'it 'im!'

Arthur shouted, between his laughs; 'Go on, scoot, get out.' Bull did not move, as if his feet had been driven into the floor with Rawlplugs. Mrs. Bull did not want shooting a second time, so she said they'd better go, adding that they'd be back soon with a copper. 'You wain't prove owt if you bring a copper,' Arthur said. 'Nobody'll find this gun, I'll tell yer that.'

They moved back, through the scullery and towards the backyard, followed by Arthur. Fred saw the old man walking down the yard with his head freshly shaved, a look of rage on his face as though he'd been cheated of a year's bonus at the factory. He met the Bulls before they reached the gate. 'Hello,' he said, 'what are yo' pair doin' 'ere?'

Arthur said they had barged into the house and started shouting something about him having an air-gun.

'Oh, did they?' the old man said, turning to Mr. Bull. They were the same height, but Seaton was broader and had a bigger, more determined head. 'I thought I towd yer never to cum into my 'ouse agen?' he said, lifting his fist.

Doors were opening. People came out to watch.

'You're a lot of bloody rogues and thieves,' Mrs. Bull screamed at the Seatons. It was an even bigger row than the empty-bellied pre-war battles. Feuds merged, suppressed ones became public, and Mrs. Robin fainted, sending her husband in for whisky, a good excuse for him to stay out of the fight because he was a man who sent his sons to join the Scouts and always voted Liberal, a traitor to the solid bloc of anarchistic Labour in the street. Mrs. Bull threatened to smack Fred in the chops when he told her that this was what came of spreading slander about Arthur carrying-on with married women. She retorted that whatever people said about her, she wasn't a gossiper, and that was a fact. The dusk became deeper, faces indistinct. Everyone was shouting that they'd drop everyone else. Mrs. Robin had been revived by the whisky but was sent back into a dead faint by the heavy curses bandied about. Someone from the scuffle gratuitously called her a bag of bones and she came to in time to see Arthur thumping Mr. Bull all the way up the yard. 'You're a bastard,' he said, knotting his fist. 'You gossipin' lot.'

'I'm not a bastard,' Bull retorted.

'Y'are.'

''M not.'

Then a big thump, like the climax of a firework display, and Mrs. Robin fainted again.

Crowds dispersed, doors slammed. It was completely dark, and the old man went back into the house to mash some tea, muttering: 'That'll settle 'em. That'll settle 'em.'

A policeman came to ask whether they had

an air-gun. He searched for it on Arthur's invitation, but found nothing. Arthur had even got rid of the black pock-marked shell-shocked poodle from the bedroom shelf, burying both dog and gun beneath a heap of coal under the stairs. They denied everything to the policeman, who saw no more than a neighbours' quarrel, saying merely that they should stop making trouble in the yard. Even the evidence of Mrs. Bull's bruise had gone down to the point where it might have been caused by a smack from her husband's fist. This appearance of the law satisfied Mrs. Bull's pride, and Arthur heard no more of her gossip.

She went on standing at the yard-end, however, but placed herself a little way into the street, where the line of fire from Arthur's window was interrupted by two lavatories. She still stood out of the way, even when Arthur left to do his fifteen days.

CHAPTER NINE

July, August, and summer skies lay over the city, above rows of houses in the western suburbs, backyards burned by the sun with running tar-sores whose antiseptic smell blended with that of dustbins overdue for emptying, drying paint even drier on front doors, rusting knockers and letter-boxes, and withering flowers on windowsills, a summer blue sky up to which smoke from factory-chimneys coiled blackly.

Arthur sweated at his lathe, worked at the same fast pace as in winter to keep the graph-line of his earnings level. Life went on like an assegai into the blue, with dim memories of the dole and school-days behind, and a dimmer feeling of death in front, a present life punctuated by meetings with Brenda on certain beautiful evenings when the streets were warm and noisy and the clouds did a moon-light-flit over the rooftops. They made love in parlour or bedroom and felt the ocean of suburb falling asleep outside their minuscular coracle of untouchable hope and bliss. From his own bed one night, when the blankets were thrown to the floor before falling asleep, he heard a dustbin lid rattled against the backyard paving, disturbed by some cat on a nocturnal prowl for food, and he remembered Fred taking him by the hand to the dinner-centre when he was six; and the assegai into the blue was only tipped with death when newspaper headlines rammed the word war with a nail-punch into the staring sockets of his eyes. The best hours to remember were those when he made love with Brenda, yearning to stay in her bed and never leave it, to keep his arms around her body and lie there in comfort until morning. But midnight was his deadline, otherwise he would be seen by Jack as he came in cold and ill-tempered from the night-shift. It must be good to live all the time with a woman, he thought, and sleep in a bed with her that belonged to both of you, that no one could turn you out of it if they caught you there.

The future meant things, both good and bad, to look forward to, like the coming of summer (good); military training at the end of August (purgat'ry), Goose Fair in October (smashin'); Bonfire Night (good if you didn't get blown to bits); and Christmas at Christmas. Then the new year swung its fist and dragged you blindfolded and by the neck-scruff on to the high crest of another wave.

Living in a town and working in a factory, only a calendar gave any real indication of passing time, for it was difficult to follow the changing seasons. As spring merged into summer or autumn became winter Arthur glimpsed the transitional mechanisms of each season only at the weekend, on Saturday or Sunday, when he straddled his bike and rode along the canal bank into the country to fish. On long summer evenings he sat on the front doorstep with a pen-knife and a piece of wood, carving the replica of a fish for his float, with a cigarette burning uselessly away on the step by his side, while he held the half-shaped fish lightwards to gauge the proportions of head, body, and tail. Later he would colour it with intricate designs, grey and red, orange for its eyes, and a belly of duck-egg blue, a strange fish that he hoped would attract live counter-parts to a baited hook. And sitting on the canal bank below Hemlock Stone and the Bramcote Hills he cast out his line over the narrow sleeve of still water, with elderberry leaves bending across from the opposite bank and white cloud-edges moving above green branches. It was a quiet and passionless place to be, where few people passed, hemmed in by steep bush-covered banks of a cutting against which, by the towpath, lay his bicycle. There

213

was no sign of the city. It lay four miles over the hills, yet distant enough when measured by silence and peace as he sat with a cigarette between his fingers watching the float near the far bank, concentric rings of water that snapped around it, and water-beetles skating gracefully like tiny rowing boats between broad-leaved water-lilies. In the khaki side-pack of his army days were sandwiches and a flask of tea and a bottle of ale for late afternoon, sufficient until the deep shade darkened and grew chill, when he would tie his rods to the cross-bar and race home against the advancing minutes of lighting-up time. So passed many Sundays of his summer, a bejewelled and multi-coloured season of the year whose borders were blacked by sleepy afternoons in the factory when he forced a rapid pace at his lathe, driving his muscles away from their natural desire for sleep. The rest was a brief glimpse of sky at midday and evening, a prison-like system pleasant enough because he could be happy in knowing that by this work he never had to worry where the next meal, pint, smoke, or suit of clothes was coming from.

At times he remembered how at eighteen-and-a-bit he had been clapped into khaki, how he had walked into the stores wearing collar-and-tie and sports-coat and had been spawned out at the other end a fully-fledged swaddie, battledress over his sports-coat and shoulders burdened by strange equipment. While polishing his webbing-buckles he thought about the way his cousins had lived during the war: tall, grinning army deserters caught time and time again by Redcaps or police, but always escaping, on the run, in hiding, living with whores, thieving for food and money because they had neither ration-books nor employment cards. A shaky game, and Arthur sometimes wondered why they had kept at bay so long, why they hadn't gone overseas to get killed and end it all. But they had been right, he knew that, because they were still here, alive, at work, earning a good living in spite of the army. He remembered Dave telling his father during the war: 'I was on the dole eighteen months ago, same as yo', Harold. We all had a struggle to keep alive, and now they want to call us up. My mother had eleven to drag up, with Doddoe only at work now and again. Then one night I broke into the back door of a shop because we'd got nowt t'eat. When I got back that night—I shall never forget it, Harold—we had the best meal we'd ever had in our lives. I was fifteen at the time, and I broke into a shop

215

every week for a couple of months, but one night the bastards got me. And do you know what I got for it? I know you do, Uncle Harold, but I'm just tellin' yer. Three years in Borstal. And then when I came out the war'd started and I got called up. Do yer think I'm going ter fight for them bastards, do yer?'

Arthur remembered Dave's face: thin and half starved, red and wind beaten after riding a stolen bike the seventy-odd miles from Manchester, over the Pennines on nothing to eat, to get away from the Redcaps. It was Thursday, and the week's rations were collected on Friday, so there was only bread and jam and tea in the house. Seaton offered to put him up for a week. He stayed for three. One afternoon, when he was out, the police came for him, and while they were looking around the house Arthur got a wink from his father and so walked out of the house. He met Dave coming down the street whistling a song, his long legs peddling a stolen bike. The sirens had just gone, and while Arthur was telling Dave not to come back to the house, white shell-puffs filled the sky and the stick-like shadow of a Jerry plane slid over the rooftops like a coffin. Arthur could have laughed. There was a war on then, and they were fighting the Jerries, and Churchill spoke after the nine o'clock news and told you what you were fighting for, as if it mattered. For what could you do? he thought. Do what Dave had done to get out of the army? No, all that was left to you in the world was cunning. Nothing more. Knuckle under for two years and then think yourself lucky you were out. He had begun to polish his boots, and, when the sergeant passed and saw everything all of a shine and glitter, so neat and tidy, he said that Arthur would make a good soldier. Cunning, he thought. You bastards won't get me down. The return of Ada's three sons after their short terms of army service at the beginning of the war had been witnessed and remembered by him: the burning of uniforms and equipment in the bedroom grate, smoke coming from chimney-pots not normally used.

Because Arthur was tall they put him in the military police, gave him a whistle and red cap and stood him up like a pit-prop to check the passes of the lucky ones as they went out on pass or leave. He was a Redcap. What irony! It was the joke of the family. But he fretted all the time. He was paid five bob a day, and thought bitterly of the two pounds earned at his lathe. But let them start a war, he thought, and see what a bad soldier I can be. 'Them at the top' must know that nobody would fight, and he supposed that because of this they weren't so anxious to rely on them in another war. In the army it was: 'F—— you, Jack, I'm all right.' Out of the army it was: 'Every man for himself.' It amounted to the same thing. Opinions didn't matter. Intelligent co-operation meant falling for a slip-knot, getting yourself caught in a half-nelson, though he knew a way to get free from both. The only peace you got was when you were away from it all, sitting on the osier-lined banks of a canal waiting for fish to bite, or lying in bed with a woman you loved.

They were angling for another war now, with the Russians this time. But they did go as far as to promise that it would be a short one, a few big flashes and it would all be over. What a lark! We'd be fighting side by side with the Germans that had been bombing us in the last war. What did they take us for? Bloody fools, but one of these days they'd be wrong. They think they've settled our hashes with their insurance cards and television sets, but I'll be one of them to turn round on 'em and let them see how wrong they are. When I'm on my fifteen-days' training and I lay on my guts behind a sandbag shooting at a target board I know whose faces I've got in my sights every time the new rifle cracks off. Yes. The bastards that put the gun into my hands. I make up a quick picture of their stupid four-eyed faces that blink as they read big books and papers on how to get blokes into khaki and fight battles in a war that they'll never be in—and then I let fly at them. Crack-crack-crack-crack-crack-crack. Other faces as well: the snot-gobbling gett that teks my income tax, the swivel-eyed swine that collects our rent, the big-headed bastard that gets my goat when he asks me to go to union meetings or sign a paper against what's happening in Kenya. As if I cared!

He remembered his father digging up the back garden to plant an Anderson Shelter, Arthur stumbling into the hole and getting a clout for doing so. And later the family sat on the planks inside, coughing from the damp moist soil, scratching their scabied bodies, and listening to the weird-sounding hollowness of the naval guns behind Beech-dale woods, his white-faced father rushing in at midnight, a teapot in one hand and half a dozen cups strung along the fingers of the other, having braved falling shrapnel to mash, back just in time to escape the Jerry plane that sprayed the factory with its machine-guns. In the long high-pitched whistle of a bomb the whole world was caught and suspended so that you just wondered, wondered, wondered, keeping quite still during the whistle, not breathing, not moving a finger, your eyes open wide, until the explosion on the railway yards or on a pack of houses in the next street made you glad to be still alive.

And when he came to think of it, Ada's sons had not done too badly. At the end of the war they were rounded up for the last time and dumped in the glass-house. Dave was sent to the B.L.A. six months before demob. The war was over, and in Berlin he met Arthur's sister, Margaret, who worked as a waitress with the N.A.A.F.I., and they walked arm in arm along the Unter Den Linden, pointing out the ruins, talking of old times, drinking strong beer, and laughing at the thought that they of all people should meet among the smashed streets of Berlin, of all places.

Dave was on his demob leave in forty-five, just back from Germany, and Arthur bumped into him one Saturday night near the Horse and Groom. Dave was dressed in smart, spotless khaki, and above the pocket of his battle-dress were five campaign ribbons. 'I didn't know they gave you medals for being in the glass-house,' Arthur laughed. Dave told him how Ada and the others had painted: 'Welcome Home Dave' on the air-raid shelter, and hung flags from the bedroom window as if he were a hero, and added: 'I bought these ribbons from the Army Stores. They only cost half a crown, and they look nice for my demob leave. So long, Arthur. I've got a nobble on inside.'

*   *   *

Saying good-bye to Brenda did not give Arthur much pleasure. After a subdued bus-ride to Wollaton village they walked down Bramcote Lane arm-in-arm. Wheatfields, some already close-cropped, ran before a range of low scrub-patched hills. Odours of wheat chaff in the air caused Arthur to reminisce: 'I used to come up here blackberryin', when I was a young 'un. Once with my cousin Bert we met some kids who'd already bin blackberryin', and Bert took theirn off 'em. I didn't want to, but Bert said it would save us hours o' searchin'.'

Brenda stopped to straighten the cardigan carried folded on her arm. She was critical: 'I'll bet you didn't want to pinch 'em. Not much. You're a bright one, Arthur. You never know the difference between right and wrong.'

'Well,' he said, 'I do. That's what's wrong if you ask me, because it don't pay to know the difference, does it duck?' He raised his head on the question mark, his face serious.

'Sometimes it does. It keeps you out of trouble. And you were born for trouble. Help me over this stile, love.'

He took her hand as she climbed to the first step. 'Born for trouble? Not me. If you want to know summat, I've had a peaceful life. I never did like trouble, or doing people harm. It upsets me too much, like boozing. Only sometimes I can't keep off it. Hold your skirt down, duck, or I'll see all you've got. This is where the courting couples come, and this is what starts it, when the man helps his young woman over a stile!'

She laughed: 'The things you say. It was your idea anyway, to come down here, and you know how hard it is for a woman to get over a stile without showing a bit of her underclothes. Steady, hold my hand, Whoops! That's it, now I'm down.'

He leapt over and they walked by a privet hedge, corn over the path waving like tinsel. 'It's a bastard, though, having to go back to the army every year. They won't let a bloke live.'

222

She took his arm again. 'It's only fifteen days, and you know you don't mind it. All the men like it, if you ask me.'

'Maybe they do,' he said. 'But I don't. I tell you I hate the army, and I allus have done. You can't say that about me. I'm not daft enough to like it.'

'Well, p'raps not. But I'm sure there are plenty as do. They just love to get a uniform on and go off with lots of other men. If there was a war, millions of 'em 'ud rush to join-up.'

Bramcote Hills had green fields around their ankles, clumps of stunted trees along its ridge, and crew-cut grass patches on the slopes. He imagined himself and two hundred others staggering, falling, having to run up the ankles with fixed bayonet, charging blind-drunk into trees. A few well-placed machine-guns and mortars and you could pin down a couple of battalions, he reasoned. 'But not me. I'll keep out of it. I hate it. I don't even like to talk about it, in fact.'

The prospect of parting did not bother her as it bothered Arthur. To him her face indicated happiness at the thought of a fortnight's freedom. 'Never mind, Arthur, you'll be back soon. It's only once a year. And when this is over it'll be Goose Fair, and then Christmas.

Time flies; we'll be getting old soon, I do know that.'

'Not me,' he said gruffly. 'You're as old as you feel, and I ain't got started yet on my life.'

'No more you will, either, until you get married.'

'Married? Me? No fear. I'd only marry you, because I love you, but that ain't possible. And if I can't marry you, duck, then it's not likely as I'll marry anybody else.'

She liked his forthrightness, but replied: 'That's what they all say, I suppose. But in another year you'll have changed your mind. Everybody thinks they'll never get married at your age. So did Jack, he told me. You think you can go on all your life being single, I remember he said, but you suddenly find out that you can't.'

'Well,' Arthur said with a sly smile, 'I don't need to get married, do I. Don't get married until you've got to, that's my motto.' He stabbed her playfully in the ribs with his fingers, then caught hold of her to kiss her.

'Stop it,' she cried. 'You'll squeeze the life out of me. Don't kiss me here, there's a man walking on that hill, and he'll see us.' She was irritated.

'No, he won't,' he grinned.

'And anyhow, do you think you get married just for that? If you think so, you're wrong. Some people do, I suppose, but most of 'em get married for other reasons.'

'You sound like a know-all,' he said, the sparks from either tinder-box waxing hot enough to set both their angers alight, 'but I know a thing or two, as well. I'll know when I'm ready to marry, and I'm not ready yet.' He turned on her truculently: 'I suppose you'd like it if I did get married?'

'Don't be daft,' she said, happy now that she had angered him. 'That's just what I don't want to happen, you know that. But if ever you want to, don't let me stop you. Yes, laugh if you like, but you know what I mean. I know you love me now, but you might not in six months.'

Aye, he thought, we might all be dead in six months. So he danced on the path before her, laughing, bending his long legs up and down, disappearing into the tall corn and suddenly rushing out to try and frighten her. She had to laugh as well. 'Go on,' she cried. 'You're daft. I can never make you out.'

'Well,' he said breathlessly, his arm around her waist, 'That's what I think about you as well. But it don't bother me much because I never tek much trouble to mek people out.

225

That's summat else as don't pay.' The gladness left him feeling as if the world's gigantic wheels had turned in his particular direction with the intention of crushing him. Fifteen days in khaki were brandished before him like a knob-kerrie. The fact that Brenda did not seem very pained about him going away, and the wide blue sky of a summer evening, found no response in him, made him feel empty at the landscape's colours and folds.

'Where shall we go then, Arthur?'

He did not know. In more ways than one it was a big question. Action, he thought. That's more my line. So he shed his morbidity in a second and steered her along the right-angled line of the hedge. Wheat hid them from view, and he kicked out at it, wanted to flatten it.

'It's wrong,' she said. 'You shouldn't trample it like that.'

'What's wrong? I enjoy doing it. Besides, what does it matter?'

'Just as I said,' she replied, faintly smiling. 'You don't know the difference between right and wrong.'

'No I don't. And I don't want anybody to start teaching me, either.'

'I suppose you've got the right idea. This is a good place,' she said, looking into a smooth hollow at the bottom of the hedge. 'I do love you, Arthur,' she added. They sat down, and kissed each other passionately.

*   *   *

He stood on the platform at Derby station waiting for the Birmingham train, planted tall and straight by a disused chocolate machine, fresh from the buffet with a cup of tea and a bun inside him, so washed and shaven that his stained uniform detracted little from his air of smartness. There was a vacant seat nearby, but he scorned to bend the razor-edged creases in his trousers by sitting on it. He dwelt on the wild good-bye he had said to Brenda, out in the field until midnight and too late to catch the last bus. They had walked home under a bright moon, with a subtle note of doom let loose in so perfect a parting, the beginning of a forlorn end that could be fought against but not defeated. Nothing had been said, but both had felt it, and had betrayed it to each other in their too hard drive for gaiety. There was a bitterness in their passion, tender words without roots, and sarcasms that threw affection down like a glove that both were in too much of a hurry to take up.

'Be safe,' she had said. 'Be good. I'll see you

soon.'

Happen so, he thought.

A porter rolled a loaded trolley along the platform. Arthur stood rigid, watching thin curtains of rain fall one after the other over the black engine sheds, a fine midsummer drizzle that gave him a feeling of boredom, and emptiness that he found intolerable. Five soldiers came noisily over the track bridge and descended to the platform, filling the cold damp air with bluff jokes. Arthur recognised them. They recognised Arthur. They clobbered towards him in their heavy boots and slung kitbags on to the seat. He was lost, embraced by their brawling noise, making it more solid with his own swearing, handshakes and backslaps. 'If it ain't owd Ernie Ambergate!' They were bound for the same camp, and knew each other from last year.

*   *   *

Arthur was drunk every night. The fifteen days was a long time, insupportable if sober, for he hated change, and hated the army more. He carried wire-cutters in his pocket to help him back into camp late at night, exulting as he lay in the ditch, snapping one strand of barbed wire after another and rolling it

228

carefully back with his hand, feeling the damp earth on his trousers, grass blades tickling his face, and brambles chafing his ankles, crawling along on his stomach to keep down from the guardroom lights, until the gap in the fence would have admitted an armoured division.

On his first parade the sergeant-major exclaimed that he couldn't make out the shape of Arthur's head because there was so much hair on it, and Arthur jocularly agreed to get it cut, intending to forget about it until the fifteen days was over, which he did. 'You're a soldier now, not a Teddy-boy,' the sergeant-major said, but Arthur knew he was wrong in either case. He was nothing at all when people tried to tell him what he was. Not even his own name was enough, though it might be on his pay-book. What am I? he wondered. A six-foot pit-prop that wants a pint of ale. That's what I am. And if any knowing bastard says that that's what I am, I'm a dynamite-dealer, Sten-gun seller, hundred-ton tank trader, a capstan-lathe operator waiting to blow the army to Kingdom Cum. I'm me and nobody else; and whatever people think I am or say I am, that's what I'm not, because they don't know a bloody thing about me.

On the second day he stood in the urinal staring at the wall's grey surface with wild eyes, as if to penetrate the obscene scrawls that he had once found so funny, and see today's racing lists and tomorrow's winners set down plainly instead. The seconds he stood there passed like days, each a goods-train in his stomach, a dynamo in his brain, an anvil in his heart, a tool-vice clamped on to his mouth that nevertheless muttered: 'Bastards. Bastards. Bastards'—until Ambergate came in from breakfast and thumped him on the back, and Arthur turned with raised fist ready to give himself the pleasure of smashing him. But he stopped in time, for he could not do it to Ambergate, his collier pal from some lonely shaft of the Derbyshire foothills.

The days and nights did not pass quickly enough. On the range he was happy with the Bren, at the thought of bullets falling into the spout from the curving magazine and at the sound of them spitting like music at the boards. He liked firing, he had to admit. It gave him satisfaction to destroy, if only the board perched up above the butts. He would rather destroy something more tangible: houses or human beings: but that was impossible, yet. When it was not his turn at the sandbags he loved to stand and listen to the total bursting of bullets from the dozen guns firing, hearing the lifting and falling of sound, the absolutely untamable rhythms that ripped the air open with untrammelled joy.

Every night he went out with Ambergate to get drunk: on the long walks he plotted private war and revolution, arson and plunder, with Ambergate, bringing to the surface impossible dreams and treating them like jokes. Coming back from the village they forgot everything in the world but their own existence, the now, the this minute of their filled bellies and walking legs and chafed thighs on khaki serge. Arthur's drunken chanting sped out like primeval madness over dark fields and woods, filling the best hours of fifteen days. They passed cottages bolted and barred to them, doors and windows spurning Arthur's made-up songs that rolled and roared along like the explosion of some half-forgotten voice in the world.

One night he did the return journey alone, having somehow been parted from his pals in the pub. The clear, blue, burning day had ended, and the night was pitch-black and filled with jostling clouds. Hands in pockets, he whistled a tune, swaying with as much drink inside him as he could hold. A lightning-flash, purple and brilliant, illuminated him in the middle of the lane. He saw trees grouped together that he had not noticed before. In the cannonade of thunder that followed his tune went unconsciously on, but the first flash ploughed a furrow through the depths of his mind into which entered the second broad wink of lightning. He felt afraid, and his legs began to tremble. 'What's up?' he said. Then louder: 'What's up?' He walked on in the dull even descent of the rain, counting each second between lightning and thunder. Then he resumed his whistling, a marching tune that kept him swinging along until he stopped to light a cigarette. The next flash seemed to tear the earth apart, giving an instantaneous explosion of thunder as though a powder factory had been touched off. The lane was arched with trees, and he was afraid of being struck down. It was the first time in years that a storm had frightened him. As a boy, when the time of summer storms came, he would run screaming from the street to hide in the darkened scullery or under the stairs, until the summer when thunder changed to bombs and lightning to gun-flashes, showing him the harmlessness of thunder and lightning. He woke up one summer night during the war to the sound of

232

explosions, and flashes crossing the bedroom window, hating to leave his bed and go to an air-raid shelter, wondering why the sirens hadn't sounded a warning, or why neither he nor anyone else in the house had heard them. Fred sat up and told him it was only thunder. Only thunder! Smashin'! To its musical rumblings he went back to sleep, and remembering it now in his fear and weariness he walked on with a laugh until he saw the camp lights close by, when he no longer needed its refuge, and could go on walking through the storm for miles more.

He kicked open the billet door, unbuckled his webbing belt, and threw off his cap. The last thing he heard before collapsing into a heap was the thunder.

Lifted from the soft pit of slumber at eight the next morning, he was in bed, undressed, with blankets over him. He opened his eyes, but could not stir an arm to scratch himself. His limbs were fastened securely to the frame of the bed. Raising his head a few inches he saw that the billet was empty. They must all be at breakfast, he thought. Sun streamed in and turned the polished floor into a mirror, flooded the stove in light, illuminated tidy heaps of kit laid out on the made beds. His head ached, and he tried to free himself from

233

the tight bonds that held him down. But they were firm, and would not give. In a few minutes he was sound asleep.

He was roused by the noise of those back from breakfast, by Ambergate stowing his tin mug in the kitbag. Moore offered Arthur a drink of tea.

'Ernie,' Arthur said in a flat croaking voice to Ambergate, 'untie me.'

Moore held the tea down for him. 'Drink this, then you'll feel better.'

'Untie me first.'

Seeing that no one would untie him, he drank the tea, gulping it down loudly. They laughed at his plight. 'What bastard tied me up?' he demanded.

'You aren't tied up,' Moore said.

'Not much I'm not. Who did it?'

Ambergate winked and explained: 'When we came in last night you were flat out on the floor, and when we tried to get you in bed you lashed out. So we were going to leave you like that all night, but the C.O. came in and said: "What's that prostrate swaddie doing huddled-up on the floor in a pool of piss?" "He's passed-out, sir," I said. "Then get 'im into bed," he shouted, as mad as buggery. "A bloody swaddie's no good on the billet floor. Get the sod to bed." "But sir," I said, "every time I get near him, he gives me a clout with his pit-boot." "Don't be a bloody fool," the C.O. said, "get him into bed. Look, I'll show you how to do it." Then, bogger me, Arthur, if you didn't kick the C.O. as well, right in the nuts. It's true right enough, ain't it, lads? There, I told you. Well the C.O. nearly had a fit. "Tie him up," he shouted like a mad bull. "Tie the bloody swaddie up. No bloody swaddie's going to kick me where I daren't show my mother. I'll settle his goat in the morning, that I will." So we had to tie you up, see? C.O.'s orders.'

'You lying bastard,' Arthur shouted. 'You should be on the Empire. You'd get fifty bob a week. Now untie me.'

'Not likely,' Ambergate said among all the laughter. 'You'll only lash out again.'

'Untie me.'

The sergeant poked his head into the billet door and screamed: 'On p'rade, yo' lot,' and in half a minute the billet was empty, except for Arthur who was tied to his bed and couldn't move. Yet it wasn't disagreeable to him, for he was tired and worn out: he closed his eyes and went back to sleep.

At eleven the Orderly Officer walked through the billet.

'Now, who's this bloody fool still sleeping

235

at this time of the day?' he called out. 'Hey, you, what are you doing?'

Arthur's eyes opened. He tried to move his arms and legs, remembered, rolled his eyes, and closed them again. The O.O. shook him, prodded him: 'For Christ's sake, man, what are you doing here? Get up. Come on.'

Arthur looked up at last. 'Yes, sir?'

'What are you doing, still in bed?' he snapped.

He thought up the first excuse: 'I'm badly. I don't feel well. I got pains in my head and stomach and I feel as though I'm tied to my bed.'

'Fine, I must say. Well, why didn't you go on sick parade?'

'I didn't wake up in time.'

The O.O. tut-tutted, as though he'd just about had enough of life. 'Bloody Terriers,' he swore. 'I'll send the sergeant in to see about getting you over to the sick quarters, then.'

The door slammed, and the billet was silent. The O.O. forgot to send the sergeant, and Arthur stayed in bed till teatime, obliviously sleeping, forgetting that he was tied up, the hours passing with such pleasant speed that he remarked to Ambergate later that they should leave him be, that he could think of no better way to spend his fifteen

236

days, provided they gave him a drink of tea and a fag now and again.

CHAPTER TEN

HE changed into draped jacket and narrow-bottomed trousers, and now stood by the door of the Match looking around the L-shaped room. Brenda and Winnie were sitting at a corner table over a couple of stouts. Brenda looked up and smiled. She hadn't expected to see him. 'Mind if I sit down?' he asked.

''Course I don't.' Her head was dipped pensively forward and she took short swallows of the stout, her throat hidden until she put the glass down. Arthur wondered what she was trying to hide, feeling somehow that he was not wanted, despite the fact that his offer to buy them drinks was graciously accepted.

'Is anything wrong, duck?' he said to her.

She looked up and smiled. 'I'm all right.'

'We'll go somewhere else if you like. This place's as dead as a graveyard tonight,' he said, turning his back on those jostling each other at the bar.

'I want to stay here,' she said mildly.

She has a date, he thought, to meet some man or other.

'Suits me, then,' he put in, and asked the waiter to bring more drinks. Winnie enquired: had he had a good time at the camp? and he praised it for a holiday, saying it was better than Blackpool because instead of salt-water to swim in there had been strong beer. He hadn't seen Winnie since Brenda's gin-and-tonic party, and she looked even more desirable now, for she was clearly dressed-up to kill, with smart white blouse and black suit and hair just permed, as if she had made up her mind to go all out for a good time after hearing that her husband Bill was making hay while the sun shone with a German woman on the Rhine. Arthur thought this a good guess, for the Match had the worst reputation in town. He couldn't keep his eyes from her, and felt like a king buying drinks for two such gorgeous and tractable women.

He leaned towards Brenda. 'You don't look very happy tonight, duck. Aren't you glad to see me?'

She finished the stout before answering. 'Didn't they learn you to write at the school you went to?'

So that was it. He hadn't written to her. 'I didn't have time, duck. I told you before I went that I might be too busy.'

'Even a postcard?' she said sullenly.

'I tell you, we were kept busy from start to

239

finish. As soon as I got my feet inside the camp they chucked a rifle into my hands and made us do a scheme. Ten miles at the trot with fixed bayonet in the pouring rain, crawlin' through woods and getting scratched to boggery in the brambles. I tell yer I couldn't even lift a cup o' tea to my lips by the time we'd finished. Then we got drill, lectures, guards, unarmed combat, map-readin', every minute that God sent, as well as going most days on the range. You got no idea how they put us through it. They got their money's worth all right. I meant to write to you all the time, but I didn't get a minute to myself, no kiddin'. I didn't even write a word to mam. She was worried to death about me and called me all the rotters under the sun as soon as I stepped in the house this afternoon, saying she thought I'd got shot in the guts or got squashed under a tank or summat like that.'

'Didn't you 'ave any time in the evening?' she asked, not quite convinced despite the earnest look on his face.

'Evenings?' he said resentfully. 'The bastards had us polishing the billet floor until ten, or pulling our rifles through. Bull we had from getting there to coming away. I didn't get out for a single drink, I was so dead beat. There was guards to do as well, nearly every

240

night. I tell you, it was the worse fortnight I've ever spent.'

He won her over, yet asked himself why he hadn't written a letter, and the truth was, he discovered, that he had forgotten. He had thought of her from time to time, true, but it never occurred to him to write. Besides, he asked himself, wouldn't it have been dangerous? Suppose Jack had picked it up from the mat one morning and read it? Jack was a good bloke, but deep in his ways and hard to weigh-up, one of the sort that might go right out of his path to make trouble if he suddenly woke up to the fact that you had been doing it on him for a long time. Apart from this, writing letters was too much like hard work.

He made no progress with Brenda. But Winnie was more pliable. However, at nine o'clock he surprised them both by saying he was going home to sleep after his hard fortnight with the army. 'It's early,' Brenda said, but she hardly objected to his leaving.

'Don't bother about us, though,' Winnie laughed, an expression of mirth that boded no good for her husband. 'We can take care of ourselves.'

The doors closed behind him. He hurried up the street, pushed his way through a gang of soldiers towards lights and main-road traffic, walking away from the obstinacy of two women who had no use for him. He cursed them in foul, well-polished language: they had come out for a night on the batter, he said to himself, and had got the shock of their lives when he walked into the Match and settled himself at their table. They had drunk his stout, and hadn't got guts enough to say he was not wanted. Not that he minded them drinking his stout. He expected it from Nottingham women who, he told himself, were cheeky-daft, and thought so much of themselves that they would drink your ale whether they liked your company or not. Whores, all of them. Never again. They'd had all they were going to get from him. Brenda wasn't worth the trouble he'd been through to keep her. As if it made any difference whether he had written to her or not. It was only an excuse to make trouble. Most likely, when he went away, she had been glad to see the back of him, and had passed the whole fortnight doing the dirty on him, not to mention on poor old Jack. Instead of boozing in the Match she should be at home looking after her two kids, the poor little sods. If ever I get married, he thought, and have a wife that carries on like Brenda and Winnie carry on, I'll give her the biggest pasting any woman ever

242

had. I'd kill her. My wife'll have to look after any kids I fill her with, keep the house spotless. And if she's good at that I might let her go to the pictures now and again and take her out for a drink on Saturday. But if I thought she was carrying on behind my back she'd be sent back to her mother with two black eyes before she knew what's happening. By God she would.

He walked towards Slab Square, his bones aching for the noise of a public house, wanting to lose himself in a waterfall of ale and laughter. The main road was lit by overhead lamps furtively shining, as if ready to fall into darkness at a moment's notice on sighting a reconnoitring member of the Lord's Day Observance Society. Sunday, he thought bitterly, even preferring Monday though it meant the first grinding day of the week. Various pubs gave signs of life, but it was not of the intense violence needed to relieve the weight of woman-trouble trying to drag him down into the bright clean gutter.

A group of people had gathered at the gate of St. Mary's. Lights still shone within the church, and a Daimler car sloped like a prize black spaniel by the kerb. Arthur pushed his way through, hoping the Horse and Groom would be a safe bet for noise on Sunday night.

Irish navvies sometimes gathered there to booze away the last of their wages before drawing a sub from the gaffer on Monday morning. His cousin once worked with them, and said that each weekend it was common that two would agree to fight for each other's wage-packets in some corner of the nearest field, the condition being that the winner must leave a pound for the loser's hostel fees. Hard-headed bastards with no feelings, Arthur thought, pushing his way into the bright lights of his selected pub, revived by beer fumes even before drawing his first pint from the counter.

'It's a quiet night,' he said to the woman as she set his jar down.

'Yes,' she answered, tightening her arms and smiling only with her thin lips. 'We had trouble here last Saturday. They started fighting'—meaning the absent navvies—'so the police came in and cleared them all out. Didn't you hear about it? We nearly lost our licence.' He explained that he had been away. 'They're a rough lot, them Micks,' he agreed.

'You should've seen 'em,' she went on, not without a certain pride, 'they fought like lions. And I hear they go to church on Sunday because they're Cath'lics. I don't understand it, I'm sure, I don't.'

'That's their way,' he remarked, 'but it ain't mine. I've never been in a church in my life. I ain't even been christened.'

'Well,' she said, 'you'll go into church when you get married, I'll tell you that much.'

'Not me,' he laughed, pushing his empty jar towards her. 'For one thing I wain't get married, and for another, if I do, I'll go to the registry office.'

'You'll have to see what your lady-friend says about that. You never can tell what she'll be like.'

'Well, if she's like that I wain't marry her. I've got an aunt who's religious, and she's got it bad now. Her lad was killed by a car when he was ten, and she's never bin the same since. Not only that, but she's drinking herself to death at the same time. She puts back bottles and bottles of stout all day. So I wain't marry a tart that's religious.'

'If you're in love, you'll marry anything,' she told him.

'Not me. Another one, duck. Black-and-tan this time.' A few tables were occupied, and he considered the noise nothing to write home about. He noticed an interesting table by the far wall from which some hilarity came. Of the four that sat there he singled out a young girl whose fingers rested by a glass of shandy.

245

Her brown hair was patterned attractively into an oval shape at the back of her head, a diamond piece of brown silk scarf came down from her coat collar, and from what he could see of the front—no rings on her fingers—she wore only lipstick and looked pale enough to be having her periods. They belong to the same family, he deduced, for though the girl didn't do much talking, she let herself say from time to time: 'But that's not right, our mam,' in quite a loud voice, then became silent again while her mother went on talking to the young man and woman with them. These two latter were married, Arthur decided. Daughter and son-in-law, though they might be son and daughter-in-law. And the girl was her daughter, certainly. Their faces showed it. He thought it marvellous that, ring or no ring, you could always tell a married from a single woman. It was a matter of intuition. You looked at her for half a second and said to yourself: 'She's married,' or, 'She's not married,' and nine times out of ten you were right. Another thing about young women was—though here you weren't always so right—that you could tell from her face, even if she was dressed in a voluminous coat, the size and shape of her breasts. With a tight-lipped whippet-faced talkative woman they were as flat as porridge-plates or tinier than pheasants' eggs, but with an open-mouthed cheeky-faced, laughing woman you always had something to get hold of. The still-waters-run-deep women were often hardest to solve in this matter: mostly they turned out well, but if by chance they didn't then they made up for it in passion. And the girl that now caught his eye as she turned to say something else to her mother, fell into the divided category of the latter class. He was served with his black-and-tan.

She looked in his direction. Thought I wouldn't have the cheek to keep on staring, he said to himself, smiling and lifting his hand to acknowledge the sign she had not yet given him. Then she smiled, and turned away quickly to argue against some story of her mother's. He lifted his drink, and faced himself in the huge mirror over the bar.

Why not? he thought. Because she's with her mother, you daft sod. So what? Because her mother wouldn't like it, that's why. But her mother isn't going to get it. I'll tell the . . . She seems a nice, friendly girl, good reason for me to do what I can. He looked again and saw her white neck. Must have taken her scarf off because it was too hot. He was sorry she was busy talking to the others. Knows I'm trying to catch her eye, he thought. Twenty-five minutes to closing time, and the sands were running out.

He turned back to the bar for another drink. The woman who served had seen him before with Brenda, and asked where his friend was.

'Friend?' he said. 'She worn't my friend. She was a cousin o' mine from Sheffield, come to see us on a visit. I was just showing her the town. She's gone back now.'

'I'm not being nosy,' she said. 'Only I thought you looked a bit lonely.'

'No fear,' he replied. 'I like being lonely sometimes. I feel good when I'm alone, because I live at home in a big family, and I wok all day wi' thousands of other people, so being alone is a treat for me. There's nowt I like better than going out into the country on my bike and fishing near Cotgrave or Trowel and sitting for hours by myself.'

'I see what you mean,' she answered. 'I feel like that as well. It's no fun, you know, keeping a pub, with people coming in and out every day and keeping you at it till all hours. But then, what can you do? It's a good living. Yes, my duck? What can I do for you?' She spoke this last piece in a louder voice, looking over Arthur's shoulder. He turned, and stepped aside so that the girl he had been looking at could come to the bar. She thanked him, and asked the woman for four packets of crisps. Her coat was open, showing a dress of deep yellow with buttons the same colour all the way down. In a sly one-second glance he noted her slim but good figure.

'Is it somebody's birthday?' he asked.

'No,' she answered readily. 'It's mam's silver wedding.'

The woman laid both crisps and change on the counter and went to the far end of the bar to serve a double-whisky. 'I can't see your dad,' he said. 'Is he dead?'

'Separated,' she replied. 'It started as a joke, mam celebrating her silver wedding, and I don't like jokes like that.'

Oh, don't you? he thought. 'Have a drink then, duck, while you're here.'

She looked over her shoulder at the others, and, seeing them still talking, said: 'All right. I'll have a shandy if you don't mind. What's that black stuff you're drinking? It looks like treacle.' He told her. 'I've heard of it,' she said. 'I think I tasted it once, but it was too strong.' She sipped her shandy. 'This is as much as I can take.'

'Well, I'm not a boozer either, only I felt like a drink tonight because I've just got back off my fifteen days. A bloke deserves a drink after that.'

'I'll bet he does. What are you in?'

'Army. But I'll be done next year.'

'Shall you be glad?'

'Not much I wain't. I can't get out quick enough.'

'My sister married a man in the air force,' she told him. 'He looked ever so nice in his uniform. He's out now though, and they've got a house up Wollaton. She's expecting a baby next week.'

'Do you live up that way?' he asked, his drink not touched.

'No,' she answered, 'up Broxtowe, on the estate. I like living in them nice new houses. It's a long way from the shops, but there's plenty of fresh air.' He suggested she take the crisps to her family and come back to the bar. 'All right,' she said. He heard her say loudly to her mother that she had met a friend from work and wanted to talk to him. He drank.

'Is your mother deaf?' he asked when she came back, offering a cigarette.

'Yes, she is. And when people hear me shouting at her in the street they think I'm a pan-mouth. No duck, I don't smoke, thanks.'

He laughed, and asked her name.

'Doreen. A rotten name ain't it?' She

pushed out her tongue, healthy, spade-shaped, and drew it back into its warm retreat.

'What's wrong wi' it? Doreen's all right. My name's Arthur. Neither on 'em's up to much, but it ain't our fault, is it?'

'Well, I can think of better names than mine, I can tell yer.'

He drew the last drop of black-and-tan from his jar. 'Nobody's satisfied wi' what they've got, if you ask me. There'd be summat wrong with the world if they was. Where do you work then?'

'Me? Harris's, the hairnet factory. All right, I will have a fag. I'd better not let mam see me though, or she'll get on to me. I've worked there four years now, since I left school.'

I thought so, he said to himself. Nineteen. 'I'm in the bike trade myself,' he told her. 'I like working at a big place: you get a bonus at Christmas, a trip to Blackpool, sports club where you can go for a drink. They look after you in a factory.' Like boggery, he thought. She had emptied her glass. 'Have another shandy. Come on, it wain't get you drunk. Shandy, missis,' he called out. 'Besides, it's your mother's silver wedding.'

'You don't have to be that nice just to get

251

me a drink. I'll have a shandy. You like your black-and-tan as well.'

'You're a sharp 'un,' he said, finishing his second since she came. 'You don't miss much.'

'It don't pay to miss owt,' she laughed.

'What do you do in the week?' he ventured. 'Do you ever go to't pictures?'

She looked at him with brown suspicious eyes. 'Only on Monday. Why?'

'That's funny, because I go out on a Monday night as well to't pictures. I allus think Monday's the best night of the week for that sort of thing, because I go for a drink and see my pals at the weekend, and on the other days I have a lot to do, mending my bike, or getting my tackle ready for fishing. And Monday night is allus best for the pictures because the new ones are on then. Which one do you go to?'

'The Granby.'

'I go there sometimes on a Monday,' he said, 'and I've never seen you before.'

'That's because hundreds of other people go as well,' she answered facetiously.

'I'll see you tomorrow night at seven, then,' he said.

'Fast worker, aren't you? All right, but not on the back row.'

'Why not? I can't see unless I sit right on

the back row. If I get near the front the picture goes all blurred. Something's wrong with my eyes, I suppose.'

'You want glasses,' she said, 'by the sound of it.'

'I know. I'll get some some day. They wouldn't suit me though. I'd look too much like a boss-eyed bookie, or a rent collector. But my eyes aren't that bad. I won't want glasses until I'm sixty, and I might not live that long.'

'Cheerful, aren't you? What makes you think so?'

'All this talk about war.'

'It's only talk. It don't mean a thing,' she said.

'As long as it don't start before tomorrow night, that's all I care.'

She shrugged her shoulders. 'Men, they're all the same. It's easy to see you work in a big factory. You're dead sharp. I suppose you talk all day to the women?'

'That's what you think. I've got too much wok to do.'

'Well, I believe you, but thousands wouldn't.'

The clock-hand crept towards five minutes to ten. 'What's on the pictures tomorrow? Owt good?'

'I thought you said you went a lot to the

Granby?' she asked sharply. 'You always know what's coming on next because they show you the trailers.'

Trapped. 'I know,' he said, 'but I never take that much notice. I forget it as soon as I come out. I have a rotten memory. I even forget the picture unless it's a real smasher, with Boris Karloff or somebody like that. I must have seen thousands of pictures, like everybody else, but I'll bet I can't remember half a dozen. I remember "Henry the Fifth" and I saw it years ago, but that's only because I saw it about six times. I read that long speech he does on his hoss before the fight. It's in my brother's book.'

'Can you say it, then?'

Some of it. Certain phrases came in the king's loud voice, but he could not speak them. For any man this day that shed his blood with me shall be my brother . . . shall in their flowing cups be freshly remembered . . . his passport shall be made and crowns for convoy put into his purse . . . I would not die . . . old men forget . . . that fought with us upon St. Crispin's day. . . . His fingers forgot the jar handle for a moment, and he stood up as if to hear better once more the destructive flight of arrows at Agincourt, the noise of two hosts destroying each other in colourful slaughter, risking an arm and a leg for promises of loot and fire.

'I've forgot it. It's too long. But if you want it I'll copy it from our Sam's book.'

'No, don't take all that trouble. I think Laurence Olivier's a good actor, don't you? He's handsome. He reminds me of a lad I once knew, who worked in our office.'

The woman put the towels on, shouting: 'Time! Time, please, everybody!'

'I'll see you tomorrow night then, duck,' he said.

'Yes. At seven. And be there. Don't let me down.'

The lights began flickering off and on to hurry them out.

'Don't say things like that. I'll be there.' Doreen's mother was calling to her. 'So long, then.'

'Cheerio, see you tomorrow.'

I've clicked, he said, stepping on to the pavement; I've clicked—walking down the street, back towards the Match. People were forming bus queues from emptying pubs, each queue the flickering tadpole tail of a weekend. Time marches on, he thought. Before we know where we are Goose Fair will be here, with dark nights and a stone-cold winter, and everybody filling their Christmas

255

clubs for chocolates, pork pies, and booze. I'll be twenty-three in December. An old man soon. Turning by the church, he saw Winnie walking alone along Woolworth's darkened window.

'I thought you'd gone to bed?' she said when he caught up with her.

'I changed my mind. Where's Brenda?'

'She got fed-up and went home.'

He detected the lie. 'Who did she go home with?'

'It's as true as I stand here,' she cried, stopping to give force to her lie. 'She got a splitting headache and took a bus home.'

'If she wants to play that sort of game,' he said, pulling her into the wall so that people could pass, 'I won't stop her, but one day she'll find it won't pay, and you can tell her that from me.'

Winnie glared at him with coal-black eyes: 'You're too bloody clever, that's what's wrong with you.'

They walked on, and he placed an arm around her waist. 'Now then Gypsy, it ain't your worry, so don't get mad.' He decided that his chances of spending the night with her would be better if they didn't take a bus. His supposition that a bright ending was after all possible for his tumultuous day seemed reasonable when she squeezed his forearm affectionately. That morning he had been in Shrewsbury, and a quick review of the day and evening passed through his mind, flickering lantern-slides of cityscape, country, and sky, smells of railway stations and train-smoke, replaced by bus fumes and beer-smells, and promising now the odours of a woman's body and bedroom to crown the end of a mobile and passionate day. As he walked silently up the hill towards Winnie's he hoped Doreen would not forget her date with him tomorrow night, that she would not keep him waiting too long at the cinema. His opinion of Nottingham women had changed slightly. Of course they were gold-diggers, he told himself, but more often than not they were of the right stuff, and you could usually get what you wanted if you were careful and went out of your way sufficiently to pick the right sort of woman.

CHAPTER ELEVEN

DOREEN, at nineteen, was afraid of being 'left on the shelf'. Her married, engaged, or otherwise firmly attached friends at the hairnet factory had teased her for not yet having a boyfriend, but since meeting Arthur she was able to talk about her 'young man' with the rest of them, her oval face smiling as she extolled his attributes of kindness and generosity, affection and industry. She created his image: a tall young man of the world, nearly twenty-three and already a long way past his military service, a man who had been a good soldier and who was now a good worker because he was earning fourteen pounds a week on piecework. He would also make a good husband, there being no doubt of this because above all he was kind and attentive. What's more, he was good-looking, was tall, thin, had fair hair. What girl wouldn't be happy with a man like that? Also, she affirmed, he loved her, and, as far as she could tell, she loved him. Sitting with the women and girls over a canteen lunch she told them of how, on their first date, a youth had shouted an unpleasant word at her, and Arthur had turned back and nearly flattened him against a wall. But the women maintained that although Doreen may have a young man, she was not yet engaged, and that was what mattered. For a young man could flit away one fine night and never be heard of again, while if you were engaged he would think twice about it. To have a young man was all very well, but it didn't mean, not by a long chalk, that you were going to be married. Doreen said that it did, and revived Arthur's portrait afresh for them each day, until they reluctantly admitted that, even if she wasn't properly engaged, she at least had a very regular young man.

Arthur's view was altogether different. A month passed since their first meeting —nights were darker, longer, colder, and were fast drawing on to Goose Fair—and he had seen her only three times—at the cinema. He liked the thought of going out with an unattached girl, but since she had told him more than once on the back row of the Granby to keep his hands to himself, and had not yet taken him into her home, he had no desire to see her more than once a week. He did not deny that she was nice, that, from as far as she had permitted his sly hands to roam during long good-night kisses, she was beautiful, but he did not want to begin a courtship, while Doreen obviously did. She was a sharp one and knew how to laugh, he told himself, and he liked walking by her side with no fear of being chased by two big swaddies for his trouble, but he realised that, by going out with a single girl he may one day— unwittingly and of course disastrously—find himself on the dizzy and undesired brink of the hell that older men called marriage, an even more unattractive prospect than coming one day face to face with some husband's irate and poised fist. It was a pity, he thought, that you always had to choose between two or more evils.

He did not see Doreen often, because his weeks and weekends were divided between Brenda and Winnie. It occurred to him later that he should have kept to the safe and rosy path with Doreen, but the pleasure and danger of having two married women had been too sweet to resist. He pondered a great deal on Brenda and Winnie as he spun and thrust and pulled at the life of his lathe. Like the tool and stops before him he played off one woman against the other, taking Winnie to the Langham and Brenda to the Rose, and wondering all the time how long it was going to last. Winnie knew all about Brenda and called him a dirty dog and a naughty boy, but

Brenda had never the agile mind to twig that he was whiling the days between times away with her sister. It was a dark life and a dark deed, and his darkest thoughts revolved upon the possibility of a clash with the swaddies. But his capacity for discretion had deepened, and so far the tight-rope neither sagged nor weakened nor even threatened to throw him off balance.

★   ★   ★

He stepped out of the drizzling rain and stood with his back to a glass-case of Technicolor stills, looking across the road for signs of Doreen. The wet highway was bordered by new pink-walled houses that gave an even gloomier appearance than the black dwellings of Radford. He turned back to the stills: a war picture and a funny picture, Korea and slapstick, first the marines having a tough time of it in a dive-bombed ravine, then Abbot and Costello chased by murderers through a thousand laughs to the common ruin of happiness; everyone finally making for the doors to the tune of God Save the Queen.

It was a few days prior to the big Goose Fair, a week before the Lord Mayor's opening speech, and huge trailers loaded with complicated roundabout components and Dodgem cars rumbled into the city from all over the Midlands, converging on a large open tract of field near the city centre. Goose Fair was the great time of the year, the one place where you met people you hadn't seen for years. It was also a tradition that every young man took his young lady there, and for the past fortnight traditional Doreen had been trying to divine whether or not Arthur would ask her to go. He suspected this, but his promise to Winnie and Brenda was of such long standing that it could not be broken even if he wished to do so, which he did not.

She rounded a corner, crossed the road, and waved an arm encased in a plastic mac. 'I was late for my tea, I'm sorry I kept you waiting.' She showed her white teeth in a smile, struggled out of her mac and coat, and, as Arthur stood at the paybox they seemed like a loving and long-engaged couple only kept back from marriage by the housing shortage.

At ten o'clock they took a long walk back to her house, by the boulevard that bordered the estate (Arthur remembered seeing an aerial photo of it: a giant web of roads, avenues, and crescents, with a school like a black spider lurking in the middle). The passed the stationary chip-van and bought a packet of hot chips smelling of vinegar and salt. Doreen mentioned the Goose Fair: 'I went for a walk on Forest yesterday and they'd already got a lot of the roundabouts up.'

'Have they?' he said, as if he had never heard of the fair.

'I saw some trailers as well,' she added, 'going over Bobber's Mill Bridge.'

'I got lost on Goose Fair when I was a kid of six,' he said. 'I had a lot of fun though, because I went on all the roundabouts for nowt. About eleven o'clock I started to cry, and when I saw a copper I towd him I was lost, and so he took me to Norwood police station. They gave me cakes and cups of tea because I was hungry, and when I'd had my fill I told 'em where I lived, and then they drove me home in a police van. I can still remember how good the cakes tasted. I must have been a crazy bogger, even then, because I pretended I didn't know where I lived till they'd fed me. Coppers are all right when it comes to a thing like that, but they worn't so good to my cousin, because he once robbed nearly every gas and electric meter in one street, and when they caught him they hit him to try and mek him tell 'em where he'd hid the money. But it was already spent. He got sent to Borstal for that, and when he came home on holiday everybody asked him if he still worked for the gas company, and where was his little brown cash-bag and his peaked-cap.' He screwed his chip paper into a tight ball and sent it rolling along the gutter.

She made no comment, and they walked for some minutes in silence. He knew she wanted him to speak first. As at other times, when faced with making a decision against his own good, he felt that his back was to the wall. She also threw her chip paper forcefully down, and took his arm.

'Are you going to the Goose Fair this year?' he asked at last, on the last avenue before the crescent where she lived.

'I expect so,' she replied tersely. 'I usually go.'

'So do I, though I don't think much to it. You ride on roundabouts till you're sick. It ain't much fun.'

'Some people like it,' she said sharply. 'Thousands of them.'

The fair lasted three days, and Saturday was the best night, when he had promised to take Winnie and Brenda. It was also the night when Doreen expected him to take her.

'Will you come to the fair with me, then?' he asked in a relenting and considerate voice.

She squeezed his arm with affection. 'That'd be lovely, duck.'

'I'll take you on Friday,' he went on. 'I like Friday night better than any other because there aren't so many people as Sat'day. In any case I can't take you on Sat'day because I promised I'd go to Worksop with my mate. He's got a motorbike and I'm goin' pillion.' Her hand stiffened. What does she think I am? he wondered. Does she think we're engaged or summat, and that I've got to tek her?

'I can't come on Friday,' she said. 'I promised to go and see my sister. She'll be having her baby in a month, and I go every Friday night to help with the house.'

Story for story, blow for blow. 'That's hard lines,' he said. 'I was hopin' I could tek yer. What about Thursday then?'

'It's not a good night,' she said. 'The fair's just got started. But I don't want to put you to any trouble.'

As if she hadn't been sarcastic he went on: 'That's all right. You won't put me to any trouble.'

They came to the gate of her house. 'I can't stay out long. I've got to go in and wash my hair.'

'What time shall I see you on Thursday then?'

He heard the disappointment in her voice: 'Half-past seven at the corner of Gregory Boulevard?' She reasoned that perhaps Thursday wouldn't be too bad, being bound to meet at least some of her friends from work and be seen arm-in-arm with her young man. Had he taken her on Saturday though, she would have been seen by everyone. There was only one good-night kiss for him that night.

*   *   *

He met Winnie and Brenda on Saturday at the place and time he stipulated for Doreen two days earlier. Brenda on his right arm and Winnie on his left they walked towards the fire-lake of the fair, dressed in their best despite the maxim saying: Wear old things on such nights so that fish, chips, candy-floss, brandy-snap, and winkle-stains would not matter. Jack had stayed in to do the pools, check the union dues and enter them in his ledger, Brenda said.

The fair lights were a sheet of pale coruscating orange obliterating the darkness. Crowds were thick along the pavement, moving in uneven intermingling streams to and from the tents and roundabouts. Children clutched Donald Duck balloons, women and girls wore paper sailor-hats saying: 'Kiss me quick' or 'You've had it'; others hugged train-sets and china dogs won at hoop-la and darts. The pungent air smoked brandy-snap and vinegar. They heard the thumping pistons of red-painted engines that gave power to Caterpillars and Noah's Arks, and distant screams came down at them from the tower of Helter Skelter and the topmost arc of the Big Wheel, noise and lights a magnetised swamp sucking people into it for miles around.

He dragged his women along, stopped to buy a 'Kiss me quick' hat for Winnie and 'You've had it' hat for Brenda, and as they swung in through the entrance he narrowly missed castration on the steel post invisible in the crush of people. Winnie held his coat-tail so that she would not be lost, screaming: 'Where shall we go first?'

'Just foller me,' he bellowed.

Brenda shouted: 'I've lost my hat.'

'Leave it then,' he answered. 'I'll buy you another.'

She pressed it down with her hand. 'No I haven't.'

Music was sweet from the Bobby Horses, a circular up-and-down movement shaking along to captivating organ music. 'The horses,' Winnie yelled. 'I want a bob on the horses.'

'They're stopping,' Brenda said. 'Let's get on quick'—she lifted her skirt and Arthur pushed her from behind, pulling Winnie after him who, when on a horse, sat clutching her paper-hat.

'An old-age pensioners roundabout,' Arthur shouted. 'Wait till we're on the rocket.' When the horses rose they saw over the heads of the crowd, a mixing ground of grown-ups and children.

On a slow advance towards the centre they mounted the Caterpillar, and when the hoods covered them in darkness Arthur kissed first Brenda and then Winnie so that when the canvas slid back and let the stars look in at them, both were laughing loudly and blushing from Arthur's passionate caresses, struggling away from his righteous and powerful arms. Not like being with Doreen, he thought, who had watched his step every minute of the way on Thursday, giving no great fun to gladden the heart, and stopping to talk for half an hour to that daft pal from her workplace.

'Try our luck,' Winnie said. 'Let's roll pennies and win a quid.' Winnie let them fall from the wooden slot over numbered squares in rapid fire and lost five bob in as many minutes, while Brenda aimed well but did no better. Arthur rolled them down slowly yet without aim and won simply because he kept shouting loudly that he was born lucky. Brenda's judgment prevailed and they came away two shillings on the right side, buying brandy-snap and starting a slow crawl of the side-shows sucking a brown tasty stick. They were turned out of the zoo when Arthur tried to throw Winnie to a pair of half-dead pythons coiled up in sleep. 'You'd mek a good meal,' he said as she struggled in his arms. 'They look as though they ain't bin fed since Christmas, the poor boggers.'

The keeper chased them down the steps waving a whip over their heads. At a darts stall Brenda won an ornamental plate. 'That's what comes of having done so much practice at the club last year,' Winnie said knowingly. 'You should be able to win sommat as well, Arthur.'

'Sharpshit,' he said. 'I'll throw you to the lions next if you aren't careful, yo' see'f I wain't.'

Sanity was out of reach: they were caught up in balloons of light and pleasure that would not let them go. The four-acre fair be-came a whole world, with tents and caravans, stalls and roundabouts, booths and towers, swingboats and engines and big wheels, and a crowd that had lost all idea of time and place locked in the belly of its infernal noise.

Winnie clamoured for the Ghost Train, and Arthur felt like a father with two children, fulfilling a promise made at the anti-climax of Christmas. They waited for an empty carriage and, once pushed into the ghost-ride, were assailed by black darkness and horrible screams from Hell, that Arthur decided came from the train in front. He stood up to fight the mock-death whose horrors had been written in large letters across the façade outside.

'Sit down,' Brenda warned him.

'Or a bogey-man will get you,' Winnie said, the most frightened though she had suggested the ride. Nothing more than darkness and phantoms conjured up from your own mind were supposed to make you afraid in the first stage, and Arthur, unattacked, swore black-and-blue that it was too dark to see anything, shouting that he wanted his money back. Girls in the train before them began laughing at his complaint, shaken from the legitimate sense of terror for which they had paid a shilling.

He stepped out and ran a few yards in front, until he came level with them, determined that they should not be disappointed in the Ghost Train. His hands roamed, and they cried out in fear. The noise of a horse about to stampede whinnied through the dark tunnel, the death-rattle of a crushed man croaked around them, and finally he gave a wild scream as if suddenly put out of his misery by a rifle bullet. He left their train and, when he gauged that Brenda and Winnie had drawn level with him, climbed in.

'Who just got in our train, Alf?' asked a female voice that he could not recognise. He stood still, hardly breathing.

'I don't know,' the man said. 'Did anybody get in?' Arthur heard him patting her thigh, trying to comfort her. 'Don't worry, Lil, duck.'

'But somebody got in, I tell you,' she whimpered. 'Look, he's standing there.'

The man stretched out his hand. It touched Arthur's leg, and drew back as if he had been a piece of live-wire. 'Who are you?' he asked.

'Boris Karloff,' Arthur said in a sombre voice.

The woman cried plaintively. 'I told you we shouldn't have come in here. It was your idea, with your dirty tricks.'

'It's nothing,' the man said, a little less comforting. 'He's only one of the mechanics. But it's going a bit too far, if you ask me, spoiling our ride like this.'

'I want a drink o' blood,' Arthur said. 'On'y a cupful, for supper.'

'Tell him to get out,' the woman moaned. 'Tell him to ride in somebody else's train.'

'Brenda!' Arthur roared. 'Winnie! Where are you?' Then he laughed. He wasn't going to walk back, so might as well finish his ride in this train. They came to a turning, and the luminous bones of a hanging skeleton dangled before them, a sight that filled the tunnel with echoing screams.

'Tell him to get out,' the woman kept saying. 'You don't know who he might be,' she chafed.

'I'm Jack the Ripper,' Arthur said, 'but I'm not ripping tonight.

'Oh what horrible thing's he's saying,' she wept.

'Now then, Lil, keep calm,' Alf said. 'You'll be all right. We're only in the Ghost Train. We'll be out soon.'

'I'm frightened,' she whined. 'He's got such a terrible laugh. He might have come out of an asylum for all we know.'

Arthur stood up taller as the train drew close to the skeleton. 'Look, missis, I'll do you a favour: if you let me ride in your train, I'll smack it on the snout.'

'Get out,' she cried, hiding her face, 'I don't want to see it.'

'Now, now,' the man said. 'Don't cry. I'll see the management about this.'

Arthur hit the skeleton, a huge piece of cloth, caught it with his hands and was trapped in it. He struggled to free himself, but it fell from diverse hooks and hung on as if it were alive, folding over him and fighting back. He was buried, he was six feet under in a sackcloth coffin with train-wheels jolting his feet, aware of the woman's screaming, feeling her boy-friend trying to thump him, hearing people running from train to train, when he shouted through the hole in the cloth: 'Fire! Fire! Run for your lives!'—with all the power in his lungs. He battled with the darkness, breaking his laughter to call on Winnie and Brenda, kicking and pummelling until his arms emerged from the heavy black cover, glistening skeleton-bones looking like tiger-streaks over his back, head, and shoulders.

'I've won!' he screamed out to everyone. 'I beat that bloody skeleton!'

The train burst into the open air, into flashing lights and music, swirling round-abouts and the thud-thud-thud of en-gines—and a spanner-brandishing mechanic rushing towards him through the uproar.

Arthur gathered the cloth quickly and hurled it over the man and, while he was struggling and cursing to break free, took Winnie and Brenda by the wrists and dragged them towards the high-speed circling magnet of the next roundabout.

At the edge of the fair they stood by a stall drinking tea. Paper hats had changed heads, Brenda's now saying: 'Kiss me quick' and Winnie's: 'You've had it', and Arthur took a kiss from each woman where the crowd was thickest and when one had her back turned. It was at one of these pleasurable moments—when they were making again for the Bobby Horses—that Doreen's face suddenly appeared through the crowd. On lifting his eyes from Winnie, with the light of ecstasy still in them, he saw Doreen looking at him from between two trilby-covered heads turned the other way. The light of ecstasy left them, to be replaced by a broad smile, and a slight acknowledgement of her presence by an attempted wave of his arm.

'Who's that?' Brenda wanted to know, turning around.

'A gel who lives in our yard.'

Brenda pushed her way towards the Bobby Horses, and Arthur looked again for Doreen, but she had been swept away into a sea of swaying heads and paper hats.

Each with an ice-cream cornet they stepped on to the Cake Walk, shuffling, jogging, laughing along the shaking rattle of moving machinery, Brenda in front, Winnie behind holding her waist, and Arthur last of all holding whatever his hand found. From the Cake Walk he suggested the Helter Skelter, a tall wooden tower with an outside flyway, smooth enough for a swift ride down, sufficiently boxed-in to stop people speeding like birds over tents and stall tops and breaking their necks. Collecting mats they entered the tower, feeling a way up narrow wooden stairs, hearing the dull sliding of passengers descending on the outside.

They emerged from a doorless opening at the top, and Arthur sent Winnie down first. 'Don't push,' she screamed. 'I don't want to go too fast'—and disappeared from view, followed by Brenda. Arthur sat on his mat, waiting for the next person to come up and give him a flying push. He looked over the lights and tent tops and people bellowing out a rough voice to the sky, at the three-day-ritual bout of forty thousand voices. He felt like a king up there with so much power spreading on all sides below him, and until two hands

275

stabbed into his back and pushed him into oblivion he was wondering how many columns of soldiers could be gathered from these crowds for use in a rebellion.

He sped along the smooth curving chute-way, round and slowly down, drawing nearer every second to an ocean of which he would soon form another drop of water. Winnie and Brenda would be waiting for him in that unclean turbulent ocean, so the prospect of splashing into it became less terrifying. He tried to create more speed by pushing himself against the walls of the chute, then straightened his back to look over the side, at the mass of tents and lights and noise into which he was descending, and as his speed increased the noise grew to a scream. His minute-long journey seemed like a life-time, and so many thoughts were trying to enter his mind that it was the least pleasurable of all his rides. He was near the earth once more, close to the chute-end, ready to slide out safely on to a pile of mats. He felt relaxed now that it was nearly over. There was nothing else to do but wait, a voice said to him. But wait for what? He turned the last bend at the height of his speed, emptied of thought, supremely purified, until he hit the pile of mats at the bottom.

Winnie and Brenda stood in front of the crowd. Jack, wearing overalls, his face expressing surprise at seeing Arthur, held Winnie's arm; to the right stood the big swaddie and his friend still in their khaki, Bill's face swelling with rage and thoughts of vengeance as he leapt out of the crowd with the clear and definite intention of strangling Arthur as soon as he could get hold of him. Before he moved, Arthur saw the danger, was on his feet, and when the swaddie came in range of his boot, kicked him and dived into the crowd, his last sight being that of Brenda and Winnie with contrite faces, his last feeling being that of the swaddie's hand sliding away from his arm near the elbow as he lowered his head and lost himself among the people.

CHAPTER TWELVE

WALKING the streets on winter nights kept him warm, despite the cold nocturnal passions of uprising winds. His footsteps led between trade-marked houses, two up and two down, with digital chimneys like pigs' tits on the rooftops sending up heat and smoke into the cold trough of a windy sky. Stars hid like snipers, taking aim now and again when clouds gave them a loophole. Winter was an easy time for him to hide his secrets, for each dark street patted his shoulder and became a friend, and the gaseous eye of each lamp glowed unwinking as he passed. Houses lay in rows and ranks, a measure of safety in such numbers, and those within were snug and grateful fugitives from the broad track of bleak winds that brought rain from the Derbyshire mountains and snow from the Lincolnshire Wolds. Grey rain splashed down drain-pipes and ran across pavements into gutters, a sweet song whether you heard it sitting by a coal fire, or whether you trod through it while on your way to pub, cinema or the clandestine bed of an uncontrite and married woman. Arthur held his cigarette down in the darkness, caught in a game of fang-and-claw with a dangerous hand of aces, feeling, after each successful foray between Brenda's or Winnie's sheets, that one pitch night the royal flush would stay at the bottom of the pack.

When he met Doreen after the Goose Fair—remembering that she had seen him with two women at a time when he should have been in Worksop—he put on a righteous expression and demanded to know why, instead of answering his greeting, she had lost herself so readily in the crowd. 'I wanted you to meet my two cousins,' he said, 'and all you could do was go off like that as if you didn't want to meet me in public.' She retorted that, even if the two women were his cousins—which she didn't believe—then why had he said he was going to Worksop on his mate's motor-bike? 'I know I said that,' he answered, still with a hurt tone, 'and it was true. But my mate's motor-bike conked out before we got half a mile, so we couldn't go. We tried to get a bus there, but they were full up. Then as I was walking home from his house—he lives on Mansfield Road—I bumped into Jenny and Lil, and they asked me to go with them to Goose Fair. So I couldn't refuse, could I, duck?' She believed him, telling herself that, after all, perhaps she shouldn't have run off like that when she saw him on the fair, for Arthur, she said to herself, was honest and straight, and it wasn't right to snub him.

★   ★   ★

With a full wage-packet safely installed in his overall pocket, he began to clean his lathe. He stood up from wiping the chucks clean, to see Jack standing by his side.

'Good afternoon, Arthur,' he said calmly. Arthur wondered why he was all dressed up, and replied by making a joke about his promotion. For Jack was a chargehand now, supervised part of the bicycle assembly process, and was dressed in a clean brown overall buttoned neatly down the front.

'How's life?' Arthur said.

'I can't grumble,' came Jack's answer, 'these days.'

'It's a long time since I saw you,' Arthur said, hiding a smile. 'On Goose Fair, worn't it?'

'Yes,' Jack replied. 'And we didn't have time to say much, did we? I wanted to ask you a thing or two, but you seemed to be in a hurry.'

'I know,' Arthur explained. 'I couldn't

stay. That swaddie had it in for me. I don't know what for, mind you, but you saw how he went for me. If it 'ad summat to do wi' me bein' wi' Winnie at the fair, it didn't mean owt, you know. I'd just met Winnie and Brenda a few minutes before, and I asked them to come on the Helter Skelter with me. I can't see owt wrong in that, can you? Who was that swaddie, anyway?'

Jack's eyes looked fixedly at the lathe. 'Bill, Winnie's husband. His unit's in England now.'

'Well, he didn't need to get so ratty,' Arthur complained, 'did he?'

'He said you'd been carrying on with Winnie,' Jack replied.

Arthur picked up a spanner and tapped it on the palm of his open hand. 'It was uncalled for, then. If you see that swaddie again tell him from me that he wants to watch his step. I don't like being accused of things like that. People shouldn't have such dirty minds.'

There was a pause, then from Jack suddenly: 'Why don't you get wise, Arthur? Why don't you meet a nice girl and settle down? It'll do you the world of good.'

He ignored the first question. 'I've got a nice girl, if you want to know. But I's'll 'ave ter think twice before settling down. I don't feel up to it yet.'

'You'll like it when you do,' Jack said, 'you take my tip.'

'Maybe I will,' Arthur smiled, 'but I don't feel like spending all my spare time with a woman. On Friday night I'd have to run home with my wages, drop 'em in her lap, and get nagged for not droppin' enough, but now I can go home, change and tek mysen off to the White Horse for a pint or two.'

Jack thought for a moment, a look of nervousness and distaste on his face, as if caught in the grip of having to make up his mind. 'I never reckoned much to the ale in the White Horse,' he remarked.

Arthur felt that the conversation was becoming more sociable. 'I don't know much about that, but on nights like these when it's either freezin' cowd or pissin' down wi' rain, the White Horse is a good place because it's on'y a gnat's nip away from our house. Anyway, the ale ain't all that bad. I'm going there tonight for a sup, I do know that.'

Jack had made his decision. 'Well,' he said, almost gaily, 'I never was one for a lot of booze, you know that. Ain't the White Horse full on a Friday night?'

'Not as yer'd notice,' Arthur said, 'but yer've got to drink summat after standin' at a lathe all day.'

Jack made a move to leave. 'Maybe you're right.'

'You didn't want to see me for owt special?' Arthur asked.

Jack frowned, took his hands from his pockets. 'No, I only wondered how you were going on.' It was ten minutes to knocking-off time. He said: 'Cheerio then, Arthur,' and walked up the gangway. Arthur felt in his pocket for a cigarette, and struck a match against the carborundum wheel on the opposite bench, wondering what was wrong with Jack, having never seen him look so shifty and embarrassed. Jack had hardly dare look at him all the time he stood there, and had cleared off as suddenly as if he had wanted to stab him in the back but had thought better of it. He took down the time-sheet to tot up his week's work.

*　　*　　*

After a tea of sausages and tinned tomatoes he sat by the fire smoking a cigarette. Everyone was out at the pictures. He stripped off his shirt and washed in the scullery, emerging to scrub himself dry with a rough towel before the fire. Up in his bedroom he surveyed his

283

row of suits, trousers, sports jackets, shirts, all suspended in colourful drapes and designs, good-quality tailor-mades, a couple of hundred quids' worth, a fabulous wardrobe of which he was proud because it had cost him so much labour. For some reason he selected the finest suit of black and changed into it, fastening the pearl buttons of a white silk shirt and pulling on the trousers. He picked up his wallet then slipped lighter and cigarette case into an outside pocket. The final item of Friday night ritual was to stand before the downstairs mirror and adjust his tie, comb his thick fair hair neatly back, and search out a clean handkerchief from the dresser draw. Square-toed black shoes reflected a pink face when he bent down to see that no speck of dust was on them. Over his jacket he wore his twenty-guinea triumph, a thick three-quarter overcoat of Donegal tweed.

On cold and deserted Eddison Road the air was damp because it bordered the Leen, a stream that meandered down through fields and collieries from Newstead, Papplewick and Bulwell. Behind throbbed veins of machinery, and from the gasworks a generator sounded like a whining cat, a ghostly noise increasing until he passed the grey office at the gate.

In the White Horse he asked for a black-and-tan, unbuttoned his coat, and took a seat beneath the window, feeling the wall vibrate whenever a trolley-bus went by outside. In a half-filled pub he felt strangely isolated from the rest of his familiar world. He did not want to go alone, and had expected to find some of his friends at the bar. To be alone seemed a continuation of his drugged life at the lathe. He wanted noise, to drink and make love. Sitting at an empty table made him feel sorry for himself, and he debated riding on a trolley-bus to Slab Square in search of noise, but rejected the idea because he couldn't be bothered. Friday was a bad time for seeing Winnie or Brenda, for they went out visiting relations—so he had been led to believe—and to seek out Doreen would, he felt, land him in no more lively a situation than the one he was in now. He thought back to more than twelve months ago, when he came here with Brenda and had rolled down the stairs like a snowball after drinking seven gins and eleven pints, a fantastic night whose memory lay near his heart's core. And since then, he had juggled Brenda, Winnie and Doreen crazily, like a man on the stage, throwing himself up into the air as well each time and always landing safely in one soft bed or another. A dangerous

285

life, he reflected.

At half-past eight his Uncle George came into the pub. Arthur knew him for a sponger and disliked him but, under the circumstances, called out and treated him to a pint. George filled his pipe, and complained that the weather was bad. He wanted rain.

'Don't come it,' Arthur said raucously. 'We 'ad about fifteen inches last week. The ground's still soppin' wet.'

'Not any more it ain't, my lad,' George told him. 'The soil sups up rain quicker than yo' can sup up ten pints o' Shippoe's ale.'

'I don't suppose a bloke like yo'd be satisfied unless it was chuckin' it down all the time,' Arthur said.

'I wouldn't grumble at that,' George said, a tall, red-faced, sharp-featured market-gardener. He was known as The Whistler, a nickname fastened on to him by the family because whenever any member of it saw him on the street he was always whistling loudly, his cheeks sunken in, lips pursed, hands in his pockets, walking quickly to some nondescript made-up tune, his blue eyes vacant and a flat cap perched on top of his greying hair. He could barely read and write, but behind his blue-eyed emptiness lay a shrewdness that gained him a fair living from the small acreage of gardens he cultivated. Arthur passed his gardens once and saw a notice posted on the gate saying: 'Fresh cut lettices sixpance 'each' and a small queue by the hut door. 'He must be all there,' his mother said about her brother, pointing to her temples, 'to make the money he makes.' 'And if I hear him whistling again,' Arthur cried, to the delight of his father who didn't like his wife's family, 'I'll send him a packet of bird-seed for a Christmas Box.'

George had changed the subject. 'Have yer read the papers lately, Arthur?' Two-thirds of the pint went in one long agony of his Adam's apple.

'I read 'em every day. Why?'

'I wondered what you thought about the big race tomorrer.'

Arthur had often given him good tips, much to his chagrin. 'Last Echo,' he said. 'Back that.'

George gasped, and finished his beer. 'But it's at twenty-to-one. It can't win wi' them odds.'

'Last Echo,' Arthur repeated, who silently agreed with him. 'I know it's twenty-to-one, but I'm having a couple of quid on it. I may have more. Put a fiver on it, Uncle George, and you'll never regret it.'

George was cautious. Smoke from his black twist went into Arthur's eyes. 'I'll see what the bookie thinks.'

Such bastards always prosper, Arthur thought. 'I don't care what the bookie thinks. I know it's a dead cert, and I'm putting all my money on it. Of course the bookie'll tell you to leave it alone, because he knows it's a dead cert and don't want to lose his lolly.'

George had to admit the logic of this, but a flicker of distrust stayed in his eyes. Arthur called out for two more pints. No good expecting George to order. You could never shame him into it, the mean bastard. You had to admire him sometimes. George asked why he thought Last Echo such a dead cert.

'Because Lord Earwig rang me up today from Aintree. "That you, Arthur?" he asked me. "Look, bein' as we've bin pals for such a long time I'm goin' ter put yer in the way of a bit of cash. I know yer can do wi' it, sweatin' yer tripes out all day at that bleedin' machine." No, Uncle George, I can't tell you how Lord Earwig knows about this, because he made me swear never to tell anybody how he gets hold of it. He'd get chucked out o' the Jockey Club if I did, and I'd never be able to give you hot tips any more. Anyway, all my other tips 'ave bin good, ain't they?'

George was appeased, though somewhat credulous about Arthur's aristocratic connection. 'All right,' he said with a wink. 'I see what you mean.' The glasses were empty once more and George gazed vacantly at the bar, a faint whistle coming from his lips. When Arthur ordered again, he swigged it down as though he'd been ten days without a drop to drink. 'What do you think of the war, Arthur?' he asked.

'War?'

'Yes. A bloke told me in the market that he'd read in the paper as a war was goin' ter start in three months' time.'

Arthur laughed. 'Don't worry about a war, Uncle George. They don't call-up blokes of your age.'

'It ain't that. I was on'y thinking about rationing coming in again. There's a terrible shortage of food in a war.'

This bright, culminating start of the conversation made Arthur splutter into his beer with mirth. The only thing George thought of was money. He was clever right enough. During the war he'd wangled his way out of the army and worked in a gun factory, making luminous black-out buttons, gas-mask boxes, and ration-book covers in his spare time as a fire-watcher, and near the war's end had saved enough to buy his gardens. Apart from vegetables, he did good business in poultry and eggs.

'I wouldn't be so happy about a war if I was yo',' Arthur said. 'If they drop an atom bomb a hundred miles away from Nottingham even, it'll make all the soil dead so that you wain't be able to grow a thing. It kills all chickens as well. They call it radiation, or summat. I heard a talk about it on the wireless the other night.'

George, sceptical in most things, had a wild fear of scientific fact. 'You don't mean it?' he exclaimed, turning pale and putting his beer back on the table. 'It's the first time I've heard owt about a thing like that.'

'That's because yer don't meet people who know such things,' Arthur said. 'All you do in your spare time is stand at the bookie's counter.'

'Nay, lad, I ain't got so much spare time as it matters. I wok hard for my bit o' money.'

'I suppose yer think I play poker all day? Anyway, I'm tellin' yer that these atom bombs poison the earth so's nowt can grow. This bit I'd read in the paper as well, by a doctor who'd bin six months testin' lettuces from the places that have been atom-bombed.'

The glasses were empty, and George stood up, sober in spite of his cadged and gobbled pints. After a long pause he remembered Arthur's sting about the bookie's counter. 'But I know what hard wok is, I can tell you.' He buttoned his jacket, adjusted his cap, and adopted a jaunty air that became him. 'I'm off to the Dog and Stag,' he said, and walked to the door whistling so loudly that he did not hear Arthur's reply to his abrupt good night.

He drank another pint in solitude, deciding to go home, have some supper, and perhaps watch the television. An early night would do no harm for once. He shouted 'Good night' to the barman.

The White Horse stood on a corner, and he went out by the main door, watched a trolley-bus descend from the station and stop at the opposite corner. 'Shall I run, and take it to town?' he asked himself. 'No,' he answered, without thinking. He heard the conductor's bell and, like a lighted greenhouse growing people, the bus trundled away up the hill. He turned into the darkness of Eddison Road, walked a few yards, heard a movement of heavy feet behind him.

'That's 'im, right enough. Sink your boots into 'im, Bill.'

What's going on? he wondered. Boots into

who?

'We've got the bastard now.'

'It's about time an' all.'

Two shadowy figures came level and took his arm. Into me, he thought, struggling to break free, wheeling his fists like windmill sails until he stood clear.

'Be careful,' he said, 'or you'll get hurt.'

His back was to the wall, fists raised, blood behind his eyes distilled to defiance and a hard-gutted core of self preservation. The war was on at last, and there was no escape from weighted fists and heavy boots, except by his own outnumbered sinews.

They lost no time. In their eagerness one came forward before the other, and Arthur smashed him with all his strength so that he ran back into the roadway holding his face. He felt the heaviness of his own breathing, and then stopped feeling anything in time to meet the second onrush with a kick of his shoe. There was no weight to it so he stepped aside and caught the man's head with his fist. Somehow the wall was no longer behind him and he did not realise it, because what he thought was the wall itself sent a shock of pain to the centre of his spine. He was caught around the neck and held fast, but made a miraculous escape from this before the other swaddie could come in. The way was open to run, but for some reason that he could never bring himself to understand, he did not run.

His back was again to the wall. They rushed him together. He piled all his strength on one and repelled him, lunging with his shoe in an attempt to lessen the charge of the second. He hit the first, then the second, then the first again reeled back, but they were still fresh, and Arthur felt a crack explode down his face that seemed to break all the bones in it, pain bursting across his eyes and throwing showers of orange sparks over him. In the same second he threw out his fists and freed himself, but a blow caught him in the back, followed by another that grazed his chin. He drove his fists back hard against one or another of them. They were undifferentiated and without identity, which put a sense of exultation into Arthur's attacks. But four fists against two began to tell, though it still did not occur to him to run. A hundred people were drinking beer or whisky in the White Horse, but the world had shrunk for him to a struggle being decided in the space of a few square yards, and his world was the colour and hue of sombre purple.

In the time between one defending blow and the next, he felt as though he were in a dream. He still held them away from him, heard their curses and advice, monosyllables and grunts that leapt about his face as he threw them back each time. Judging by the colour of one man's curses, the jolting ache at the joint of his arm, and the sting across his knuckles, he gave the biggest and best smash-hit of the night. Then he thought they were leaving. They were not leaving. He felt a blow on his chest, then another, and he stabbed his elbow into a stomach and hit out with his free hand. He was being pulled away from the wall. A blow at the side of his mouth spun him around, and the floor lifted to hit his shoulder. He kicked out, freed himself, drove his knuckles into someone's eyes, stood up again. They dragged him down, and he wrestled, lifting his head from the tangle of limbs. He pressed his fingers into a throat while his head was pulled back and back. He heard a hooter from the main road, and before its strident sound ended, a blow knocked all sense from him.

Knives and arrows went into all parts of his body. They want to kill me, he thought dimly, and tried to stand up, only to be kicked down again. He lay curled up. His thick clothes cushioned the hard core of their boots. Thinking that someone was coming along the road, they went away.

Rage helped him to get up. He held dizzily on to the wall, noticed that cement was missing from certain cracks, and picked more of it away with his fingers until he was able to stand by himself. He felt his face, tried to move forward, thinking of revenge and unwilling to tell himself whether or not he had deserved to lose his fight. His greatest wish was to hurry back to the White Horse for a double whisky before closing time. He tapped his coat: the wallet was still there. Pain leapt into his head. The world he saw stayed purple and sombre, bricks and paving stones shining lividly in the darkness, filled with rage and pain when he tried to touch them. His fingertips had a will to live. Walking slowly he came to the back-gate of the White Horse. He looked at his watch, but it was smashed, hands bending outwards from half-past nine. Seven quid gone down the drain, he said to himself, making for the lavatories. Under the dim lightbulb he turned on the tap and bathed his face in cold water, soaking a handkerchief to wipe the grime away. Two side teeth were loose. Rinsing blood from his handkerchief, he reached into his pocket for a comb. It was broken so he threw it down and sprinkled water on his hair, smoothing it back with his

295

fingers. Pain would not let him think, flaring over his face when he bent down to rub dust from his shoes.

Pushing open the saloon-bar door he walked quickly to the counter with his overcoat collar well pulled up, and asked for a double whisky. The lights were too bright, like giant magnets inflating his head to several times its size, burning his eyes into a squint so that he was hardly able to see. The whisky went into him like a sheet of flame, and he was about to ask for another, wondering how it was that no one could see the blood that seemed to be running down his face, when someone tapped his elbow. He turned and saw Doreen.

'Hey up, duck,' he said with a smile.

'My God,' she said, 'what's the matter with you, Arthur? You do look a mess.'

'Where did you spring from?' he asked, ignoring her question.

'I've been to my sister's and brother-in-law's and we came here for a drink. They're sitting over there, look.' He didn't follow the finger she held out, so she turned back: 'But what's happened to you? What's wrong with your face? How . . .'

Her words trailed off and, with a grin, he slipped down in a dead faint, feeling the world pressing its enormous booted foot on to his head, forcing him away from the lights, down into the dark comfort of grime, spit, and saw-dust on the floor.

PART TWO

SUNDAY MORNING

CHAPTER THIRTEEN

HE lay in an apathetic state and, sitting up to move his pillow, stared without recognition at the pink wall of the bedroom. Then he fell back, to sleep his troubles away. On waking up he ate voraciously the meals his mother set on the bedside chair, becoming surly when she asked what was the matter and why he lay there for days on end like a dead dog.

'I'm badly,' he answered.

'Well let me get you a doctor.'

'I'm not that badly.'

He didn't much care whether he lived or died. The wheels of change that were grinding their impressive tracks through his mind did not yet show themselves off in him to advantage. He stared at the pink-washed bedroom wall above the fireplace, plagued by crowding and inexpressible thought, thinking that he was going mad. He heard the rattle of plates and cups from downstairs, the dull thumping of factory turbines at the end of the terrace, people walking the street, children playing under lamp-posts, wireless sets piercing the air from neighbouring houses, an aeroplane flying low overhead like an asthmatic man playing a comb-and-paper—but they had no meaning and he only vaguely noticed the combined pandemonium rolling over the black cloud of his melancholy. He told himself that he would be able to go back to work soon, to the pub again in the evening, to the pictures; would be able to take a bus to town and walk around Woolworth's to see what was on the counters for Christmas—but nothing could drag him out of the half-sleep in which he lay buried for three days.

They seemed like a hundred years, wheeling their brilliant Goose Fairs and Bonfire Nights and Christmases around him like branding irons in a torture chamber. When he stopped looking at the wall he lay back to sleep, and awoke after violent yet unrememberable dreams to see the grinning frantic face of the cheap mantelpiece clock telling him that only two minutes had gone by. He knew it was no use fighting against the cold weight of his nameless malady, or asking how it came about. He did not ask, believing it to be related to his defeat by the swaddies, a fact that did not call for much speculation. He did not ask whether he was in such a knocked-about state because he had lost the rights of love over two women, or because the two swaddies represented the raw edge of fang-

302

and-claw on which all laws were based, law
and order against which he had been fighting
all his life in such a thoughtless and unorgan-
ised way that he could not but lose. Such
questions came later. The plain fact was that
the two swaddies had got him at last—as he
had known they would and had bested him on
the common battleground of the jungle.

He ate, but did not smoke, did not fight the
tumultuous lake and whirlpool in his mind.
He never thought to do so, but waited unknowingly for the full flood to diminish and
cast him unharmed on to dry banks, cured of
brain-colic and free to carry life on where he
had left it. Every bone in his body seemed to
have its separate and private pain, and he
knew that his despair had acted as an anaes-
thetic when he came out of it and felt the
actual sharp pains that forced him to stay in
bed for another week.

On Saturday morning he had not replied to
his father's gruff call that he should get up for
breakfast. He heard the voice each time, distinct and peremptory, rolling up the stairs
and through the closed door, but he stared at
the wall wondering how many times his
father would call before giving him up as a
bad job.

Fred came in later and asked if he was all

right.

'Why?' Arthur demanded, as best he could.

'I just wondered,' Fred said. 'I thought you might want a doctor if you're feeling badly. You don't look good.'

'No,' he said.

'Did the swaddies get you?'

'Yes. Leave me alone. I'm not getting up for wok on Monday. I'm all right. Shut the door when you go.'

'Who was that girl as brought you 'ome las' night?' his brother wanted to know.

'What girl? Leave me be.'

'Do you want a doctor?'

'No. Bogger off.'

Fred left, and closed the door. Arthur fell back into a half-sleep. What girl? It must have been Doreen that gave me the brandy when I conked out in the White Hoss, and walked me back later, propping me up along Eddison Road, one step at a time. He remembered trying to talk to her, and wondered what he had told her when she asked him how he came to be looking so black-and-blue. He didn't doubt it was something that sounded true, for even when you were dozy-daft it was easy to make up lies and excuses, he thought.

When he could think more clearly he asked himself a question and, because he couldn't answer it, he was angered. It was this: How had the swaddies known he would be drinking at the White Horse that night? Neither of them had looked in at the door, and it was impossible to see through the windows because the curtains were well drawn. They had known he would be there and had waited outside, so who had told them? Had anybody told them? Perhaps not. Perhaps it was a coincidence that they had been standing outside when he turned the corner on to Eddison Road. But he didn't think so. They had lounged around in the darkness, waiting for him to come out.

On the fourth day sun shone through the bedroom window and made a javelin-point of light across his rumpled bed. He sat up and read the *Daily Mirror*, and at eleven o'clock shouted for a cup of tea. His mother came up with a plate of cream biscuits and set them down on a chair. Watching him dip one in his tea, she said: 'You're in a fine mess, I must say. What did you do to get like that?'

His blue inflamed eyes looked at her. He spoke with swollen lips, with graze marks scarring the side of his face. 'I fell down. You know how I am when I'm drunk. Do you want a biscuit?'

'I've had some. Fell down! You don't get all

305

that wi' fallin' down.'

'I fell off a gasometer for a bet,' he said.

'More likely some woman's husband had it in for yer. If he did, let it be a lesson to yer. You can't play wi' fire wi'out gettin' yer fingers burnt.'

He grimaced, and set his empty cup down. 'I suppose Fred's bin opening his big mouth. You can't even trust yer own brother now.'

'Nobody needs ter tell me owt about yer,' she said, standing well away from his bed as if to see him clearer. 'I can tell what's wrong wi' yer. Ye'r my own son, aren't yer?'

He couldn't deny it. 'I'll stay in bed for a day or two more. I don't feel well. I've got a bad back again, and my guts are rotten.'

She folded her arms, pride and tenderness in her eyes. 'Shall yer 'ave another cup o' tea?'

'In fact I wain't go back to wok till nex' Monday,' he decided.

She took his cup. 'Don't be mardy. You can go to wok tomorrow.'

All she wants is to get me back to wok, he thought. 'I'm not mardy. I've got pains in my stomach.'

'I'll get you some Indian brandy, and some oil to rub your back. Shall you have some more biscuits? I got half a pound from the shop.'

So he changed his mind: it ain't true that she's pushin' me back to wok, and he wanted to kiss her and put his arms around her. 'Good owd mam,' he said, doing so. 'Yes, I'll 'ave some more biscuits.' And she went downstairs to get them.

He lay back, pains burning his swollen eyes, his head aching as if his brain lay open to the sky. Thinking increased the pain, but he couldn't stop thinking now. He sensed that though he had merely been beaten up by two swaddies—not a very terrible thing, and not the first time he had been in a losing fight—he felt like a ship that had never left its slipway suddenly floundering in mid-ocean. He did not move his arms to swim, but gave himself up to rolling buffeting waves and the stabbing sharp corners of jetsam that assailed him. The actual blows of the swaddies were not responsible for this, because by the fifth day their effect had gone.

He felt a lack of security. No place existed in all the world that could be called safe, and he knew for the first time in his life that there had never been any such thing as safety, and never would be, the difference being that now he knew it as a fact, whereas before it was a natural unconscious state. If you lived in a cave in the middle of a dark wood you weren't safe, not by a long way, he thought, and you had to sleep always with one eye open and a pile of sharp stones by your side, within easy reach of your fist. Well, he realised, I've allus done that, so it wain't bother me much. He had often dreamed of falling from the top of a cliff, but could never remember smashing himself as he landed. Life was like that, he thought, you floated down on a parachute, like the blokes in that Arnhem picture, pulling strings this way and that so that you could put out your hand to reach something you wanted, until one day you hit the bottom without knowing it, like a bubble bursting when it touches something solid, and you were dead, out like a light in a Derbyshire gale.

Well, that's not for me. Me, I'll have a good life: plenty of work and plenty of booze and a piece of skirt every month till I'm ninety. Brenda and Winnie were out of his reach, penned in by Jack and Bill, but there was always more than one pebble on the beach, and more than one field in which clover grew. He went back to sleep, taking to it as though he hadn't had any for years. And it was true now that he thought of it, that he had never in his life stayed in bed for more than three days, ever.

Margaret came on Friday night and ascended the narrow stairs with a child on each arm. William trailed behind, dressed in woollen leggings, and a cap that Arthur snatched from his head and held up for him to reach. But William was surprised and shocked at seeing Uncle Arthur in bed at such a strange time of the day, and did not leap up for it. Margaret sat down and told Arthur that she'd had a television set installed. 'It's marvellous, our Arthur. I never thought I'd be able to afford one, but Albert don't drink so much any more, and he said he'd pay the thirty-bob a week. So whenever he gets on to me, I can just switch on the pictures and forget him.' She even forgot to ask why Arthur was in bed.

Television, he thought scornfully when she'd gone, they'd go barmy if they had them taken away. I'd love it if big Black Marias came down all the streets and men got out with hatchets to go in every house and smash the tellies. Everybody'd go crackers. They wouldn't know what to do. There'd be a revolution, I'm sure there would, they'd blow-up the Council House and set fire to the

309

Castle. It wouldn't bother me if there weren't any television sets, though, not one bit.

'Arthur,' his mother shouted. 'There's a young lady to see you. Can she come up? she wants to know.'

He supposed it was Fred playing a joke on him. 'Send her up,' he called out with a laugh. 'But tell her to watch out!'

He knew the particular tread of everybody's feet in the family as they ascended the stairs, but the footsteps coming closer to his door were those of a stranger, the light hesitant footsteps of a woman. What sort of a joke was this? Were they passing one of his aunts off as a young woman? Or was it Winnie? Or Brenda? No, they wouldn't have the cheek to come and see him. His heart stopped beating at the thought. He switched on the light as his visitor fumbled with the latch.

'That's it, duck, that room there,' his mother called up from behind. He heard laughter downstairs, and silently swore at them.

The door opened, and it was Doreen.

'I've come to see how you're getting on,' she said, apparently wondering whether she was doing the right thing.

He was shocked, not having thought about

310

her for days, but lifted himself up on the pillows, saying: 'Come in, duck, and sit down. I didn't expect you to come and see me.'

'I can see that,' she remarked wryly. 'You look as though a ghost just walked into your room.'

'No, I'm sure I didn't.' He leaned back on his elbows and looked at her distrustfully.

'I like your room,' she said, her eyes on the open curtain of his wardrobe. 'Are all them clo'es yourn?'

'Just a few rags,' he said.

She sat up straight, hands in her lap. 'They look better than rags to me. They must have cost you a pretty penny.' She wore lipstick, and some perfume whose pleasant smell gave more life to the room.

'I get good wages,' he said, looking at the coloured headscarf on her knees, 'and spend 'em on clo'es. It's good to be well dressed.' He felt uneasy, ashamed at having been caught in bed. Them bastards downstairs really played one on me this time. 'Did you see a good picture this week?' he asked, grudging even this small chip to the conversation. When wounded he liked to be alone in his lair, and he felt intimidated by her visit, as if he would have to pay for it with his life.

'Oh yes,' she said eagerly, pleased to see

him less truculent. 'It was ever so good. "Drums in the Jungle." You should have been there, Arthur.'

'I would have, only I couldn't get out. My crutches were at the cobblers being soled and heeled. They promised 'em for Monday morning so's I could 'obble to my lathe, but they worn't ready.'

She laughed. 'Perhaps you'll be able to come next week,' she said, too unsure of herself to make it a definite hint. He looked morosely towards the window. 'It's a cold night out,' she ventured, little else to say.

'Not in bed,' he said. 'It's warm in here with all these blankets.' Then with inspiration that he could not reject: 'You should come in and try it.'

'No fear,' she smiled. 'What do you take me for?'

'I bet it wouldn't be the first time,' he said with a grin.

'Don't be cheeky.' But he knew from the look on her face that it wouldn't have been the first time. Other words came to her lips, less revealing of herself, but galling for him:

'Tell me how you feel,' she asked. 'You really were in a state when I brought you home from the White Horse last Friday.'

'I feel better,' he said, non-committally.

'You look better, I must say.' The conversation lapsed for a few minutes, then: 'What happened to you?'

'I towd yer,' he answered gruffly, having forgotten what he had told her. 'I got run over by a horse and cart. I didn't see it till it was almost on top of me. I thought I was a goner.'

'You're very secretive,' she said, unsmiling. 'You won't tell anybody anything.'

'Why should I? It pays to keep your trap shut.'

'No it don't,' she said. 'You talk to me as if I was the dog's dinner.'

'I towd yer how it was,' he said, resisting her wiles.

'Ye'r fibbin',' she retorted. 'You know you are.'

I am a bit of a bastard, he said to himself, after she's been so nice to me. 'You wain't like it if I tell you,' he said aloud.

She laid her hand on his wrist. 'I won't mind.'

It don't much matter whether she minds or not, and he said: 'I got beat-up wi' two sowjers. I'd bin knocking-on with two married women for a long time. So they bested me. Two on to one. I'd have flattened them if they'd been one at a time.'

She took her hand from his wrist. 'Were

313

you going with these women while you were taking me out?'

'Sure,' he said, glad to hurt her for asking this. Can't she put two and two together? he thought.

She turned her betrayed expression away from him. 'I think you might have said something sooner.'

He hated her for this, and hated himself more for having told her. It might not have been a very nice trick he had played, but there were no promises between them, he told himself. 'Never mind,' he said soothingly, 'it's all over now.'

'Maybe,' she said, turning to him, wanting him to say something else, to say he was sorry. But he thought he had said enough already, too much. Though perhaps it's better to have it out now, and be done with it.

'That's how it was,' he said. 'But I wain't see either of the women again. It ain't much of a paying game.' He lifted a hand to one of his bruises.

'So them two women on Goose Fair with you weren't your cousins?'

'Yes,' he said roughly, 'they were my cousins. I'm not that much of a liar.' He had given her an inch and she wanted a yard.

'They weren't,' she said, 'but you don't

need to tell me. It upsets me when you tell such big lies.'

He was angry. 'Well, I've been through the mill as well. And we worn't engaged or owt like that, don't forget.'

She saw the wicked logic of his remark. 'Even so,' she began.

'But I'm glad you came to see me,' he said cheerfully. 'I think I'd 'ave stayed down in the dumps for good if you hadn't.'

'I wondered how you were getting on. You were half dead last week.'

He came closer to her, so that he was lying near the edge of the bed. Her coat was open, showing a green blouse, and he put his hand inside, but she drew back. 'It'd tek more than two swaddies to kill me,' he said with bravado.

'I suppose so,' she went on, evading his ubiquitous hand again, 'but I wanted to see what was happening to you because I was worried. I like you Arthur and I kept on hoping you were all right and that you weren't dead or something. When I brought you home last week your mother looked at me gone-out, as if I'd made you like that. She was so sharp I felt I was in the way, so I left straight away. This week though, she was nice.'

He held her wrist, and they talked for another hour.

'We'll go to the pictures on Monday,' he said, as she buttoned her coat to leave. 'I'll meet you at seven, earlier if you like.'

'No, at seven, because I want to get my tea. I'm allus hungry when I've finished work.' She bent down to kiss him, and he held her firmly around the neck and waist, both hands out of bed.

'Come in, duck,' he whispered, feeling the passion she put into the kiss.

'Later, Arthur, later.'

Monday was not far off, and perhaps time would pass quickly.

CHAPTER FOURTEEN

HIS finger jumped back from the drill and a mound of blood grew from his sud-white crinkled skin, broke, and ran down his hand. He wiped it away with a bundle of cotton-waste: a small cut, but the blood poured out, over his palm and down to his wrist. He drew a dry finger across and diverted it to the floor, away from his bare sinewy forearm. He cursed the lost time, and set out for the first-aid department, to have his finger hockled and bandaged. It meant going from one end of the factory to the other, so he walked quickly across the main lane-way, his finger held down, blood dripping freely on to the grease-soaked floor of the corridor. At the turning of a corner, he met Jack.

Arthur stopped, and watched him lighting a cigarette. He struck the match slowly, and lit-up with care, so that the cigarette, now that Jack had set his mind to lighting it, didn't stand a chance. It was a slow and efficient operation, like all his other jobs. He threw the match down and looked up before continuing his journey, then saw Arthur standing before him. For some reason he was shocked and turned pale.

Without knowing why it was, Arthur did not feel friendly towards him. He didn't greet him, but only said: 'What's up wi' yo'?' when he noticed the heightened pallor of his face. 'Do yer want some smellin' salts?' In the split second before the reason for it fully came to him, he had made the first words of a sarcastic demand: 'Or did you think they'd killed me?'

Jack could not speak, looking as if a rope were about to be fixed around his neck. Who else but Jack could have told the two swaddies where he would be at a certain time on a Friday night two weeks ago?

'Killed you?' Jack said. 'I don't know what you're talking about.'

'I didn't think you would,' Arthur said. 'That's the sort of bloke you are. Until you get bashed in the face, then you'd squeal like a stuck pig.' The corridor was empty, and both realised it at the same time. Arthur clenched his hand, now covered in blood from the cut. He didn't think it was worth it: an eye for an eye and a tooth for a tooth, but he had had more than his fair share of both. He said: 'Why don't you have the guts to admit it, you sly spineless bastard?'

Jack drew back at this outright statement and mumbled some answer that Arthur didn't

318

bother to understand. They stood against the wall to let a trolley-load of chromed handle-bars go by. They looked at each other in silence, Jack unable to unclamp his eyes from Arthur's finger, at the jewels and diamonds of blood dripping copiously on to the floor, his eyes blinking as each drop fell.

'Well, what if I did tell them where you were?' Jack said at last, with some show of truculence. 'You shouldn't have gone out with Brenda like that. It worn't right.'

Arthur had an impulse to hit him, to smash him again and again, from one end of the factory to the other. Jack felt this, and looked away, at the back-end of the trolley now rounding a corner. Not here, Arthur thought. I can get him the same way as the swaddies got me, in a dark street at night. 'You don't need to tell me what's right and what ain't right. Whatever I do is right, and what people do to me is right. And what I do to you is right, as well. Get that into your big 'ead.'

Jack had let his cigarette fall, and now lit another, his eyes turned from Arthur's close, granite-set face. 'I might as well tell you,' he said, 'that Winnie's husband is still after you. He's on leave over Christmas, so watch your step.'

Arthur fumbled with one hand for a cigarette, but could not reach the packet.
'Thanks for telling me. But if he's on his own,
he'll regret it. I'm warnin' 'im now: if I get
him, I'll break him, so don't forget. And I
mean it.'

Jack saw that he did. 'You're too much of a
trouble-maker, Arthur,' he said mildly.
'You're too violent. One day you'll really cop
it. And you'll ask for it as well.'

'And you're too narrow-gutted ever to get
into trouble,' Arthur responded, feeling no
kind words for him.

'That's as it may be,' Jack said. Seeing
Arthur struggle with his one hand: 'Have one
of my fags,' and he thrust the packet forward.

Arthur reached his own at that moment.
'Don't bother,' he said, covering the match-
box with blood before getting a light.

Jack wanted to go on his way, but for some
reason, he couldn't. 'Are you still working in
the turnery?' he asked, unable to stand the
silence between them.

'Where do you think I got this cut? I'll be in
it till Doomsday. Unless I go barmy first.'

'No fear of that,' Jack said. 'You'll get a big
bonus this Christmas from the firm. How
many years have you been working here
now?'

'Eight. It's a life sentence. If they make it twenty-one I could have done a murder.'

Jack laughed hollowly. 'That's right.'

'Not that there's anybody I'd like to murder. I don't think anybody in the world's worth murdering, unless it's for fun. Not yet, anyway.'

'Don't think like that,' Jack said in a friendly forbearing voice, giving him an intimate piece of advice. 'You won't knuckle under, Arthur. If you would, you'd enjoy life.'

'I do enjoy it, mate,' he said loudly. 'Just because I'm not like you, don't think I don't. Yo've got your life an' I've got mine. Yo' stick ter your managin' and the races, an' I'll stick to the White Hoss, fishin' an' screwin'.'

'I've got my way, and you've got yourn,' Jack acknowledged.

'That's right. And they're different.'

Jack stood in silence.

Arthur said: 'I'll get crackin' to't first-aid before I bleed to death.'

'And I've got to go to the stores for some spares,' Jack said with relief. 'I'll see you again sometime.'

'Maybe,' Arthur said, walking away.

*   *   *

321

On Friday night he went home with thirty pound notes in his pocket: bonus and wages. On Saturday he bought toys for Margaret's children, and presents for the rest of the family, returning from downtown with full arms and a cigar between his teeth. A bet on Fair Glory in the two-thirty won him twelve pounds. He hid twenty in his room and stuffed his wallet with what was left to see him through Christmas.

As he walked across the market square on his way to Aunt Ada's a blanket of dark cloud lay low over the city as if, were God to pull a lever, it would release a six-foot blanket of snow.

He pushed his way in through the defective back door and Aunt Ada launched into him because he had missed the midday meal, saying that now it was stone-cold in the scullery and fit only for the cats to eat. Arthur dipped his hand into his overcoat pocket and threw sixpenny bits to the children and gave cigars to Bert, Dave, and Ralph, so that the four of them filled the already warm room with clouds of smoke. All that day, Ada told Arthur, they had been expecting a coloured soldier from the Gold Coast. Sam was his name, a friend of Johnny's who was with the R.E.s in West Africa. Johnny had told Sam to visit them while on his mechanics course in England. A telegram came the day before saying: 'Arrive twenty-fourth Sam'—and Ada pictured him wandering about the cold city like a lost soul, unable to find his way to the house.

'He thinks all telegrams are sent by tom-tom,' Bert said, his face bursting into a laugh at his own joke. 'You wain't be able to miss him though. All you have to do is look for a black head wrapped up in a khaki coat.'

Arthur went with him to search the railway and bus stations, and an hour later they stood at a tea-stall near the market without having seen him. It was late, and cold, and they wanted to hear the football results at home on a full belly and a fag by the roaring fire. 'It's gone five,' Arthur said, pushing his cup aside. 'If he gets lost it's too bad. I'm not going to freeze to death running around after a Zulu.'

They went back to the house. Sam was already there, a stocky negro with a calm intelligent face, who explained that he had come in on a morning train and spent the day exploring the city. Dressed in well-pressed khaki, with three large stripes prominent on his battledress arm, he sat stiffly in a cane-bottomed chair by the fire looking as if about to stifle in the hot crowded kitchen. His blancoed webbing belt, neatly folded, rested on the sofa beneath the window. He was the centre of attention, and stood up to shake hands with Bert and Arthur when they came in, Arthur noticing the tight warm grip of his black hand as he said: 'I'm pleased to meet you.' Two ginger-haired daughters were trying not to laugh at the ordeal of numberless introductions that Sam was undergoing, for Dave came in five minutes later from the football match and pretended to jump with surprise on seeing for the first time in his life a Negro sitting in the living-room. The two girls shouted that the second battalion would be in any minute now, and Ada threatened them and told them to be quiet. Ralph, hudged-up by the fire, ignoring the noise, locked in his own warm world, turned only to ask Dave what team had won.

'County lost four none,' Dave said. 'Everybody's talking about it. They've never had such a run of rotten luck.' He threw his cap at the girls who were now laughing at him, then lifted a neatly folded football *Mirror* from his pocket and tossed it across to Ralph, saying: 'You'll get the half-time results from there.' The paper unfolded in mid-flight and Ralph caught it near the range as it was about to land in the fire.

Arthur sat at the table with a cup of tea, enjoying the banter, and the questions showered on simple and unselfconscious Sam. Could he read and write? Who taught him, then? Did he believe in God? How was Johnny going on in Africa? Did Johnny look well in such a hot place? Was he enjoying himself? Did Sam miss West Africa? (Of course, Bert said in a loud whisper, he misses the tom-toms. Ada gave him a stern look.) How long had Sam been in the army? Seven years! Did it seem a lifetime? And wasn't he glad he had only another three to do? How old are you, Sam? Only thirty-two! And do you like England? Well, I expect you'll get used to it soon. And do you have a girl-friend on the Gold Coast? Is she nice? (Is she as black as the ace of spades, Bert whispered in Arthur's ear.) Will you get married at church? Arthur dug his fork into a piece of meat-pie, glad to be in Ada's house for Christmas and showered under by jokes that fell like sparks on the relaxed powder-barrel of each brain. He went with Dave and Bert to lounge in armchairs by the parlour fire, smoking, listening to people walking by outside whose feet punctuated the empty weekend hours between football matches and opening time. The door-knob

325

rattled, and Jane came in, a thin-faced ginger-haired woman of thirty who balanced herself on the arm of Dave's chair. 'I want half a crown from everybody towards a crate of ale, for when we come back from the pub tonight.'

Uncomplaining, they dug their hands into their pockets. 'What about Sam?' Dave asked.

'He ain't giving owt,' she said. 'He's a guest.'

'It's just as well,' Bert remarked. 'He'd on'y pay in beads.'

She turned on him fiercely. 'You shut up. He's going out wi' yo' lot ternight, and you'd better be nice to 'im, or Johnny'll gi' yer a good thump when 'e comes 'ome from Africa.'

Later the house functioned like the neck of an egg-timer: visitors came in through the backyard, and were disgorged with gangs of the family by the front door. Ada, Ralph, Jim, and Jane went out with the first batch. The under-sixteens were despatched to the last house at the pictures.

Arthur left with Bert, Dave, Colin, and Sam. All wore overcoats, though Sam shivered. They walked up the bridge-slope in twos and a boy coming in the opposite direction carrying a parcel of fish and chips was swept off the pavement. The marshalling yards below were covered in mist; ascending

326

sounds of jangling trucks were enveloped and dulled by its dampness before floating up to the lighted road. Over the opposite parapet orange lights glowed around the great station clock, and black outlines of grain warehouses stood up around it.

The Lambley Green was almost empty. Dave ordered pints and they played darts, Arthur siding with Sam against Colin and Bert, Dave keeping scores. Sam possessed an uncanny eye and hit whatever he aimed at— Bert accounting for this as a legacy left over from throwing assegais. In the next pub, more crowded because it was nearer the town centre, Sam offered to buy a round of drinks but was shouted down. Arthur caught hold of the brass rails and called for five pints. While passing them back one by one over his shoulder some beer trickled on to a woman's coat, and she turned on him menacingly: 'Can't yer look what ye'r doin'?'

'Sorry, missis,' he said gaily.

Her husband stood nearby, a tall man with thick lips, black moustache, and hair swept back from a low forehead until it touched the white scarf tucked into his black overcoat collar. 'Butterfingers,' he exclaimed. Arthur ignored him and continued passing the beer. 'Are yer deaf?' the man demanded. Arthur clenched his fists, ready to smash him.

'He must be,' the woman put in, showing bitter lips and haggard vindictive eyes. Arthur said nothing. Dave pushed his way to the man's side: 'Looking for trouble, mate?' Sam and Colin looked on from the wall. 'Drop him one, Arthur,' Bert called out.

'I'm not looking for trouble,' the man said, turning away from Arthur's cold stare, backing out with maximum belligerence. 'He just wants to look what he's doing, that's all.'

'It was an accident, worn't it?' Dave said loudly, standing over him, his face red and tight with anger.

'Bash 'im, Jack. Why don't yer bash 'im?' the woman said, sipping her port.

'It's yo' as wants bashin', missis,' Dave said. 'It's your sort as causes all the trouble.' The publican moved up from the other end of the bar. 'Now then, I don't want any fights in here.'

'What's the matter?' Sam asked Arthur.

'I don't like people spilling ale all over my wife's coat,' the man said truculently.

Arthur relaxed his fists.

'If it'd a bin whisky she'd a lapped it up,' Bert said. 'This place's like a graveyard. It's full o' dead-pans.'

They crossed Slab Square and, fresh from

328

a pint in the Plumtree rolled to the Red Dragon and from there pushed into the Skittling Alley and the Coach Tavern and finally elbowed through the squash of people packing the Trip to Jerusalem, a limpet of lights and noise fastened on to the carcass of the Castle Rock.

Sam tried to count those jammed into the parlour, but gave up at twenty, when he thought he was counting people already counted. Jane poured beer into cups and glasses. 'Come on, Arthur, grab hold of this. Having a good time, Sam?'—she swung around as he came into the room. 'This is good beer, Sam,' she told him in her bright intoxicated voice. 'Jim and me got it from the pub next door. A couple of years ago,' she told Sam, 'Bert and Dave went down into our cellar with a hammer and chisel and knocked a few bricks out of the wall and got two crates of beer out of the pub cellar next door. Then they cemented it up again so that nobody found out. We had a good booze-up from that.'

Arthur's great laugh rang out with the others at the memory of this because he had been in on it, remembering the bricks that he had numbered with a piece of chalk as they were passed to him.

Ada came in with a large white meat dish heaped over with leg-of-mutton sandwiches. 'Come on, Tribe, get summat to eat. We want you to 'ave a good time, Sam,' she said to him. She turned abruptly to Colin: 'Where's Beatty? I thought she'd be up tonight, being as it's Christmas Eve.'

'You shouldn't fill her up so often, Colin,' Dave said to him.

'You've only got to look at Beatty and she drops a kid,' Bert said, filling his glass and helping himself to a sandwich. Ada wore a gaily coloured dress. 'How do you like my parlour, Sam?' He looked around at the walls and up at the ceiling, at the Christmas cards on the marble mantelshelf that hid the clock but for a walnut dome. 'Arthur and Bert papered it for me a couple of years ago. It'd 'ave cost me five quid with a decorator, and they did it just as good.'

'Except for them big creases,' Arthur said, coming out of a long mistletoe kiss with one of his ginger-haired cousins. Ralph, wearing a coloured paper hat, and Jim in his pilot-officer's uniform also wearing a paper hat, did a song-and-dance movement into the room, with the second ginger-haired cousin behind flaunting her brother-in-law's air force cap. 'Don't be leary,' Ada said to her.

'I want some ale,' she cried.

Ada said she would bat her tab if she touched a drop. Sam sat on the settee and someone pulled a pink paper hat down over his black grizzled hair. Tubercular Eunice came in with Harry, her young man with a broad sallow face and brown curly hair combed back flat over his head, who worked as a welder in one of the Meadows factories. Eunice wore a maroon coat padded at the shoulders to hide her thin body, betrayed though by hollow cheeks and stick-like wrists. Mutton sandwiches and drinks were thrust into their hands, and Arthur, by now well-soaked, started the whole room singing, while Bert, Colin, and Dave played desultory rounds of Solo at the table. Ada told Sam to sing louder, but he said he didn't know these songs. 'Do you know "Everybody Likes Saturday Night" Sam?' Bert shouted from the table, and Sam beamed with happiness at the universal sympathy around him. One by one they went into the kitchen, until Harry and Eunice were left alone. They switched off the light and sat in the bay of the window watching traffic pass along the road.

When the fire died out in the kitchen everyone went to bed, and doors could be heard slamming all over the house. Arthur, feeling his way up the unlit stairs behind Sam, was to sleep in the big bed with his two cousins, while a special camp bed had been made-up for Sam by the window. The others went immediately to sleep, but Arthur was kept awake by noises in the house. He heard a door bang, the laugh of a female voice, an animal cry of protest, the snore of his cousins. A dull heavy jangle of trucks, like the manacled advance of some giant Marley over Trent valley, came from the nearby railway line. Window-panes rattled as a car went by. A man's footsteps passed the door, and from the city centre a few melancholy clocks struck the half-hour.

*   *   *

Sam was awakened by curses from Bert and Dave as they fought to pull the bed clothes from each other. Children were running barefoot about the corridors, and sun shone through the windows. Sam was left to dress in privacy, and the smell of fried bacon became stronger as Arthur, Bert, and Dave descended to the kitchen. Jane and Jim were talking in their bedroom, and Ralph turned over with a snore behind his closed door. They washed one by one at the scullery sink. Sitting down to breakfast Bert joked about

332

Sam: 'Hey, mam, there's a Zulu in my room.' Ada told him not to be daft and to leave Sam in peace. When Sam came down he was served with three eggs, and the girls grumbled and said this wasn't fair. But Ada showed them her fist and told them to shut-up. They sat in the parlour after breakfast, roasting themselves before the fire. A wire from the kitchen wireless was run through to a speaker, and the whole house was shaken by the chosen blasts of Family Favourites, part of a Bach concerto roaring like the tumult of a sea into every room.

They walked into town. A bitterly cold wind came from the east, and Dave prophesied snow, teasing Sam who had seen it on postcards but never in the streets. The pub noises were subdued and reflective, as if people were spending two hours of silence in memory of the previous night. One moment the sun was in their eyes, the next they were almost blown over by the wind. They had a pint in the Horse and Groom, and Arthur took five minutes explaining to Sam what an 'awker was: 'A man who sells fruit from a barrer on the street.' Back at the house a special table was set in the parlour, and the fire had been kept blazing for them. They were served by the girls with baked potatoes, roast pork, and cauliflower, and no one spoke during the eating of it. Plates of Christmas pudding followed, rivers of custard flowing down the escarpments of each dark wedge. A noise like a dark sea-tide came from the kitchen, where the family was feeding under the stern dictatorship of Ada. Everyone gathered in the parlour to play Ha'penny Newmarket, the kitty of a glass fruit-dish set in the middle of the table, soon filled with money as the games went on. A dozen played, including Sam and Ada whose big arms rested on the table. Orders were snapped out when cards didn't fall fast enough, coins slid across the polished table-top to start a new round, and some gleeful hand scraped the kitty-dish clean when the round was over. A ten-year-old girl scooped up the three-and-ninepence. 'Dirty little twister,' 'Rogue.' 'Dead lucky.' She refused to chance the money back into play, said she was going to see a pal now, and the air was filled with threats. 'I don't have to play if I don't want to,' she shouted. And the door slammed. Ada turned to one of Beatty's children and asked when her mother would come. Dave fanned out his cards and threw down a two of hearts: 'She's got too many kids to look after,' he said sympathetically. 'It's impossible to feed 'em all at one time. I don't know where they all sleep in that house. Colin must 'ave rigged bunks up in the cellar.' 'I've never seen such a tribe,' Bert chipped in. 'Whenever you go in by the back door you squash a couple of kids against the wall.' Sam was puzzled at their private jokes, though laughed with them. Tea was served in three relays, with Ada the dominant organiser, lording it over her two unmarried sisters. Annie was small and pinched after too many years in a lace factory, a woman of forty with fading and braided hair, wearing a dusk-green frock and a coal-black cardigan. Bertha was taller and older, with a full bosom, a booming voice, and more becoming clothes. Ada came in from the scullery with a dish of salad followed by Bertha with a bowl of trifle and Annie with a Christmas cake whose pink band made a crown for Ada. Bert reached out for a slice of bread and butter, shouting to Annie for the ham. 'Tek yer sweat, our Bert. You can see I'm busy mashing the tea.' Arthur heaped salad on to a plate, balancing slices of tomato on his fork across the white cloth. Bertha was stationed at the table-end with teapot poised, ready to bear down on anyone whose cup was empty. Her eyes rested on Sam: 'Sam knows how to eat. He's filling his belly all right.' Sam looked up and smiled.

'Do you get snap like this in the army?' Bert asked. 'I'm sure he don't,' Ada said before he could answer. 'Do you Sam?' 'No, but sometimes the food is good in the army,' he replied with an instinctive sense of diplomacy.

'When I was wi' the army, in Belgium and Germany,' Bert called out, reaching for the mince-pie plate that Annie laid down, 'we ate pig-swill.' Dave laughed: 'When I was in the army I got bread and water, when I was lucky.' 'Do you know what regiment he was in?' Bert said to Sam, who answered: 'No.' 'He was in the R.C.Ds.,' Bert went on. 'Do you know what the R.C.Ds are, Sam?' Sam asked what regiment the R.C.Ds. were. 'The Royal Corps of Deserters,' Bert boomed across the table. 'We're all going back into that regiment as soon as a war starts, ain't we Arthur?' Dave called out for another cup of tea, and Ada shouted that they should make haste because another two sittings were still to come. So they filed back to the parlour, and while Sam went across to the lavatory, Jane entered and held out her hand for more half-crowns. 'It's for beer,' she said. When they paid she demanded: 'Where's Sam?' Arthur told her, and Bert added: 'Wi' a blanket round 'im.' 'He's got to give half a crown as well.' 'I thought he was a guest?' Dave said, throwing two lumps of coal on the fire. 'He's got to pay up, just the same,' she said indignantly. 'He's got enough money.' 'What about Annie and Bertha then?' Dave said. 'Have them two spongers paid?' 'Yes,' Bert cried, 'what about them Biblebacks? They're allus there wi' their ha'penny. They put enough money in the church kitty every Sunday.' 'Don't worry,' she said, 'they'll pay.' She waylaid Sam in the corridor and collected half a crown.

After a round of pubs in the evening they ended at the Railway Club drinking with Ada and Ralph. It was a long low hall with rows of tables like a soldiers' mess, with a bar and stage at one end. Housey-Housey was in progress. Arthur, Sam, Bert, and Dave bought cards and watched their counters. Near the climax of the game a man wearing a cap suddenly jumped up and screamed with all his might, as if he had been stabbed: 'HOUSEY!' Sam shuddered with fright; the others groaned at their bad luck. 'Christ!' Ada exclaimed 'I only wanted two to win.' 'I only wanted one,' Arthur said. 'What a shame,' she said. 'You'd 'ave won a bottle of whisky.' At ten-thirty the Tribe streamed out, over the railway bridge, and home. Overcoats were piled in heaps on the kitchen table, and the hall racks were so overloaded that they collapsed. Beer for grown-ups, orangeade for children, with sixteen the dividing age, and Jane discriminating at the parlour bar. Beatty, tall and noisy, sat with Colin on the settee; Eileen, Frances, June, and Alma took chairs by the window and were trying to start an opposition song to annoy the others; Arthur, Sam, Bert, and Dave dominated the space around the fire; Ralph, Jim, and Ada stood by the door; Annie and Bertha were giving out meat sandwiches; Frank, Beatty's twenty-two-year-old son by her first husband, was persuading his fiancée to be sick outside and get it over with; Harry and Eunice, and a girl in khaki, occupied the settee; and various children were hanging on to table-legs for safety. Alma, a girl of fifteen with chestnut hair, wearing a low-necked cotton dress that showed the white skin of plump round breasts, was fair game for Bert who forced her into a kiss beneath the mistletoe. She ran out of the house when he tried to make her kiss Sam. Balloons exploded; coloured streamers floated from the ceiling, Bert pushing his way around the room with an uplifted cigarette. Above the uproar Jane's voice was heard saying to Jim: 'I don't believe it. It ain't true. You want to mind what you're saying, you dirty bleeder'—in a voice of hard belligerence. Bert succeeded in getting Annie and Bertha kissed by Sam under the mistletoe, and Bertha asked Sam afterwards if he would write to her from Africa. 'And give my love to your girl, won't you?' she said, the slight cast in her left eye glazed by too much drink. 'Yes,' he answered, 'I will.' Ada asked if he had enjoyed his Christmas. 'Very much,' he answered solemnly. 'And will you tell Johnny all about us when you get back?' she wanted to know. Sam said he would. 'I wish Johnny was here. He's a good lad to me,' Ada said. 'I've never known him to say a bad word to me. I remember one day a man in Waterway Street said sommat to me that worn't nice and Johnny chased him all the way down the street. The man ran into his house and locked it but that didn't stop our Johnny. He ran agen it wi' his showder until the man had to open it for fear it'd be broke down, and then Johnny chased him round and round the table till he caught him and thumped him against the wall. The man was allus as nice as pie to me after that.' She passed Sam a glass of beer, and kissed him beneath the mistletoe, so that Beatty cried out: 'Well, that's not the first time she's bin kissed by a black man, I'll bet.' Someone suggested that Ralph would be jealous. 'Jealous be boggered,' she said. 'Sam's like my own son.' The girls squealed when more balloons exploded. 'Do you like England then?' Jane asked Sam. She had been out of the room for a few minutes. 'I like it very much,' Sam stammered. She threw her arms around him and kissed him, turning her back on the rabid face of her husband near the door. Two girls went home, several children were taken to bed by Frances and Eileen. Frank at last took his fiancée out to be sick. Eunice left with Harry. Annie and Bertha put on their coats and went home. Jane and Jim sat on the sofa with empty glasses, Jane sullen, Jim subdued. Sam announced that he would go to bed. 'Because I want to be up early in the morning to catch my train.' He stood up and took his webbing belt from the chair. The room went suddenly quiet. Jane was standing up, staring at Jim with tight, angry lips. 'You aren't going to say that about me,' she cried loudly. Arthur saw a beer-glass in her hand. 'What did he say, then?' Ada asked of everybody. Jane did not reply, but struck her husband on his forehead with the glass, leaving a deep half-inch split in his skin. Blood oozed and fell down his face, gathering speed until it dropped on to the rug. He stood like a statue and made no sound.

The glass fell from her hand. 'You aren't going to accuse me of that,' she said again, her lips trembling. 'Why did you hit me?' Jim asked at last, with a dazed cry of shock and regret in his voice. 'Because you want to be careful what you say,' she cried, drawing back at the sight of so much blood. 'What did I say?' he pleaded. 'Tell me, somebody, what did I say?' 'It serves you right,' she said. Dave led him to a chair. Arthur went into the scullery and held a clean handkerchief under the running tap. Sam still stood, but seemed about to faint. The cold water ran over Arthur's hand and woke him up. He pressed the cold wet handkerchief to Jim's head, feeling strangely and joyfully alive, as if he had been living in a soulless vacuum since his fight with the swaddies. He told himself that he had been without life since then, that now he was awake once more, ready to tackle all obstacles, to break any man, or woman, that came for him, to turn on the whole world if it bothered him too much, and blow it to pieces. The crack of the glass on Jim's forehead echoed and re-echoed through his mind.

CHAPTER FIFTEEN

ONCE a rebel, always a rebel. You can't help being one. You can't deny that. And it's best to be a rebel so as to show 'em it don't pay to try to do you down. Factories and labour exchanges and insurance offices keep us alive and kicking—so they say—but they're booby-traps and will suck you under like sinking-sands if you aren't careful. Factories sweat you to death, labour exchanges talk you to death, insurance and income tax offices milk money from your wage packets and rob you to death. And if you're still left with a tiny bit of life in your guts after all this boggering about, the army calls you up and you get shot to death. And if you're clever enough to stay out of the army you get bombed to death. Ay, by God, it's a hard life if you don't weaken, if you don't stop that bastard government from grinding your face in the muck, though there ain't much you can do about it unless you start making dynamite to blow their four-eyed clocks to bits.

They shout at you from soapboxes: 'Vote for me, and this and that,' but it amounts to the same in the end whatever you vote for because it means a government that puts stamps all over your phizzog until you can't see a hand before you, and what's more makes you buy 'em so's they can keep on doing it. They've got you by the guts, by backbone and skull, until they think you'll come whenever they whistle.

But listen, this lathe is my everlasting pal because it gets me thinking, and that's their big mistake because I know I'm not the only one. One day they'll bark and we won't run into a pen like sheep. One day they'll flash their lamps and clap their hands and say: 'Come on, lads. Line-up and get your money. We won't let you starve.' But maybe some of us will want to starve, and that'll be where the trouble'll start. Perhaps some'll want to play football, or go fishing up Grantham Cut. That big fat-bellied union ponce'll ask us not to muck things up. Sir Harold Bladdertab'll promise us a bigger bonus when things get put right. Chief Inspector Popcorn will say: 'Let's have no trouble, no hanging around the gates there.' Blokes with suits and bowler hats will say: 'These chaps have got their television sets, enough to live on, council houses, beer and pools—some have even got cars. We've made them happy. What's wrong? Is that a machine-gun I hear starting up or a car back-firing?'

Der-der-der-der-der-der-der-der-der-der-der-der-der. I hope I'm not here to see it, but I know I will be. I'm a bloody billy-goat trying to screw the world, and no wonder I am, because it's trying to do the same to me.

* * *

Arthur became Doreen's young man. There was something of sweetness in it, and if he was not pursuing his rebellion against the rules of love, or distilling them with rules of war, there was still the vast crushing power of government against which to lean his white-skinned bony shoulder, a thousand of its laws to be ignored and therefore broken. Every man was his own enemy, and only on these conditions of fighting could you come to terms with yourself, and the only tolerable rule that would serve as a weapon was cunning, not a quiet snivelling cunning—which was worse than being dead—but the broad-fisted exuberant cunning of a man who worked all day in a factory and was left with fourteen quid a week to squander as best he could at the weekend, caught up in his isolation and these half-conscious clamped-in policies for living that cried for exit.

Violent dialogues flayed themselves to death in his mind as he went on serving a life's penance at the lathe. The scarlet gash in Jim's forehead and the tight-lipped frightened face of Jane at Christmas had showed him, as it were, through an open chink of light, that a man could rarely play for safety if he was to win in the end (at the same time thinking that if any woman had bashed him as Jane had bashed Jim he would have thumped her back). To win meant to survive; to survive with some life left in you meant to win. And to live with his feet on the ground did not demand, he realised fully for the first time, that he go against his own strong grain of recklessness—such as striving to kick down his enemies crawling like ants over the capital letter G of Government—but also accepting some of the sweet and agreeable things of life—as he had done in the past but in a harder way—before Government destroyed him, or the good things turned sour on him.

*   *   *

On a fine Sunday at the beginning of March, with sun shining on ground that had recently felt the cold touch of snow, the air smelling cool and fresh, he met Doreen on the outskirts of the housing estate. Few people were about because it was still too soon after dinner. Arthur wore a suit, collar, and tie, black shoes, and Doreen, who was waiting for him and keeping an eye on the bus stop from which he would walk, wore a light-brown coat with the Sunday additions of stockings, elegant shoes and a green jersey within.

He walked across the road, tall and thin, with short fair hair combed neatly back, one hand in his trouser pockets. They agreed to go for a walk, Doreen wanting to go into the city, Arthur into the country. 'I'm cooped up in a factory all week,' he argued, 'and Sunday is they walked Arthur reflected on the uniqueness of his goings-out with Doreen, on the

She saw a vague plot in this, to get her among isolated fields, but gave in to him. As they walked Arthur reflected on the uniqueness of his goings-out with Doreen, on the absence of danger that had tangibly surrounded him when he formerly met Brenda or Winnie. Each outing now was no longer an expedition on which every corner had to be turned with care, every pub considered for the ease of tactical retreat in case of ambush, every step along dark streets with his arm around Brenda taken with trepidation. He missed these things with Doreen, so much so that when out with her he felt a tug of excitement at the heart on approaching a corner, and conversation would lapse for a few minutes until they had turned it and he saw with a strange feeling of frustration mixed with relief that an avenue of safety lay before him.

The day seemed timeless, was handsome with its rare high clouds. Lime trees were coming to life by the laneside, tiny erectile buds emerging to enjoy the spring and shining like emeralds, fresh enough to quench one's thirst. Looking back from the lane, the last houses of the estate appeared drab and haphazard, as if sprinkled over the earth from a madman's lap.

She held his arm, and they walked to where the bridle path divided by Strelley church, one way forking through fields to Ilkeston, the other for pit-shafts of Kimberly and Eastwood. Arthur was happy in the country. He remembered his grandfather who had been a blacksmith, and had a house and forge at Wollaton village. Fred had often taken him there, and its memory was a fixed picture in Arthur's mind. The building—you had drawn your own water from a well, dug your own potatoes out of the garden, taken eggs from the chicken run to fry with bacon off your own side of pig hanging salted from a hook in the pantry—had long ago been destroyed to make room for advancing armies of new pink houses, flowing over the fields like red ink on green blotting paper.

They walked slowly towards Ilkeston along a narrow stony path with a low fence on one side and a privet hedge on the other, talking little, taking the fork towards Trowel when the track widened. Arthur, after a lifetime of wandering on summer nights after school and work, knew every path and field in the country. They came to a house, a window of which showed chocolate and lemonade for sale. He had called there before, had tackled the stony path on his bicycle, enjoyed the jolts and skids on his way to do some fishing in the Erewash Canal, had often screeched-on his brakes and drawn in at the same window to buy something to eat.

Doreen chewed a bar of chocolate and drank a bottle of lemonade. The woman of the house remembered Arthur, and asked slyly: 'You aren't going fishing today?'—searching in the window for his particular brand of chocolate.

'That bar with nuts and raisins in, duck,' he stipulated. 'You'll like this sort,' he said, turning to Doreen. 'Not today,' he answered the woman. 'I'm courtin' now, can't you see?' He hugged Doreen around the waist to prove it.

'Courtin'?' the woman exclaimed. 'Oh well, the fishes can rest in peace from now on.'

He paid her, and she shut the window. 'There'll still be time for fishin', I expect,' he said.

They came to a swing-bridge over a stream, and stood against the rail. 'I know a short cut back to the estate from here,' he said. 'We needn't bother wi' a bus.' His arm was around her, and they looked down at the dark-green rushes only a few feet away. It was hardly a stream, but an aborted branch-line of the nearby canal. The water was very still and shallow, and reflected the clouds. They stood in silence, no one else in sight. His arm moved over her back, and rested on the warm nape of her neck. He tried to kiss her. She pulled her face away.

'Nobody's lookin'.' He held her fast round the waist, and was cast into sad reflection by staring at the water below, a rippleless surface where minnows swam gracefully in calm transparent silence. White and blue sky made islands on it, so that the descent into its hollows seemed deep and fathomless, and fishes swam over enormous gulfs and chasms of cobalt blue. Arthur's eyes were fixed into the beautiful earth-bowl of the depthless water, trying to explore each pool and shallow until, as well as an external silence there was a silence within himself that no particle of his mind or body wanted to break. Their faces could not be seen in the water, but were united with the shadows of the fish that flitted among upright reeds and spreading lilies, drawn to water as if they belonged there, as if the fang-like claws of the world would come unstuck from their flesh if they descended into its imaginary depths, as if they had known it before as a refuge and wanted to return to it, their ghosts already there, treading the calm unfurrowed depths and beckoning them to follow.

But there was no question of following. You were dragged down sooner or later whether you liked it or not. A ripple appeared in the middle of the water, expanded in concentric rings, and burst by a timeless force of power. Each line vanished into the reed-grass near the bank.

'I feel tired,' she said, breaking the silence.

'Come on, Doreen.' He took her arm and led her on to a footpath. They followed his short cut towards home, and came to the loneliest place of the afternoon where, drawn by a deathly and irresistible passion, they lay down together in the bottom of a hedge.

*   *   *

After a bout of Saturday-night pictures he said he wanted a pint before going back to her house. It was raining, he said, and so reason enough for them to get a bit of shelter in a pub. She suggested they take a bus, which would keep them dry, but he replied that he could not stand queues of any sort. 'I've never queued in my life,' he said, 'and I'm not going to start now.'

'You on'y queue for five minutes,' she said, piqued.

'It's too long. Besides, I said I wanted a pint, didn't I?'

'What do you want a pint for?' she asked, pulling up her collar to avoid the cold needles of rain. 'Let's go back to my house where it's warm. Mam'll have some supper for us.'

He felt a hard stubborn force of resistance against her. 'I want a pint,' he maintained, 'and I see nowt wrong wi' that.'

'Well I do,' she said. 'You drink too much.'

'No I don't. I don't drink half enough since I met you. So don't try and stop me having a pint when I want one.'

351

The smoke and noise of the pub assailed them. 'Only one, then,' she said as they went in.

'You have something as well,' he offered.

She agreed to a shandy, but refused to sit at a table, saying that he would stay till closing time if she did. 'Are you trying to keep me in check?' he laughed. 'We aren't married yet, you know.'

'No, nor even engaged,' she said ironically.

'Well,' he said, 'we've on'y known each other for a few months.'

'And do you call that courting?' she said, pulling a face. 'Some people might, but I don't.'

'Not like the last fortnight?' he suggested.

'Pig,' she cried, 'always throwing it in my face.'

He laughed softly and grinned, looking at her: 'Well, you know I like to see you arguing and telling me off.'

'You should take it as it's meant,' she said, 'like other people.'

'I would,' he said, 'if I didn't love you.'

'Love,' she exclaimed. 'You don't know what love is.'

'Not much, our Doreen. I know a bit more than yo', I'm sure.'

'You're a crack-pot,' she said, 'that's what

352

yo' are.'

'Ah!' he called. 'All this fuss because I wanted a pint and you didn't get your own way. And just look at yourself supping that shandy down. Anybody'd think you were born in a public house. I'd be ashamed to own you if I didn't love you, watching you drink like that.'

She bit her lips and glared at him. 'Anybody'd think we were already married,' she threw out, 'the things you say, and the way you carry on. You get your own way all the time.'

'And aren't you glad when I do?' he demanded in the same light-hearted infuriating manner. 'Don't you love it? And it's only right that I should always get my own way, you know that.'

'My God,' she said, 'if we weren't in a pub I'd crack you one, a good one as well.'

'I bet you would, Doreen Greatton. I'd like that too. But I'd crack you one back. You know that, don't you?'

'A lot of good it would do you,' she said, but in a milder tone. Then remembering his previous remark: 'Besides, who says I love it? It's not you that makes me love it, I can tell you.'

'Yes it is, and stop telling lies. Have you forgotten all them nice things you towd me, about how you liked it? I don't know, you allus say one thing and then tell me you meant another.'

She fell silent, and watched him ask for more beer. He offered her a cigarette and, when she refused it, lit his own with an exaggerated striking of the match. 'You think you're the cock o' the walk,' she said, implying: 'But I'll tame you, you see if I don't.' Turning to drop his match he noticed that the man nearby was wearing army uniform. He was tall and well-built, good-looking in a soldierish way, though his face was too flushed below dark hair and would soon become florid, and the moustache was clipped too short above livid red lips. His cap lay on the counter, beside an empty beer-mug. He looked at Arthur long enough for mutual recognition, then turned away.

'Ain't your mate wi' yer tonight?' Arthur demanded.

'Who's that?' Doreen asked, pulling at his elbow.

The handsomeness fell from the swaddie's face when he said with a wrathful sneer: 'What's it got to do wi' yo' whether my mate's wi' me or not?'

'If yer still want trouble yer can come outside,' Arthur said. 'Keep quiet,' he said to

Doreen. 'He's an owd pal o' mine.'

The swaddie did not move, leaned against the counter, with brows wrinkled and eyes half closed, as if he had drunk too much. 'I'm not looking for trouble,' he said, beaten by Arthur's iron stare.

'What do you mean?' Doreen cried in a sudden high-pitched frightened voice. 'Saying he's a pal o' yourn?'

'Well I'm warnin' yer,' Arthur said to the swaddie, 'if ever yer want trouble, yer can 'ave it.' He'll never say he's sorry, and I'll never say I'm sorry. If he worn't a sowjer he'd be on my side, grabbin' 'is guts out at a machine like mine, thinking about making dynamite to blow up the Council House. But no, he's a brainless bastard. I can't see what Winnie sees in him, the poor sod. I'll bet a bob he's having more trouble with her. I'll ask him to have a pint on me: 'Have a pint, mate,' he said.

'No thanks,' the swaddie answered.

'Come on,' Arthur said in a friendly way, 'have one.' He ordered it, and another for himself, and the jars were placed side by side on the counter. The swaddie looked at it suspiciously, as if it were a mug of poison.

Arthur lifted his glass: 'Cheers. Drink-up, mate. I'm getting married next week.'

The swaddie came out of his bitter trance, saying: 'Good luck to you then,' and finished off the beer in one swallow.

*   *   *

They took a bus out to the estate, sitting silently during the ride like two people in an aeroplane for the first time and too frightened of its motion to say much. When they were walking along the crescent she asked: 'Who was that soldier?'

'An old pal of mine,' he answered. 'I knew him in the army.' And he would say no more.

They walked down the garden to the back door, entering the narrow porch between coal-house and lavatory. Arthur followed her into a kitchen smelling of stale gas and washed clothes. The living-room was untidy. It'd get cleaned up if I lived here, Arthur thought. A line of dry washing hung diagonally across the room, and both dresser and shelf were crowded with old recumbent Christmas cards, snapshots standing against hairbrushes, clocks with no hands, and cigarette packets. A twenty-year-old wireless crackling from the dresser was switched off by Doreen's mother as soon as they came in. The table was set for supper: teapot and cups, sugar, a tin of milk, bread, cheese, and some knives and forks.

Mrs. Greatton sat by the fire reading a newspaper, and a Bombay Indian crouched opposite by the coal-box, smoking a cigarette through his clenched hand. Doreen's mother was deaf and wore glasses, and Arthur guessed her age to be about fifty. He wondered what her Indian friend saw in such a big loosely built woman with no beauty, whose hair had gone thin and grey near the forehead. The Indian had not spoken a word to Arthur on his previous visits to the house, merely nodding to him because he apparently knew not a word of English. Doreen's mother said he worked at an engineering factory in town, and that after three years he would go back to Bombay with a thousand pounds saved, where, she said, you could be a millionaire with a thousand pounds. The Indian wore overalls and a jacket, and a cloth-cap that Arthur had seen him take off only once—when he followed Mrs Greatton upstairs to bed, showing himself to be completely bald. He was a man of about forty, good-looking in an Indian way, though Arthur did not like him. He always sat silently gazing at the pictures in some magazine, smoking cigarette after cigarette very slowly and meditatively through his hand, his lips never touching the tip of the cigarette. Mrs. Greatton would occasionally look up from her newspaper and make some affectionate remark to him that he did not understand but that he acknowledged by a grunt and a nod or a word of his own language that she did not understand.

Mrs. Greatton folded her newspaper and served them supper, doing every action with a cigarette in her mouth, looking down over her glasses, moving in slow cumbrous movements so that Arthur was surprised when food was finally set out neatly before them in the short time of ten minutes. Neither was hungry. They sat facing each other, munching slowly at bread and cheese and tinned meat, Arthur winking at Doreen when Mrs. Greatton's head was turned, and putting outstretched fingers to his nose at the Indian when he was looking down.

'Your mother teks all night to read that newspaper,' he remarked quite loudly because Mrs. Greatton was deaf. 'Does she read slow, or is she looking at the adverts?'

'She reads every word of it,' Doreen replied. 'She loves the newspaper, more than a book.'

Mrs. Greatton looked up. Her sharp eyes

358

told her that they were talking. 'What are you saying?' she asked with interest.

'I was telling Arthur you read all the adverts in the paper,' Doreen shouted.

'They're interesting,' she said briefly. The Indian—Arthur had never heard them use his name, as if they hadn't troubled to ask him what it was—looked up and smiled at hearing them speak.

'He's a lost soul,' he said to Doreen as she smiled back at him.

'What?' Mrs. Greatton wanted to know.

'He's a lost soul,' Arthur bellowed.

'Not so lost,' Mrs. Greatton said. 'He's all right. He's a good bloke.'

'Ain't he got a name?' he asked Doreen.

'I don't think so,' she answered, 'but we call him "Chumley" because that's what it sounded like when we asked him what it was. Didn't it, Chumley?' she shouted across to him. He turned and stared at her, as if she were trying to get some secret from him, then turned back to the fire.

'He ain't mad,' she explained, pouring Arthur another cup of tea. 'He likes us to talk about him.'

'He looks lonely,' Arthur said, as if obsessed by this fact.

'He's not really,' she said, 'mam and him

359

get on well together. He don't have too bad a life.'

'Well, he looks lonely to me,' he said. 'He should go back to India. I can tell when a bloke's lonely. He don't say owt, see? And that means he misses his pals.'

'He's got mam,' Doreen said.

'It's not the same,' he answered, 'not by a long way.'

They finished eating, but stayed at the table talking. Arthur was waiting for Chumley and Mrs. Greatton to go to bed, out of the way, so that he could be alone with Doreen, who spoke less and less, as if impatience was gnawing at her also.

Chumley stood up and, cap in hand, bald head shining beneath the strong electric light, walked towards the door. Mrs. Greatton's shield of newspaper rustled and lowered when she sensed his movement. 'I'll be up soon, sweetheart,' she said.

'Let's hope so,' Arthur muttered.

They heard Chumley treading slowly up the stairs, and Mrs. Greatton went on reading, as if she would stay at it doggedly all night. Arthur passed a lighted cigarette to Doreen, then lit one for himself. He broke the match-stick into little pieces and set them out along the edge of his plate, then flicked them one by one towards the piece of cheese in the middle of the table. Doreen asked him again about the soldier in the public house. 'I'll tell you what went on,' he said. 'You see, he was my mate in the army. He got put on a charge once, and I put him on it. I couldn't help doing it, you see, because an officer was with me, and he got seven days' jankers. Well, when he'd finished his jankers he met me in town and set on me, and we had a fight, and ever since then we ain't bin such good pals. But now I suppose it's all right. He's a good bloke, and we had some good times together before I had to put him on this charge. Now you can see why we was mad at each other when we met tonight.' He went on to elaborate the details of their adventures together, until Doreen was convinced of his story by the sincere narrative tone of his voice, which took some minutes to acquire.

Mrs. Greatton rustled her paper on to the back page. Sports news, Arthur thought, I'm sure she won't want to read them.

'Does your mam do the crossword puzzle?' he asked with magnificent disinterestedness. 'If she does, she'll be at it until four o'clock.'

'No, she tried 'em once, then gave it up because all them black and white squares hurt her eyes.'

Relieved to hear this he watched Mrs. Greatton's eyes travelling up and down the paper. Chumley had been upstairs for twenty minutes. When will she bloody well get up and move? he wondered. She'll sit there all night at this rate. He caught and killed a fly that walked on his wrist. Mrs. Greatton looked up at the sound of the smack, then went on reading. I'll sit her out, Arthur thought grimly, if she stays in that chair till morning. A car drove by along the road. 'That's the fish and chip van going back to town,' Doreen informed him. It was a quarter to eleven. They heard the insistent stomp of Chumley's stockinged feet on the bedroom floor. 'She'll go now,' Doreen said.

But she did not go. Get up them stairs, for Christ's sake, Arthur said to himself. Mothers are so bloody-well awkward when it comes to a thing like this. Why don't you go?

At eleven o'clock she stood up and folded her newspaper. 'Well,' she said, looking at them both, 'I'm off to bed. And don't be long yourself, Doreen.'

'All right, mam. Only ten minutes. Arthur's got to go now. He's got a long walk home.'

'I 'ave an' all,' Arthur shouted. 'I'll get crackin' in a bit.'

'And I'll wash the pots, and clean up before coming to bed, our mam,' Doreen said as she went out. When her footsteps sounded on the loose board at the top of the stairs Arthur held Doreen and kissed her passionately. 'I thought she'd never go.'

'Well, you were wrong,' she said reprovingly, slipping away from him. She moved clothes and newspapers from the settee so that they could sit down and kiss there undisturbed, a Saturday-night routine already well established by the few Saturdays that had gone before. A few minutes later she broke free and stood up: 'Let's make as if you're going now.'

'The same old trick,' he said, following her through the scullery to the back door.

Doreen opened it with a loud click, calling out forcefully:

'Good night, then, Arthur.'

'Good night, duck,' he shouted out so that the whole estate must have heard. 'I'll see you on Monday.'

The door slammed so violently that the house shook, Doreen making sure that her deaf mother's ear reacted to the noise. Arthur, being still on the inside, followed Doreen tip-toe back into the warm, comfortable, well-lit living-room.

363

'Don't make much noise for a while,' she whispered in his ear.

He smoked a cigarette and lay back on the settee, whistling softly to himself, spread out at his ease while Doreen cleared the table and washed the dishes in the kitchen, making discreet but appropriate noises that floated through the house, hoping they would lull the mother to sleep, or at least into believing that her daughter was safely doing her work in an empty downstairs.

She came out of the kitchen and took off her apron, standing by the table in her dark-green dress that showed the curves of her breasts and slender body so well that Arthur said: 'I've never seen anybody look so nice as you do.'

She smiled, and sat down by him. The room was warm from fire still in the grate. He threw his half-finished cigarette into the coal bin. 'I love you,' he said softly.

'I love you, too,' she replied, but flippantly.

He put his hand on her shoulder. 'I'd like to live with you.'

She gave a wider smile. 'It would be nice.'

'How old did you tell me you were?' What the bloody-hell's that got to do wi' it?

'Twenty, soon.'

'I'm twenty-four. You'll be well off with

me. I'll look after you all right.'

Her face grew radiant: 'I shan't forget that walk we did that Sunday,' she said quietly, taking his hand, 'when we looked into the water near Cossal, and then went into the fields.'

'You know what I mean, though?' he demanded sternly.

'Of course.'

They did not speak. Arthur was subdued, his mind blocked with questions and unsatisfying answers, fighting the last stages of an old battle within himself, and at the same time feeling the first skirmishes of a new conflict. But he was good in his heart about it, easy and confident, making for better ground than he had ever trodden on before. I must be drunk, he thought. No I'm not. I'm stone-cold sober.

They sat as if the weight of the world had in this minute been lifted from them both and left them dumb with surprise. But this lasted only for the moment. Arthur held her murderously tight, as if to vanquish her spirit even in the first short contest. But she responded to him, as if she would break him first. It was stalemate, and they sought relief from the great decision they had just brought upon themselves. He spoke to her softly, and she nodded her head to his words without knowing what they meant. Neither did Arthur know what he was saying: both transmission and reception were drowned, and they broke through to the opened furrows of the earth.

CHAPTER SIXTEEN

He sat by the canal fishing on a Sunday morning in spring, at an elbow where alders dipped over the water like old men on their last legs, pushed by young sturdy oaks from behind. He straightened his back, his fingers freeing nylon line from a speedily revolving reel. Around him lay knapsack and jacket, an empty catch-net, his bicycle, and two tins of worms dug from the plot of garden at home before setting out. Sun was breaking through clouds, releasing a smell of earth to heaven. Birds sang. A soundless and miniscular explosion of water caught his eye. He moved nearer the edge, stood up, and with a vigorous sweep of his arm, cast out the line.

Another solitary man was fishing further along the canal, but Arthur knew that they would leave each other in peace, would not even call out greetings. No one bothered you: you were a hunter, a dreamer, your own boss, away from it all for a few hours on any day that the weather did not throw down its rain. Like the corporal in the army who said it was marvellous the things you thought about as you sat on the lavatory. Even better than

367

that, it was marvellous the things that came to you in the tranquillity of fishing.

He drank tea from the flask and ate a cheese sandwich, then sat back to watch the red and white float—up to its waist in water under the alder trees—and keep an eye always close to it for the sudden indication of a fortunate catch. For himself, his own catch had been made, and he would have to wrestle with it for the rest of his life. Whenever you caught a fish, the fish caught you, in a way of speaking, and it was the same with anything else you caught, like the measles or a woman. Everyone in the world was caught, somehow, one way or another, and those that weren't were always on the way to it. As soon as you were born you were captured by fresh air that you screamed against the minute you came out. Then you were roped in by a factory, had a machine slung around your neck, and then you were hooked up by the arse with a wife. Mostly you were like a fish: you swam about with freedom, thinking how good it was to be left alone, doing anything you wanted to do and caring about no one, when suddenly: SPLUTCH!—the big hook clapped itself into your mouth and you were caught. Without knowing what you were doing you had chewed off more than you could bite and had to stick with the same piece of bait for the rest of your life. It meant death for a fish, but for a man it might not be so bad. Maybe it was only the beginning of something better in life, better than you could ever have thought possible before clamping your avid jaws down over the vital bait. Arthur knew he had not yet bitten, that he had really only licked the bait and found it tasty, that he could still disengage his mouth from the nibbled morsel. But he did not want to do so. If you went through life refusing all the bait dangled before you, that would be no life at all. No changes would be made and you would have nothing to fight against. Life would be as dull as ditchwater. You could kill yourself by too much cunning. Even though bait meant trouble, you could not ignore it for ever. He laughed to think that he was full of bait already, half-digested slop that had certainly given him a share of trouble, one way or another.

Watching the float so intently made him sleepy: he had been with Doreen until two the night before. They spoke of getting married in three months, by which time, Arthur said, they would have collected a good amount of money, nearly a hundred and fifty pounds, not counting income-tax rebate, which will probably bump it up to a couple of hundred. So they would be sitting pretty, Doreen replied, because Mrs. Greatton had already offered to let them stay with her for as long as they liked, paying half the rent. For she would be lonely when Chumley left. Arthur said he would be able to get on with Mrs. Greatton, because living there he would be the man of the house. And if there was any arguments, they could get rooms somewhere. So it looked as though they'd be all right together, he thought, as long as a war didn't start, or trade slump and bring back the dole. As long as there wasn't a famine, a plague to sweep over England, an earthquake to crack it in two and collapse the city around them, or a bomb to drop and end the world with a big bang. But you couldn't concern yourself too much with these things if you had plans and wanted to get something out of life that you had never had before. And that was a fact, he thought, chewing a piece of grass.

He fixed the rod firmly against the bank and stood to stretch himself. He yawned widely, felt his legs weaken, then strengthen, then relax, his tall figure marked against a background of curving canal and hedges and trees bordering it. He rubbed his hand over the rough features of his face, upwards over thick lips, grey eyes, low forehead, short fair hair, then looked up at the mixture of grey cloud and blue patches of sky overhead. For some reason he smiled at what he saw, and turned to walk some yards along the towpath. Forgetting the stilled float in the water he stopped to urinate against the bushes. While fastening his trousers, he saw the float in violent agitation, as if it were suddenly alive and wanted to leap out of the water.

He ran back to the rod and began winding in the reel with steady movements. His hands worked smoothly and the line came in so quickly that it did not seem to be moving except on the reel itself where the nylon thread grew in thickness and breadth, where he evened it out with his thumb so that it would not clog at a vital moment. The fish came out of the water, flashing and struggling on the end of the line, and he grasped it firmly in his hand to take the hook from its mouth. He looked into its glass-grey eye, at the brown pupil whose fear expressed all the life that it had yet lived, and all its fear of the death that now threatened it. In its eye he saw the green gloom of willow-sleeved canals in cool decay, an eye filled with panic and concern for the remaining veins of life that circled like a silent whirlpool around it. Where do fishes go when they die? he wondered. The glow of long-remembered lives was mirrored in its eyes, and the memory of cunning curves executed in the moving shadows from reed to reed as it scattered the smaller fry and was itself chased by bigger fish was also pictured there. Arthur felt mobile waves of hope running the length of its squamous body from head to tail. He removed the hook, and threw it back into the water. He watched it flash away and disappear.

One more chance, he said to himself, but if you or any of your pals come back to the bait, it's curtains for 'em. With float bobbing before him once more he sat down to wait. This time it was war, and he wanted fish to take home, either to cook in the pan or feed to the cat. It's trouble for you and trouble for me, and all over a piece of bait. The fattest worm of the lot is fastened to the hook, so don't grumble when you feel that point sticking to your chops.

And trouble for me it'll be, fighting every day until I die. Why do they make soldiers out of us when we're fighting up to the hilt as it is? Fighting with mothers and wives, landlords and gaffers, coppers, army, government. If it's not one thing it's another, apart from the work we have to do and the way we spend our wages. There's bound to be trouble in store for me every day of my life, because trouble it's always been and always will be. Born drunk and married blind, misbegotten into a strange and crazy world, dragged-up through the dole and into the war with a gas-mask on your clock, and the sirens rattling into you every night while you rot with scabies in an air-raid shelter. Slung into khaki at eighteen, and when they let you out, you sweat again in a factory, grabbing for an extra pint, doing women at the weekend and getting to know whose husbands are on the nightshift, working with rotten guts and an aching spine, and nothing for it but money to drag you back there every Monday morning.

Well, it's a good life and a good world, all said and done, if you don't weaken, and if you know that the big wide world hasn't heard from you yet, no, not by a long way, though it won't be long now.

The float bobbed more violently than before and, with a grin on his face, he began to wind in the reel.